THE ATTENDING PHYSICIAN

A JOAN KAHN BOOK

The Attending Physician

by
R.B. DOMINIC

HARPER & ROW, PUBLISHERS
New York, Hagerstown, San Francisco, London

I

In Washington, D.C., most of the local disasters are man-made. This does nothing to lessen their danger. After all, volcanoes can smolder harmlessly for a long time, but elections take place every other year. And, to add insult to injury, there are special prosecutors, ethics committees and the *Washington Post*.

As a result, politicians who become fixtures are politicians with survival skills. While new restaurants, new press secretaries and new policies attract all the attention, old Washington hands lean back, watching them come and go.

Congressman Benton Safford (D., Ohio) had won enough elections to qualify as a veteran, particularly in the current House of Representatives, where he was unmistakably on the balding side of the generation gap. But, as luck would have it, he served on a sub-committee that was a veritable bouquet of hardy perennials.

Congressman Eugene Valingham Oakes (R., S. Dak.) had represented his hard-working, teetotaling, God-fearing constituents since time immemorial. "Yes, I believe I could use a little topping up, Ben," he said, studying the bourbon level in his glass. "Nothing like drafting a report to give a man a thirst."

His fellow Republican, Elsie Hollenbach of California, was made of sterner stuff. She accepted her second martini with a gracious nod, but stuck to the subject at hand. "I think we are submitting a fair survey of Medicaid abuse. Hearings in four cities—"

Congressman Anthony Martinelli, who came from Providence, Rhode Island, groaned aloud. "Passaic, Cedar Rapids, Scranton and Bangor! God, I hate these road shows." He did not wait for Safford to offer hospitality, but applied himself to the bottle at his elbow.

"Congressional committee hearings outside of Washington are an invaluable aid in bringing government closer to the people," said Mrs. Hollenbach, who had sailed around the circuit without visible wear or tear. "Although I was glad to get back to Washington yesterday."

She then dispelled this suggestion of weakness by continuing: "I want to keep an eye on what's happening over at Treasury. I don't like the way things are developing at all."

"What do you mean, Elsie? There hasn't been time for things to develop, at Treasury or anywhere else," said Ben, dutifully defending his party.

Six months earlier the American public had put a new man in the White House and, by extension, in every corner of the Executive branch. There were Democratic rookies everywhere you looked.

Martinelli, too, suspected partisan sniping. "Tell the truth, Elsie," he said with friendly malice. "Passaic, Cedar Rapids, Scranton and Bangor got to you, too, didn't they?"

"Certainly not," she replied. "I found our investigations very rewarding."

Val Oakes chose to take issue. "Rewarding? We knew before we started that half the doctors in the country are getting rich off Medicaid. What's rewarding about traipsing from state to state hearing them deny it?"

Mrs. Hollenbach ignored him to address Ben. "And I am not discussing Treasury proposals, although I don't like what I hear about them. No, it's Sumner Fenton. I understand he may have to resign because of conflicts of interest."

"So soon?" Ben commented unwisely.

Oakes was with him in spirit. "This resignation business is getting out of hand," he declared. "People used to stick to their guns through thick and thin. Now, every little thing—and they roll over and play dead."

As always, there was salty wisdom in what he said. But Tony Martinelli had his own political savvy. "What little thing has Fenton been caught at?" he inquired.

Mrs. Hollenbach, sometimes described as the Conscience of the

House, said: "There are allegations of improprieties in a bank he owns. Or I should say what appear to be improprieties."

This stung Congressman Martinelli. "Dammit," he exploded, "Republicans are supposed to own banks, not Democrats!"

"Times are changing, Tony," Ben told him.

"Not in South Dakota," said Val Oakes. "The only Democratic banker I ever heard of was run out of town forty years ago. Of course, back then we didn't call it impropriety. We called it robbing the cash box. And there wasn't any hogwash about appearances, either."

Again he had voiced the sense of the meeting. Even a moralist like Mrs. Hollenbach blanched at recent demands for nonstop displays of virtue. Not that she had anything to fear. Elsie was the embodiment of public and private rectitude, from her disciplined gray hair to her well-shod feet.

Martinelli hailed from a different political tradition. Removing an infinitesimal speck of lint from his Italian silk sleeve, he said: "It's bad enough we've got priests in Congress. Now they want saints!"

If so, Benton Safford was out of luck. He was no saint. He was not even a campaign manager's dream. Still, he suited Ohio's Fiftieth Congressional District, possibly because he was reassuringly human —rumpled clothes, thickening waistline and all.

Val Oakes, on the other hand, was an unabashed sinner. "This, too, shall pass," he declared sonorously.

Elsie did not care to go that far. "Naturally, I support stricter requirements for public office—including complete financial disclosure."

"Sure, sure," said Martinelli.

She eyed him. "The public should have access to the income-tax returns of every candidate. There is no legitimate reason they should not."

"I can think of a few."

Sparring between Martinelli and Mrs. Hollenbach was an old story. It was more a product of their mutual respect and affection than of their profound political differences.

"Besides, why pick on politicians?" Tony continued. "Why not doctors, for example? We could recommend that doctors with Medicaid patients have to publish *their* income-tax returns, huh, Elsie?"

Given the subcommittee's recent trek from Passaic to Bangor, this was a timely if unscrupulous thrust. Mrs. Hollenbach was taking a deep breath when Ben Safford stepped into the breach.

"I guess we'd better start work," he said.

He drew fire from all sides.

"On what?" asked Tony, while Val Oakes shook his head ponderously.

Mrs. Hollenbach abandoned Martinelli to quash Ben Safford. "You haven't forgotten that we are simply submitting the testimony with a letter of transmittal, have you? We all agreed—" she shot a look at Tony—"that recommendations would be premature."

"One hundred percent correct, Elsie," he said with a flashing smile.

"Best thing for you to do, Ben, is fill 'em up again," said Val, easing into his real message. "Blessed are the peacemakers when they know what they're doing. Otherwise they get blown out of the water."

Grinning, Ben complied with the suggestion. "Yes, Elsie. I remember it's a letter of transmittal—period."

Reform of the Medicaid system of assistance to the poor and the elderly was long overdue. But the strategy in Congress was to approach new legislation cautiously and to begin with the accumulation of data proving widespread abuse. The recent subcommittee hearings had been so much spade work, necessary but uninspiring.

"Let's look on the bright side," said Martinelli jauntily. "We send this damn thing off and we're finished with Medicaid and touring circuses—at least for the time being."

No sooner had he spoken than L. Lamar Flecker (D., Ala.), the subcommittee chairman, bustled into Ben's office. As always, he looked too harried for his own good.

"Sit down and take a load off your feet, Lou," said Val Oakes expansively.

Flecker sat and accepted a drink. But he lacked Val's genius for relaxation. "I've just come from the Speaker," he announced after a gulp.

"How's he settling in?" Ben inquired.

The House was undergoing changes, too. The new Speaker was not, of course, an unknown quantity. For over thirty years he had represented Cook County, Illinois, with bibulous charm and unswerving party loyalty.

"He enjoys being Speaker," said Flecker after giving the question due thought.

A vestigial sniff from Mrs. Hollenbach made him add: "And I think he's going to do a real fine job."

The loyal opposition struck back. "Don't tell *us,* Lou," said Oakes. "Tell the White House."

Flecker was too preoccupied to notice this mild jibe. His kind, worried eyes rested on Ben Safford. "The leadership just told me about a change in plans," he said, apologetically enough to produce an uneasy silence. Into it, his next words fell like millstones. "They want us to hold one more set of hearings out of town—before we submit our report."

Ben Safford did not join the chorus of dismay. Instinct told him that Flecker was holding something back, and instinct was right. Finally, when Elsie's measured cadences trailed off, when Martinelli stopped boiling over, when Val finished quoting Ecclesiastes, Ben seized his opening.

"Lou, where are these new hearings going to be?"

Flecker could not face him. "In Newburg, Ben."

"Newburg—Ohio?" Ben asked hollowly.

There was no way to soften the blow. On Tuesday the subcommittee was scheduled to hold hearings on Medicaid abuse in Newburg, Ohio—the Fiftieth Congressional District, which Benton Safford had the honor and privilege of representing in the Congress of the United States.

"Why?" he was still demanding an hour later. "Why dump this on me? I've cooperated with the leadership! I've done my committee work! Hell, I even backed the rebate!"

Madge Anderson, Ben's highly competent and knowledgeable secretary, treated his questions literally. "I think it's just bad luck," she said.

He stopped pacing up and down before her desk, transfixed by the inadequacy of her response. "Bad luck?" he repeated. "Good God, Madge, do you realize what a can of worms they're handing me? Dear old Dr. Whatsit—in my own backyard."

"It's going to be tricky for you," she said with a small frown.

"Thanks for that much sympathy," he said grumpily.

Madge was unmoved. A slim, attractive young woman, she was

spiritual kin in Washington to Ben's sister Janet back in Newburg. Her attachment to Ben's interests was wholehearted, quasi-maternal and more astringent than indulgent.

"By bad luck, I simply meant the coincidence of the timing."

"What coincidence?" he demanded.

Genuinely surprised, she said: "Didn't Congressman Flecker tell you?"

"No, he had to rush off to Ways and Means."

"And you haven't read the newspapers?"

Ben was getting tired of admitting his own inadequacy. "Look, Madge, I just got back from the wilds of Maine."

"Well, you'd better read them now," she said, indicating the display of Ohio newspapers adorning the table by the window.

On the whole, the Cincinnati *Inquirer* put it as pithily as anyone else.

NEW MEDICAID REVELATIONS BY HEW
7 NEWBURG MD's PAID $1,000,000

2

In Newburg, Ohio, the Department of Health, Education and Welfare occupied two floors of the Federal Building. When Congressman Flecker and the rest of his subcommittee descended two days later, the regional director there was almost too cooperative. Quentin Trumbull was deeply shamed by the corruption over which he found himself presiding. Yet, at the same time, he could not help taking perverse pride in its magnitude.

"Now, this one you won't believe," he predicted, brandishing another file.

Val Oakes corrected him. "After Scranton, we'll believe anything."

Tony Martinelli concurred. "They've got crooks there like nothing you've ever seen."

"Just take a look," Trumbull pleaded. "I don't say Newburg doctors are the biggest crooks in the world, but they've got to be the sloppiest."

By now the subcommittee knew more about Medicaid swindling than they wanted to. Even hometown pride could not make Ben Safford interested in further squalid detail. Only Mrs. Hollenbach remained indefatigable. She glanced through the folder, then frowned. "This is a vasectomy billing by a Dr. Yarborough," she commented. "As I recall, there is no Dr. Yarborough on the published list."

"He's not one of the Newburg Seven because he died ten months ago," Quentin Trumbull explained. "He'd practiced here for forty-five years, and for a while they wanted to name the new wing of the hospital after him. I seem to remember hearing you talk at the kick-off dinner, Congressman Safford."

Ben cast his mind back over the worthy causes that had called on him to eat a bad dinner and make a worse speech. "What did I say?" he asked warily.

Trumbull was enjoying his own private joke. "Among other things, that we'd never forget how Ned Yarborough gave of himself to the poor. His sons told everybody they were particularly touched by that remark."

Ben was resigned. "And I suppose he was in this swindle up to his ears?"

"He sure was. Yarborough may have spent time with poor patients, but that was to get their Medicaid numbers. They're the one essential for this racket. But what really makes me laugh is that it was the sons who let the cat out of the bag."

Martinelli was beginning to wonder if a childhood on the back streets of East Providence had left him too innocent for the world of modern medicine.

"You mean they fingered their old man?" he asked hoarsely.

Trumbull was able to reassure him. It had all been an accident. "And no one regrets it more than the Yarboroughs," he reported. "But they got into some squabble over the old man's estate, and the younger brother went to court to demand an accounting. So a lot of stuff became a matter of public record, including Yarborough's final year of Medicaid billings. It was the first time that anybody added them all up, and they came to over a hundred thousand dollars. Well, that made HEW think."

"Good," said Elsie militantly.

"Particularly," said Trumbull, sweeping on zestfully, "particularly when I remembered that Yarborough took six months off that year —to visit Tahiti and Hong Kong. I decided we'd better take a closer look."

"That's when you hired some computer time?" Ben asked.

"Not right away," said Trumbull. "We've got something better than a computer. Her name is Charlene Gregorian. She works downstairs in Social Security, and she's been there for years. The computer is okay for numbers, but Charlene knows all about the people involved—you know, everybody on old-age pensions, everybody who's blind or disabled. So I asked her to glance through the Yarborough file. When she pulled out that vasectomy billing, Mrs. Hollenbach, I thought she'd die laughing."

This daunted everybody but Mrs. Hollenbach. "Why is it so funny? Naturally, I'm assuming that Yarborough never performed the operation—"

With a happy yip, Trumbull interrupted. "He'd have had a hard time trying. The patient, Sidney Kincaid, is a forty-eight-year-old welfare mother."

Congressman Oakes was the first to recover. "You mean the doctors you keep around here don't even check on *that?*"

"I told you they were sloppy," Trumbull boasted. "They've got their little black book of Medicaid numbers. Whenever they need extra cash, they dash off a billing—for the first thing that enters their heads. They can't be bothered to simply pad their bills."

"But why not reduce the odds?" Tony Martinelli persisted. "Make it an appendix? At least everybody qualifies for that."

Trumbull shrugged. "For all I know, they like a little variety. Anyway, Charlene had a field day with Yarborough's records. Patients who were dead when he claimed he was treating them, people who'd moved to Florida. She found enough to justify our requesting computer print-outs on every doctor in town. And you know what came out of the woodwork."

"We sure do," said Ben Safford ruefully. "You found seven doctors in town who made over a hundred thousand each from Medicaid last year—and you gave their names to the papers."

Val Oakes reverted to an earlier point. "Could be I was wrong. Newburg may be worse than Scranton. Then again, it may be that Scranton just doesn't have a Charlene Gregorian handy. I'd like to meet that little lady."

"You're going to," Trumbull promised, consulting his watch. "I told her we'd drop by this afternoon. She'll give you a real eye-opener about what goes on around Newburg."

"Cheer up, Ben," said Val as they trooped out into the hall. "All this will come in handy for you—someday."

But in the reception area of the Social Security office, the first eye-opener to come their way was the welfare system as it works at street level. The whole room was filled with people, all gesticulating, all shouting. At first glance, Ben spotted a clergyman, two students in

Ohio State sweatshirts and a middle-aged woman sitting slightly apart, fanning herself with a magazine. A sudden rift in the tangle of activity revealed the eye of the storm, an elderly woman who was alternately sobbing and drumming the arms of her chair with her hands. The moment that the visitors saw her, she saw them. Levering herself to her feet, she pointed a gnarled finger at Congressman Martinelli and burst into a shrill foreign language.

"Hey!" Tony protested, backing away in alarm.

Supporters rallied around the principals. The clergyman bent over the crone with nervous reassurance. Mrs. Hollenbach courageously moved in front of Tony. The middle-aged woman froze in midsweep, and Quentin Trumbull settled back on his heels and bawled: "Charlene! Charlene, are you there?"

A flapping hand appeared from the turmoil. "Take them into my office, Quen. They're just making things worse."

Val Oakes led the retreat.

"It's always a madhouse down here," Trumbull apologized when they had reached safety. "I should have called first to make sure the coast was clear."

Mrs. Hollenbach was not used to treatment like this. "Things have come to a pretty pass when Congressmen need convoys to get through Federal offices."

"That was Italian she was shouting, wasn't it, Tony?" Ben asked. "What was the old lady saying?"

Martinelli was reluctant to interpret. "She confused me with someone else," he hedged. "But I'll tell you one thing—that woman was raised in the gutter."

Charlene Gregorian breezed in ten minutes later, treating the whole incident as part of a day's work. "We've got Mrs. Bertilucci squared away," she announced. "Sorry about her yelling at you. She thought you worked here."

"Tell her we're from Congress," Tony suggested.

"That would make it worse," Mrs. Gregorian said cheerfully, clicking her way around the desk.

She was a roly-poly woman, about fifty-five years old, who radiated bouncy practicality. Her hair had been so artfully streaked that the faded blond, the gray and the chemical frosting all blended into a silver-gilt aureole framing her round face with its slightly protuberant blue eyes. Neat little feet teetered precariously atop high heels transforming her natural four-foot-eleven into a statuesque five-foot-two. She was totally unimpressed by the arrival of a Washington delegation in her tiny office.

"Charlene," said Trumbull by way of introduction, "knows more than anybody in Newburg about Social Security."

"And a fine mess it is," she said stoutly.

The rest of the subcommittee could take a detached view of her comment. But Ben Safford got elected by the people flowing through Charlene's hands.

"What exactly was Mrs. Bertilucci's problem?" he asked.

"Oh, the usual thing. She's over sixty-five, but she doesn't have a birth certificate to prove it. In the old days, we'd scramble around and dig up her immigration papers or her marriage license. But these days . . ."

Lou Flecker thought he heard an accusation. "Now, Mrs. Gregorian, I know a lot of people don't like the new Social Security regulations we've passed. But how have they made it harder for Mrs. . . . Mrs. Bertilucci to prove she's eligible?"

"Oh, it's not you," she said promptly. "It's the others—the ministers, the students, the volunteers. Helping senior citizens has become very trendy. That's fine, I suppose, but it's also trendy to wage war on bureaucrats. Fifteen years ago Mrs. Bertilucci would have come in here with her daughter and we would have settled everything in no time."

Flecker conscientiously followed every word. He still did not see the problem. "Why can't she do that now?"

"Because she can't even get out of her own house without attracting a—a—" Charlene's plump little paws fluttered graphically—"a swarm of do-gooders. Everyone is ready to champion her when we try to grind her under our heel. By the time the whole gang gets here, the daughter's lost control—that was her, fanning herself—the old lady's hysterical and nobody will listen to a word we say."

Mrs. Hollenbach was less shaken by this vision of unbridled emotion than her male colleagues. "It's regrettable," she said, "but it makes no real difference, does it? Mrs. Bertilucci ends up with her Social Security checks."

Charlene was a good-humored woman. "It doesn't make any difference to Mrs. Bertilucci," she agreed. "And I suppose you could say that all the wasted time doesn't cost us more than three GS-10 salaries a year."

Having scored her point, she contemplated her visitors genially.

"But why complain? What we're losing is peanuts—compared to the way Medicaid is being ripped off. Quen, did you tell them about the nursing homes . . . ?"

By the time Ben Safford reached home that evening he was a troubled man. His brother-in-law took one look and sympathetically handed him a glass without asking questions. His sister Janet, however, had hospitality on her mind.

"I'm sorry we're not getting to see the others until tomorrow," she said, bustling in with a tray. "We could have arranged dinner tonight."

"It's just as well," Ben said. "After what we learned about Medicaid in this town, nobody was in any mood for a party."

Janet was ruffled. The Safford seat in Congress was very much a family affair. Ben not only continued to maintain bachelor quarters in the big old house that he and Janet had inherited, he also relied on his sister, his brother-in-law and his tribe of nieces and nephews to mend fences, hit the campaign trail and provide political intelligence. Anything happening in Newburg that escaped the attention of one Lundgren or another was a rarity.

"Well, what did you expect?" she demanded with asperity. "You just spent a month looking into Medicaid abuse everyplace else. Did you think Newburg would be different?"

Ben hated to admit it, but that was exactly what he had thought. "I knew there'd be hell to pay once the Cincinnati papers started running stories naming the Newburg Seven. But it isn't just Medicaid, Janet. You wouldn't believe what goes on at the Social Security office."

"Oh, wouldn't I?"

Belatedly, Ben recalled the network of activities that took Janet into hospitals, schools, churches—and, presumably, welfare offices.

"All right. But you can't say that I don't do a lot with Social Security. Whenever I get a complaint, I do something, don't I?"

She sniffed. "You mean Madge calls somebody at headquarters. Forget about the Washington end, Ben. It's high time you saw what goes on at the Newburg level."

"Oh, let the man enjoy his drink," urged Fred Lundgren, a large, peace-loving man. "Like it or not, Ben's going to be seeing plenty of the seamy side of Newburg life."

"That's what the woman at Social Security kept saying," Ben told them without enthusiasm.

"Charlene?" said Janet. "I work with her quite often. She's got a lot of sense, Ben."

"I was afraid of that," he said with a groan. "I suppose you know all these damn doctors, too. Seems to me you spend half your time lining up medical attention for people, or finding nursing homes."

His relatives stared at him, then laughed aloud.

"You really do lead a protected life in Washington, don't you?" Janet finally said. "Doctors don't do things like that anymore. It's all social workers now."

Fred flourished his glass. "You don't see a doctor these days until you're lying there waiting for him to start cutting. Or," he added in the interest of greater accuracy, "unless you're selling something they want."

Ben had recently accumulated some information of his own about the medical profession. "I thought they all drive Cadillacs."

Fred Lundgren owned the Ford agency in Newburg, the largest dealership in southern Ohio.

"Sooner or later, plenty of them switch to Lincolns," he said comfortably. "And the younger ones give me a lot of business in four-wheel drives. Yes, I bet I've met every single doctor in Newburg."

"Including the Newburg Seven?" Ben asked provocatively.

"See them all the time. Hell, they've got to spend that money somewhere, don't they?"

Ben did not argue. "Have you seen them since they hit the headlines, Fred?"

After thinking about it for a moment, Fred said, "Only in passing. Now that you mention it, they've been making themselves scarce. I suppose they don't want to do much talking about this mess."

The oven bell brought Janet to her feet. But she paused at the door for a final observation:

"They don't want to discuss it with outsiders. But I'm sure they're doing a lot of talking among themselves, aren't you? I wonder what they're saying."

3

While the Newburg Seven might not be talking to the outside world, they were making sure to be seen by it. The next evening, the head of the local AMA showed the flag by accompanying two of the elect, and their wives, to a symphony performance in Cincinnati. Two other doctors hauled their wives out to the Trianon, Newburg's fanciest restaurant, for an extended meal designed to prove that they had nothing to be ashamed of. The remaining three were on display in the dining room of the Newburg Country Club. They were placed at a table for five because Dr. James Rojak was one of Newburg's swinging singles.

Except in giant cities, doctors are almost forced to socialize together. Who else can afford the price tag of their amusements, who else can arrange to play golf regularly at noon on Wednesdays, who else can close down an office for a week's medical convention, a two-week jaunt to Hong Kong, a four-month vacation in South America? They learn to live with each other in spite of different tastes. Howard and Connie White, in their late forties, were tanned enthusiasts of the beach life, from Cape Cod to the Bahamas to Acapulco. Arnold Deachman, while only a few years older, gave the impression of belonging to another world and another generation. White was lean, but Deachman was thin to the point of emaciation. White was wearing a navy-blue blazer and a white turtleneck;

Deachman's three hundred dollars' worth of tailoring was formal enough for a funeral. Both men projected an aura of success, but White normally exhibited an innocent satisfaction in this state of affairs, while Deachman was always alert for imperfections in his universe. He had found one that very afternoon.

"That lawyer of mine claims we have no case against these newspapers," he reported angrily. "Well, I certainly am not taking his word for it. I'll get another opinion, and if he thinks I'm going to pay some fat bill for that kind of help, he's in for a surprise."

His old friend had some advice for him. "You'll be wasting your time, Arnie. I went to mine yesterday and he said the same thing." White was pleased to have a new nugget of information. "It seems that reporters have the right to print government statistics."

"They don't have the right to defame me," Deachman retorted roundly. "There must be some way to stop them."

Neither Deachman nor White was pleased to discover that the third doctor was grinning sardonically. "Why don't you both wise up? The damage is done now. We know that we're simply beating the establishment at its own game. But newspapers don't raise their circulation by being realistic. They've got to pretend to be on a moral crusade. So there's no point in whipping yourself up about it. They're just doing their thing."

This authentic voice of the seventies had been a familiar instructor in modern values for over a year now. The Deachmans and the Whites had been spending most of their spare time together for two decades. Jim Rojak, fifteen years their junior, was a comparative newcomer to the group.

Connie White was always telling her husband that Rojak helped keep them abreast of the times. But today she had her own reasons for thinking that he had gone too far.

"It's all very well to be so detached, Jim," she protested, "but people are beginning to pay attention to these stories. Quite intelligent people, too. Do you realize that the Sierra Club is hesitating about reappointing me to the education committee?"

Rojak laughed outright. "Use your head, Connie," he urged, "and your clout, too. Why do you think you got on that committee in the first place? Just tell them you're reconsidering your annual donation and they'll get back into line fast enough."

Connie half admired, half deplored this frankness. Her husband rose above it. "This is more important than Sierra Club committees, Jim. And you can't fool me that you enjoy being painted as some sort of crook any more than we do."

"It will die down." Rojak shrugged indifferently. "In the meantime I can live with it."

"That's right," Nesta Deachman said coolly. "This is just a cheap publicity gimmick. As soon as the next sensation comes along, the papers will forget all about us. Everybody knows that."

Connie stiffened. Like many a middle-aged woman before her, she welcomed guidance about the brave new world from an attractive younger man. The same tuition from a younger woman raised her hackles. When Arnold Deachman, two years earlier, had divorced his wife to marry his beautiful nurse, he had disrupted Connie's life almost as badly as Margaret Deachman's. From the day he led Nesta to the altar, Connie was doomed to sit across tables listening to Nesta dismiss housewives, their children, their recipes. When the talk turned to fee scales or prepayments, Nesta did not withdraw into the PTA. Oh, no, she was right in there, a professional among professionals. Then in the powder room, while Connie vigorously brushed her sun-bleached crop, Nesta would comb a luxuriant cloud of black hair and provocatively moisten a finger to smooth the dark eyebrows that arched over astonishingly blue eyes.

And, to top it all, Connie had to watch Nesta coax displays of uxoriousness from Arnold that Howard White would never match in a million years. Luckily, on this occasion Nesta had rubbed her husband the wrong way.

"You forget, Nesta, that, unlike Jim here, I have a family to consider. They're just starting out in the world and they're being exposed to all this filth, they're reading these innuendoes." Deachman paused to make the strongest possible effect. "I not only have to think about my children, I have to think about my grandson."

Nesta was careful about some children. "If little Trigger is reading any innuendoes, he's making headlines himself," she said indulgently.

This sally elicited reluctant smiles, even from Connie White. Arnold Deachman Taggert had been born only six months ago, but he had already achieved a hammerlock on his grandfather's affections.

"That's beside the point," Deachman said with the fretful authority that was second nature to him. "I can tolerate passing discomfort as well as anyone. This may have permanent consequences."

"You're right on the button, Arnie." White's forehead was creased by an unaccustomed frown. "We've worked hard to establish our reputations and we've been looked up to in this community. If you ask me, it's a crying shame to have all that go down the drain because some reporter wants a front-page byline."

In many ways Jim Rojak was the most straightforward person there. As long as he could keep his license to steal, he did not insist on public acclaim.

"Who cares what the bastards in Newburg think?" he demanded. "They're probably all ripping off something on the side themselves. What gives them the right to be so superior?"

"Nobody has suggested this is a question of moral superiority," Deachman snapped.

Rojak nodded approvingly. "That's just it. This is a question of power. We're the doctors and we've got the power to run our practices any way we want. All the talking in the world isn't going to change that. We run the hospitals, we run the whole damn health-care system. People may not like our methods, but if they want any treatment, they've got to come to us. It's that simple."

Deachman could not disagree, so he cast around for some other target. "All this worry is playing hell with my stomach, and I don't even have my pills," he complained, fussing through the contents of his pockets. "Nesta, you know I shouldn't leave the house without them. Why in God's name didn't you remind me?"

"Because you resent being reminded almost as much as not having them. So *I* brought them." With a flourish she produced a small container from her evening bag. "I may not be able to stop the pressure, dear, but I can see that you take proper care of yourself."

This display of wifely solicitude mollified Deachman. "Tit for tat," he said with creaking playfulness. "You remembered to bring my tablets and I remembered to deposit the money for your coat."

"Oh, Arnie!"

But even as Nesta rhapsodized, her eyes slid sideways to Connie White and her lips folded in a secretive smile of satisfaction. Connie bit down hard. When Nesta's mink coat had first been mentioned, Connie had instinctively reminded everyone of her commitment to the preservation of wildlife. She forgot what she had managed to produce in honor of the diamond bracelet and the Mercedes convertible, but even to her own ears these protestations were beginning to sound like sour grapes.

"Aren't you lucky, Nesta?" she said, forcing herself into feminine enthusiasm. "I can hardly wait to see it."

But now that Howard White had begun his career as a worrier, he was finding material in unlikely corners. "For heaven's sake, I hope you're going to be tactful, Nesta. This isn't the best time to flaunt thousands of dollars' worth of fur in Newburg."

Rojak was amused. "That's good, coming from you, Howard. Whose boat was on the front page this morning? And how much did that yacht set you back, anyway?"

"Dammit, that picture is over a year old. There wasn't anything I could do about it. And it's not a yacht, it's just a sailboat."

"Try explaining that to some of the clowns who've got to make do with a Sunfish." Rojak leaned forward persuasively. "Christ, Howard, I don't have anything against your boat. They may dig up an old picture of me with my plane any day. That's why I say it's no use sucking up to every would-be critic that comes crawling along. We're rich, everybody knows it, and instead of trying to hide it, we should be using it like a hammer. I'll tell you one thing: there isn't a merchant in this town who doesn't know that, long after the stories have stopped, we're still going to be big customers."

Howard White chose to think that yacht brokers warmed to him personally. He wouldn't believe that his money had anything to do with their cordiality.

"You're leaving a lot out, Jim," he said quietly. "There are plenty of people who aren't trying to sell us something. Like those Congressmen who are investigating us. You can afford to relax. You're third down their list of witnesses, and plenty can happen before they get to you. But I'm the one who has to testify tomorrow."

Deachman, who was second on the roster, naturally sympathized. "It's disgraceful that we should be pilloried in public this way. I told Perrin that it was the AMA's job to stop these hearings. But you know him—he has the backbone of a rubber band. He said it wasn't his job to get involved."

"He was absolutely right."

The four outraged gasps that greeted Rojak's statement brought an involuntary grimace to his lips. "Look, whose side do you think I'm on?"

"I sometimes think you forget when you're trying for an effect," Deachman said tartly.

Rojak shook his head. "You're not facing this sensibly. There's been a big story with headlines screaming corruption. Nothing in God's name could choke these pols off from their grandstand play. They've got to make themselves look good at our expense. Perrin would just be wasting leverage trying to stop the subcommittee."

"That's wonderful," White said sarcastically. "So you're saying I go on the stand tomorrow morning and it shouldn't bother me because nothing can stop it from happening. Even though anything I say may be wrong and there's everything at stake."

"Like what?"

White stared.

Rojak repeated his challenge. "Like what? Oh, I admit it may be embarrassing at the time. I don't expect you to enjoy it, and I won't either when my turn comes. But it's all a bunch of hot air. What do you think they can do to us? Take away our license to practice medicine?"

From the uproar, he might have suggested the House of Representatives could have them drawn and quartered.

"For Chrissake, Jim," exclaimed White, "what are you talking about?"

Connie was just as shaken. "They can't do anything like that."

"I should think not," Deachman said. "Laymen have no call to interfere with professional standards."

Nesta alone did not bite. "Oh, for heaven's sake, don't let Jim get you going. Congressmen don't have any jurisdiction to yank medical licenses."

But nobody was listening to her, and Rojak went on enjoying the tumult he had created. "No, I haven't lost my marbles. I'm simply reminding you that this subcommittee can't stop us practicing. So what's the next thing bugging you?"

They were now on delicate ground and Howard White had difficulty choosing the right words.

"Of course I was never worried about practicing as such. But I don't want any interference either." For a moment he stalled, unable to get over the hump. "The thing is, we've all worked out the routines under which we do our best work. I don't say there isn't an occasional clerical error. But what's that compared to the cures we effect? My office is set up for a certain flow and I don't want anybody tampering with it."

Jim grinned understandingly. He had no trouble following his colleague's thoughts. "You mean you don't want HEW claiming we can't submit any more Medicaid billings? Well, that's the point at which Perrin comes into his own. That's when he does his work. Medicaid and Medicare give the patient the right to choose his own doctor. That hands the AMA all the ammunition they need if any dummy in Washington thinks he can blacklist us. They can scream their heads off about not depriving the patient of his rights. Perrin will like it because he doesn't have to sound as if he's covering for us, and every MD in Newburg will back him. Give these bozos the right to select doctors and we might as well have socialized medicine and be done with it."

Part of the gloom oppressing White and Deachman had been the sense of isolation from their fellows. At this prediction of professional solidarity, they both brightened.

"I suppose HEW might try to recover some of the past billings." Deachman was quasi-judicious now, all signs of temper dissipated.

"Don't you believe it!" Rojak snorted. "Why do you think they published those totals? First, it's all they've got. There aren't any breakdowns they can use. Second, they can't lay a finger on us and they know it. So they try and embarrass us into being good little boys. Well, they need more than that, as far as I'm concerned."

Nesta was right in step with him. "All it takes is enough guts to outface them. They're used to dealing with people who run if you say boo. Well, that's not us, is it, Arnie?"

While her husband accorded only tempered enthusiasm to this view, Howard White was more responsive.

"Here, boy!" he called. "Get me the wine waiter. We're going to have some champagne to this."

The sommelier was living proof of Rojak's thesis about merchants and customers. The wine waiter was almost reverential as he sold White the most expensive magnum in the cellar.

When it came, White could hardly wait for it to be chilled. "You've been right all along, Jim," he said with heartfelt relief. "That damned subcommittee can't touch us at all."

Rojak was watching the bubbles rise in his glass with dreamy content. "It's better than that, baby. Nobody in the whole world can touch us."

4

Champagne produces a glow, not a roaring fire. Jim Rojak was coaxing the last drops out of the bottle when Arnold Deachman pushed back his chair.

"Time for us to be going, Nesta," he announced. "Jim, Howard—I'm glad we had a chance to talk this thing through."

"Calling it a night already?" Rojak protested. But he obediently jammed the bottle down into the ice bucket and rose to assist Nesta.

"Arnie and I are real early birds, Jim," she murmured. "Howard, the champagne was just lovely. Thank you so much."

This reminded Deachman of a nicety. "Howard," he said, "good luck with the subcommittee tomorrow. Remember, you've got a lot of friends rooting for you. Coming, Nesta?"

Rojak was about to follow the Deachmans when he saw that neither Howard White nor Connie had budged.

"We're staying on for a couple of dances," explained White.

For a moment Rojak suspected champagne-inspired bravado. But Connie, who had a harder head than her husband, was determinedly cheerful, too.

"You're absolutely right, Jim," she said. "About not letting them embarrass us. Howard and I love to dance, and that's what we're going to do any time we please—including right now!"

"Enjoy yourselves," said Rojak, indifferent to the gesture and to dancing at the sedate Newburg Country Club. "Give me a call tomorrow, Howard, and let me know how it goes."

"Absolutely," White said, tapping his foot to the energetic rhythms that the three-man combo was striking up.

Connie jumped to her feet and tugged at him. "Come on, Howard —or Jim! How about you?"

"No, I'd better be moving," he said, with a hasty farewell salute.

The Whites danced extremely well, especially with each other. They executed intricate maneuvers with flawless timing and swirled smoothly around the dance floor while others shuffled through two-steps. Their performance was more athletic than graceful, but it was skilled.

However, they were always having trouble with duffers. A dazzling twirl at the finale of "Galveston" cannoned them into another couple steering a more modest course.

"Oops—sorry!" said White, breathing heavily from his exertions. "Fred Lundgren! What brings *you* here?"

Fred Lundgren had belonged to the Newburg Country Club for years, but he didn't find it necessary to say so. He greeted Fred Astaire and Ginger Rogers civilly and waited for them to twinkle away.

Unfortunately, Connie White had to demonstrate how unembarrassed she was. Brightly she said: "Janet! I've been meaning to call you for weeks! Margie Flannery told me that you're organizing the WNCH Telethon—"

Fred interrupted to introduce his partner. "Mrs. Hollenbach, may I present Mrs. White—and Dr. White."

Elsie placed Howard White instantly. Medicaid bills of one hundred seventy-three thousand dollars. She nodded courteously but silently.

Connie's contrition was exaggerated. "Oh, dear! My awful memory for faces. You know, I blame it on Howard having so many patients. It's hard to keep everybody straight!"

"Well, it's good seeing you here, Fred," said Dr. White with meaningless geniality. "Nice to have met you, Mrs. Hollenborn—"

There were limits to Fred's good nature. "Congresswoman *Hollenbach* is here in Newburg for the subcommittee hearings," he said firmly enough to break up this unfortunate encounter.

Mrs. Hollenbach was ready to second him. "It's been a pleasure," she said, preparing to yield the dance floor.

The Whites, however, could not leave well enough alone. In rapid succession they passed from surprise to consternation.

"Congresswoman Hollenbach! Of course," said Dr. White with chagrin. "I beg your pardon."

"Not at all, Doctor," said Elsie, moving faster.

But Mrs. White trailed after them. "That's right, your brother-in-law's on the subcommittee, too, isn't he, Mr. Lundgren? I suppose you know that Howard will be testifying tomorrow morning, don't you, Mrs. Hollenbach?"

Talking compulsively, she dogged Elsie, leaving Fred with no alternative but to bring up the rear with Dr. White. The whole caravan arrived at the table where Janet, Ben and Val Oakes were enjoying their after-dinner coffee as only non-dancers can.

"Mrs. Lundgren!" Connie cried. "Can you imagine! I mistook Mrs. Hollenbach for you when we bumped into her—literally bumped into her, didn't we, Howard?"

"Yes, we certainly did," said Dr. White with a hearty smile that didn't reach his eyes.

For once, Janet's composure was not equal to the occasion. She stared blankly at the Whites, then at her husband. Fred, who had an unpredictable sense of humor, said, "You can never tell who you'll meet when you're dancing. Want to try this one with me, Janet?"

The situation was getting out of hand when Elsie Hollenbach intervened. "Ben," she said with a sympathetic look at Janet, "I don't know if you know the Whites . . . ?"

This broke the trance. Janet pulled herself together, introductions were performed and somehow the Whites were sitting down. Fortunately, Mrs. White's nervous vivacity seemed to have subsided, so they were spared relentless small talk. Dr. White, in fact, opted for a certain openness.

"I expected to see your committee down at the Federal Building tomorrow morning, Mr. Safford—not here at the club tonight. If I'd known you were all going to be here, I'd have brought my lawyer along."

"We're off duty right now," Safford replied briefly. He did not want to disconcert Dr. White, but he was not encouraging familiarity either.

"Besides, we're not all here," said Val Oakes with deceptive easiness. "You're safe for the time being, Doctor."

With a stickler's precision Mrs. Hollenbach enlightened White. "As you perhaps know, there are two other members of our subcommittee. But they were not able to accept Fred and Janet's hospitality tonight."

"Oh," said White. Then, with an effort: "Well, I wish I looked forward to meeting them. I suppose I shouldn't say that. Tomorrow isn't going to be too bad, is it?"

He struck only one responsive chord. "For heaven's sakes, of course not," said Connie White vigorously. "You don't have anything to hide, so what is there to be afraid of?"

Val Oakes, of all people, took pity on Dr. White. While everybody else pretended not to hear Connie White's challenge, he tackled it head on: "Nothing I admire more than a wife who sticks up for her husband. The Angel in the House—isn't that what the Poet calls her? Her price is above rubies, isn't it, Ben?"

This magniloquence naturally flabbergasted Mrs. White. Satisfied that there would be no more trouble from her, Val contemplated the doctor.

"And your good wife is right. All we're going to do tomorrow morning is ask you a few questions. You'll get the opportunity to tell the truth and shame the devil."

Unexpectedly, White responded to the substance, not the flourishes. "I know you're going to have questions," he said, "but I'm planning a prepared statement that I want to read."

Ben was willing to encourage a pedestrian discussion of procedure. "You can read a statement, or you can just submit it for the record."

White was stubborn. "I want to present it myself."

"I'm sure the chairman will consider it," said Ben cautiously.

White wanted to argue further, but thought better of it. "Well, we'll be going over all this tomorrow, won't we?"

"We sure will," said Val Oakes largely.

White acknowledged him ruefully. "I repeat, I wish I could say I was looking forward to it. Connie . . . ?"

The Whites' departure left a silence waiting to be filled. Fred Lundgren obliged. "He's not the brightest guy in the world. But White's got more on the ball than you might think."

Connie White knew this better than anyone else. Unlike his patients and his fellow doctors, she alone heard the true Howard White. Tonight his monotone filled the car all the way home.

". . . sometimes Jim Rojak is too damned smart for his own good, but this time he's right, Connie. I can handle them. I can handle them with no problem at all."

For some reason, this made her nervous all over again.

5

The Subcommittee on Medicaid Abuse assembled at nine o'clock the following morning and summoned its first witness thirty minutes later. Dr. Howard White requested and received Lou Flecker's permission to read a statement, and did so with relish. The script had been prepared by the lawyer at his elbow, but White enjoyed reviewing his qualifications, his experience, his dedication. In the audience, Mrs. White clasped her hands in her lap and watched him worshipfully.

". . . doctor-patient relationship. This calls for long and arduous training on the part of the physician, and trust and confidence from the patient. . . ."

By now the subcommittee had heard such self-serving outpourings from Bangor to Passaic. A fog of boredom descended as White turned page after page, lifting only when he finally shuffled his papers into a neat rectangle. Wearily, Lou Flecker said: "Thank you, Doctor. We're happy to hear your introductory remarks. Now, since it's getting on toward noon, we'll take a luncheon recess and begin our questions to you about specific billings at two o'clock."

As the gavel fell, a nondescript man in gray strode to the witness table and thrust a folded paper at Dr. White. White, who had been frowning at Flecker, glanced at it distractedly. Then he turned to his lawyer.

"Stayman," he said, too bewildered to lower his voice, "does this mean somebody's suing me?"

That roused Stayman. Jerking a warning thumb at the committee table, where Elsie Hollenbach, at least, was showing an interest, he began propelling White down the aisle. He could not keep his client quiet.

"Malpractice? What do they mean, malpractice? Stayman—"

The man in gray had stepped aside to let them pass. When the pneumatic door-closer cut Dr. White off in mid-sentence, he approached the subcommittee table.

"Are you a process server?" Flecker demanded severely.

"Not exactly. I'm the attorney for the plaintiff. Theodore Karras is my name and I think I may owe you an apology, Mr. Chairman."

Ben, standing to get the stiffness out, decided that there was some justice in Janet's claim that Congressmen lead protected lives. It was years since he had seen a lawyer like Karras. In Washington they all wore expensive clothes, carried attaché cases and flourished Philippe Patek watches. Attorney Karras' hard, shiny suit could have come from a discount store. A battered red accordion envelope held his papers.

Testily, Flecker said: "You could have served your summons someplace besides this hearing room."

Karras was unawed. "It's not easy to catch Dr. White in Ohio. For all I know, he's heading to Cape Cod as soon as he's testified. But that's not why I want to apologize."

"Oh?" said Flecker.

"You see, White's usefulness to you as a witness may be limited," Karras continued serenely, "now that he's the subject of judicial proceedings. And I'm going to need some HEW records that you may have planned to use. I don't like to wreck your timetable, but naturally my client's interests come first."

Congressmen have grown leery of a reporter's duty to his sources and an attorney's duty to his clients. Lou Flecker swallowed hard. But Val Oakes was less inhibited.

"It's a convenient time for your client's rights to surface," he observed. "Maybe you ought to apologize to Dr. White's lawyer. *He's* going to have to face the jury."

"Stayman? Oh, he doesn't have to worry. He'll be out of this. And, for that matter, a jury may be, too." Karras picked up his envelope with a half-smile. "I won't keep you from lunch. I just wanted to make sure you knew the score."

Then, with a gesture that was more benediction than farewell, he drifted toward the hall, where he was lost in the shuffling throng.

Tony Martinelli waited until the coast was clear. "Does that joker think we're dumb? Tell us the score? Hell, we still don't know the half of it."

Mrs. Hollenbach shook herself briskly as she rose. "Don't worry about it, Tony," she advised. "I have a strong feeling that people will be falling over themselves explaining this situation to us."

There were, as she predicted, explanations on all levels for several days.

One of the first came from the director of Newburg's HEW.

"I'm sorry to ask you down on such short notice. I hope I'm not disrupting your schedule," Quentin Trumbull began.

"What schedule?" Martinelli asked realistically. "Once Dr. White was back in the witness chair yesterday, his lawyer socked us with the need for a week's recess—"

"I got a subpoena, too," Trumbull said in agitation. "For documents in the HEW files. And Theo Karras is going to be dropping by any minute now to pick them up."

Lou Flecker scented danger. "Trumbull, if you've asked us to come down here to help figure out how HEW and this plaintiff can stick a knife into Howard White, you can think again. We have other fish to fry."

There was a stranger sitting by Trumbull and at this he intervened. "No, no, Mr. Congressman, I don't work for HEW."

Belatedly, Quentin Trumbull performed introductions. Lawrence Fournier was a vice-president of Great Lakes Insurance Company. And, as Fournier himself amplified grimly, Great Lakes carried Dr. Howard White's malpractice insurance, and most of the malpractice insurance in Newburg County.

"So Larry here will be representing Dr. White's interests, and Karras of course is acting for the patient," said Trumbull to allay any suspicions on that score. "But that's not what worries me. It's this subpoena by Karras. He knows exactly what to ask for—the dates of billings, the amounts, our own file and document numbers. I don't see how he can have all that information unless he's actually been in our files."

The sanctity of files rarely worries outsiders. "Just what are these billings that Mr. Karras is using against Dr. White?" Mrs. Hollenbach demanded, brushing aside the lawyer's source of information.

Over Fournier's objection, Trumbull said: "Dr. White billed HEW on three separate occasions for performing a complete hysterectomy on Mrs. Wanda Soczewinski. Then, this year he billed us for an abortion on her."

Val Oakes turned to Lawrence Fournier. "And Great Lakes is handling White's defense?"

Stiffly, Fournier concurred.

"It should be a lulu," said Val jovially.

Fournier remained unsmiling. "There isn't going to be any defense if HEW hands those documents over. I'm here to ask Trumbull to demand a hearing."

Genuinely curious, Ben Safford asked: "On what grounds?"

"The confidentiality of medical records," said Lawrence Fournier.

"But Mrs. Wanda Soczewinski *is* the patient," Trumbull protested. "Anyway, this isn't HEW's fight. The court has ordered us to hand over the records, so that's what we're doing."

Their wrangle might have continued, but Trumbull's secretary entered, ushering in Theodore Karras. He lost no time. Leaning over the desk, he painstakingly checked items on his list. There was a liberal residue of cigarette ash on his jacket, and his eyeglasses were ancient steel-framed spectacles. But being the shabbiest man present did not impair his spirits.

"Fine," he said at last. "Everything I need is here. Thanks, Trumbull."

Fournier could not restrain himself. "You're putting the screws on White and on Great Lakes even though you know he never went near your client. That's a great touch."

"And new, I think," said Karras mockingly. "But you never can tell—it may catch on."

"Like hell it will!" Fournier shot back. "You're not going to make a career of suing these—" Abruptly, he decided on a new tack. "Now look, Karras. Think of the hardship this is going to cause a lot of innocent bystanders. The committee here can't hold its hearings. HEW is going to get raked over the coals about security. Great Lakes is going to be bled. Dr. White—"

"Crap!" Karras interrupted harshly. "You don't know what you're talking about. Sure, the committee and HEW will have to make some adjustments. And Great Lakes will cover its losses by raising rates. But if you want to know what hardship is, you ought to see what Mrs. Soczewinski has to put up with."

"Save your eloquence for a jury," Fournier said sourly.

But Karras' emotion had subsided. "If Great Lakes is as smart as it's cracked up to be, there won't be any jury, Fournier."

"We'll see about that."

Fournier's defiance lasted long enough for Karras to make an offhand farewell and depart.

"He's right," Fournier grunted. "We can't take this thing to court."

Lou Flecker, meanwhile, was putting two and two together. "And you think Karras managed to buy his way into HEW files?" he said to the unhappy Trumbull, who shrugged helplessly. "You know, I'm getting curious about him. Ben, this is your hometown. Is he some kind of crook?"

"I never heard of him," said Safford, shaking his head. "I'm going to ask around. But, Lou, if he's a crook, he's a pretty smart one—no matter how he got his hands on HEW files. He's got White and Great Lakes over a barrel, doesn't he?"

Congressman Martinelli was appreciative. "It's beautiful," he said, disregarding the feelings of others. "White bilks Medicaid for operations he never performed. But those fake records for hysterectomies, then an abortion, let the patient claim that the doctor bungled the hysterectomy. White can't come out and say he was just ripping off HEW. So the patient gets the judgment. And unless the patient's a real dog, Fournier, Karras is going to take you for a bundle."

His ebullience infected Quentin Trumbull. "I called Charlene Gregorian to find out about the patient," he said, grinning as he named his authority. "Wanda Soczewinski was a nice, hard-working girl who married her high-school sweetheart, who was a nice, hard-working boy. They had two children and they were a credit to the community." The grin faded. "Then the husband got multiple sclerosis. He's back home, slowly wasting away, while Wanda supports the family with a welfare check. Karras wasn't far wrong when he said we didn't know what hardship is."

Fournier responded defensively. "What am I supposed to say? Sure, Karras has a dream client. And I'll go further: he's got a dream case. No, as much as I hate to admit it, Karras is right. There won't be any trial."

Insurance companies may deserve sympathy, but they rarely get it.

"Karras was right about something else, too," said Tony Martinelli robustly. "You'll pass your loss along by raising rates—and that will be the end of it."

Suddenly, Lawrence Fournier went on the attack. "There's where you're wrong, Mr. Congressman. It won't be the end by a long shot, except for Dr. White. Because Great Lakes will yank his malpractice coverage. And I personally will see to it that no other company touches him with a ten-foot pole. Believe me, it won't be hard."

6

Dr. Howard White's lawyer was trying to deliver the same message.

"But, Stayman, that's why I've been shelling out a fortune for malpractice insurance, isn't it? To protect myself against shakedowns like this."

Morton Stayman studied his client. He was still not altogether sure where the boundary between deception and self-delusion lay. "It's a little more complicated than that, Howard," he said slowly. "Just let me take it from the top. Great Lakes will certainly settle this Soczewinski suit out of court—no, let me finish—because you don't have any defense. Are you with me so far?"

Fright made Howard White shy at this sticking point again. Blustering, he said: "But I've paid through the nose—"

Stayman held up a hand. "And," he said implacably, "Great Lakes will decide that because of your fraud—"

"They're crooks! Her and that lousy lawyer!"

Patiently, Morton Stayman waited. "If you say so, Howard, but let's stick with fraud. Now, Great Lakes may or may not try to recover from you."

They were, at last, pushing onto new ground. From Howard

White's sudden stillness, Stayman guessed that he was only now facing the full implications of the disaster.

"Time will tell," Stayman continued briskly, "but I advise you to prepare yourself. And, Howard, you'd better brace yourself for something else: no matter what they decide about recovering, Great Lakes is almost certainly going to cancel your malpractice insurance."

All of White's attention was fixed on the immediate financial threat. "Then I'll have to go to some other company," he muttered absently.

"If Great Lakes cancels, no one else will give you malpractice insurance—ever." Stayman underscored each word, using his pencil as metronome.

A full minute passed. Then, almost petulantly, White said: "But then I couldn't practice medicine."

"That's right."

Other Newburg lawyers were dealing with their clients. Dr. Arnold Deachman was doing the talking to one of them.

". . . no, I am *not* ready to testify before the committee—and you can tell them so. Look, you tell the committee to go jump in the lake. I've got more important . . . Yes, I'll be in your office at ten. . . . Right. . . . You're damned right it's an emergency."

Nesta Deachman, still in a peignoir, was drifting past the phone. Of all the luxuries Deachman had presented to her, leaving the breakfast dishes on the table for somebody else was one she never stopped enjoying. So, nine times out of ten, she was perfectly willing to play the adoring little woman.

But Nesta had been Arnold Deachman's nurse for four years before she married him. She knew far more about him and his affairs than Margaret ever had. And she knew, none better, the close connection between those affairs and the good things of life she was learning to enjoy so much.

"Arnie," she said when he hung up, "wouldn't it be better to have it over and done with, like Jim said?"

With tight self-control he said, "The situation has changed radically, Nesta."

Suddenly alert, she stood stock still. "Radically? But the subcommittee still can't do anything, can they?"

He looked at her dully and shook his head.

"What is it?" she demanded, her voice edged by alarm.

Suddenly Deachman's feelings overcame him. Forgetting his dignity, his position, his caution, he found himself talking and talking. Everything bottled up inside came spilling out—Theodore Karras, the HEW files, Great Lakes' threats.

Nesta stared at him, aghast. Even during the bitterly fought divorce she had never seen him like this, not even when he had realized how much the property settlement was going to cost him if he wanted Nesta.

"I'm sorry, Nesta," he mumbled, mopping his brow. "But you might as well know what we're up against. Testifying to the committee—well, that's nothing. But this suit against Howard is a time bomb for us all."

She was light-years ahead of him as he continued, "If Karras can get his hands on HEW files whenever he wants to, he's got a malpractice suit against me as well as Howard. He could blackmail every single one of us. And, Nesta, if that happens, I could face what Howard's facing." Breaking off, he averted his eyes. "I could lose everything."

Neither of them noticed that it was *I*, not *we*.

Nesta, in fact, was not listening at all. She was struggling with a sudden, overpowering dismay. With an effort, she pulled herself together. What Arnold needed now was support. She reached out to touch his arm. "It won't happen, Arnie. Don't torture yourself! It won't happen. It can't!"

Dr. James Rojak knew that it could happen. So he did not want explanations, he wanted preventive action.

"You're my Congressman, aren't you?" he said with a quirk of his lips. "Well, I want some protection. I'm not going to sit still and be a patsy—"

"Whoa," said Benton Safford. "Why don't we both sit down and talk it over?"

This response to a heated constituent was automatic. In his office, in Washington or out on Plainfield Road, it was reasonably effective. It did not work so well in the lobby of the Federal Building in Newburg, which Ben had just entered.

"Look," Rojak told him, "I've been upstairs talking to that creep Trumbull—"

"Why don't you tell me who you are and what this is all about?" Safford said bluntly. He had a deep-seated dislike of bullies.

The scowling young man facing him was taken aback. "Dr. Rojak," he snapped arrogantly. "Dr. James Rojak."

"Oh, yes," said a new voice. "One of our witnesses."

The arrival of Elsie Hollenbach defused the confrontation only superficially. Glancing from one to the other, Rojak said: "Yes, one of your witnesses. But *not* one of your sitting ducks."

"Precisely what does that mean?" asked Mrs. Hollenbach with glacial dignity.

Ben Safford answered for Rojak. "I think the doctor is worried about a possible malpractice suit, in light of what happened to Dr. White. Right, Rojak?"

Rojak did not conceal his hostility. "The doctor wants to know how some cheap lawyer got hold of confidential HEW information. Aren't you supposed to guard citizens' rights? Or do you and that guy Trumbull think you can play God?"

"Mr. Trumbull assures me that he does not know how HEW information reached Mr. Karras," said Elsie. "He is investigating."

"Oh, sure!" said Rojak with a contemptuous laugh. "Well, if you think I'm going to stand still, you've got another think coming."

With that, he stormed out, leaving Elsie and Ben free to continue upstairs.

"We may not be getting through to these doctors, but this guy Karras sure as hell is," said Tony Martinelli when Dr. Rojak's outburst was described. He stared out before him with lackluster eyes. There were lawyers pleading extenuating circumstances, requesting delays, protesting procedure. "Not a doctor in sight. They're scared to death. None of them mind robbing the Federal government blind, but mention a malpractice suit and you've got them where they live."

"Look on the bright side, Tony," Val Oakes told him. "Ben's friend Karras may have found a rough-and-ready way to reform medicine in Newburg. God knows it's more than Congress has been able to do."

Ben felt constrained to repeat that Theodore Karras was not a friend. "But here's to him anyway. I can hardly wait to hear the next installment—although I can do without more of Dr. Rojak."

As he was to learn within twenty-four hours, they came in the same package. The morning news carried the story into breakfast all over Newburg.

". . . attorney Theodore Karras. According to authorities, Karras was shot in his office on River Street. The body was discovered early this morning by Dr. James Rojak, a prominent allergist. The police are still investigating at the scene of the crime. . . ."

7

"Maybe you'd go over your story again for the stenographer, Dr. Rojak," Lieutenant Doyle suggested.

Rojak pinched the bridge of his nose with thumb and forefinger. "Why not?" he said with exaggerated weariness. "I've told it to everyone else."

"Thank you," said Lieutenant Doyle, unmoved, as he continued to inspect his witness.

Of medium height, Dr. Rojak conveyed an impression of driving strength. He was a blocky man with solidly set shoulders, a square head, a square face and even square hands. A quick check at Police Headquarters had already told the Lieutenant about the customized Porsche (three speeding violations), the six-seater Cessna at the airport (one citation for failing to file a flight plan) and the impressive collection of guns (all duly licensed).

At the moment, however, nobody would have envied Rojak.

"There isn't much to tell," he began. "I had an appointment with Karras. When I got here, I found him dead."

Doyle held up a hand. "Let's take it a little slower. This appointment of yours was for eight o'clock this morning? Isn't that pretty early to see a lawyer?"

"Not if you have hospital rounds to make. I can see you don't know much about doctors."

"I'm willing to learn," Doyle said mildly.

For an instant Rojak frowned. "When I got here, the maintenance man told me that Karras was in Room 201," he continued. "So I came up the stairs and walked in. You know what I found."

"Tell me anyway."

"Karras must have lived for several minutes after he was shot. At least, that's how it looked to me. I'd guess that he was hemorrhaging badly right from the beginning. Anyway, there was blood all over the place—the desk, the floor, the chair. I crossed into the room just far enough to make absolutely sure he was dead, but that was a formality, believe me. Then I ran downstairs and phoned you people from the drugstore next door."

Lieutenant Doyle was nodding like a mandarin as he consulted his notebook. "And Headquarters logged in your call at eight-oh-seven. So that accounts for your time, all right. And we appreciate it when public-spirited citizens get us on the scene as soon as possible—instead of just high-tailing it." He paused and smiled blandly. "But then you didn't have much choice, did you? The maintenance man saw you arrive."

Rojak took up the challenge immediately. "What difference does it make who saw me? It didn't need a medical degree to see that Karras had been dead for hours before I showed up. I don't know what kind of games you're trying to play, Doyle, but as soon as they do the autopsy, your own men will tell you that I couldn't have had anything to do with Karras' murder."

This was scarcely news to Doyle. The police doctor had already delivered the unofficial opinion that Theodore Karras had been shot during the previous evening. But innocent witnesses are usually unnerved by a corpse. Not this one, however. It was Jim Rojak's unnatural assurance that was holding Doyle's interest.

"There's one thing that puzzles me," he continued, "and that's the phone on Karras' desk. You couldn't have helped seeing it. So why go out to the drugstore?"

"For Christ's sake! Sure I saw the phone, but there was blood congealed all around and Karras' hand was brushing up against it. I knew the static I'd get from you people if I disturbed all that. It seemed safer to use another phone."

"Most people don't manage to keep their heads like that in an emergency."

The remark could have been congratulation or condemnation, but Rojak simply brushed it aside.

"Hell, it would have been different if the guy had a spark of life left. Then I suppose I would have just yanked the phone up and yelled for an ambulance. But with him already dead, a couple of minutes more didn't make that much difference."

"Probably not. As you say, he'd been shot hours earlier. By the way, Doctor, I see that you have a permit to carry a handgun in Newburg."

Rojak did not let him go any further. "Me and every other doctor in town. You know what that parking lot at the hospital is like at night. And it gets worse every year."

Doyle knew that doctors had a high rate of gun permits. This was not entirely due to police negligence, however. By and large, doctors were wealthy men with a predilection for cash. They lived in homes stuffed with jewels and furs. They operated out of offices stocked with drugs. And occasionally they were called to the hospital at night. They were prime targets.

No hint of these thoughts showed on Doyle's face. "Got the gun on you?"

"No, it's where it always is. In the glove compartment of my car."

"Mind if we take a look?"

Rojak reached into his pocket and produced a key ring, which he tossed over to the Lieutenant. "Be my guest," he said sarcastically. "It's the Porsche parked by the corner."

After that performance Doyle knew that the gun would be clean. It was with genuine pleasure that he pressed forward into an area where Rojak might be more vulnerable.

"While we're waiting, Doctor, let's talk about something else. You've explained why your appointment was so early and what you did when you got here. But you haven't told me what business you had with Karras in the first place. Or is that covered by the attorney-client privilege?"

Jim Rojak snorted. "Listen, when I need law work, I go to a reputable attorney, not some shyster. And let's not kid each other. I'll bet you know all about Karras' suit against Howard White."

"I've heard it mentioned," Doyle admitted.

He could scarcely have helped it. When Theodore Karras had served his summons inside the Federal Building, he had alerted the entire Courthouse fraternity of Newburg. Within minutes lawyers, judges, clerks, bailbondsmen and court reporters were buzzing.

Doyle had known all about *Soczewinski* v. *White* before Great Lakes or even Dr. James Rojak.

"Then you know he was pulling a fast one," said Rojak flatly. "It was no accident that the suit was filed after the Cincinnati papers did a job on us."

"I didn't think it was."

"Hell, that's why all seven of us had a meeting yesterday afternoon. We figured we were all in the line of fire. And that's why I wasn't surprised when Karras called me after dinner last night."

Doyle leaned forward intently. "Just out of the blue?"

"We'd never met, if that's what you mean. But, as I said, I was half expecting him to try and shake me down."

"Now, wait a minute. Is that what he said?"

"Of course not." Rojak was impatient. "He said he thought it was advisable for us to have a meeting to discuss something that had come up. So I said I'd see him at eight this morning."

Doyle expelled his breath in a long sigh. "So you're not sure what he had in mind?"

"Come off it! You only have to look at this dump." Rojak gestured expansively at the battered file cabinets, the old-fashioned paneling, the worn carpet. "What kind of lawyer practices out of an office like this? And everybody knows Karras greased some file clerk at HEW. He *had* to be pulling a fast one."

Lieutenant Doyle bit down hard as he recalled Dr. Rojak's billing methods. That was somebody else's problem.

"All right. We can't prove it, but let's assume that was what Karras had in mind. What were you going to do about it?"

Rojak stared back defiantly. "It depended how cheap he came. If he could be bought off with a couple of thousand bucks, I was going to pay him. But if he had big ideas, I wasn't. You know, I can pull up stakes and go practice someplace else. I don't say I want to. But I'd do it before I let myself be bled—and certainly before I shot somebody!"

Doyle doubted if the options were that simple, but he deferred the point in favor of a new idea. "Still, the mere possibility that Karras might file a malpractice suit was enough of a danger to bring you here pronto."

"It wasn't a danger, it was an inconvenience."

"Okay." Doyle accepted the correction amiably. "Call it an inconvenience. But then it would be an even bigger inconvenience if he already had filed suit."

Rojak narrowed his eyes instantly. "I don't know anything about that," he said.

Doyle's next witness did not see the implications quite so swiftly.

"It was a case of harassment, pure and simple harassment," Dr. White said firmly.

Jim Rojak carried his confidence with him wherever he went, but Howard White preferred to answer police questions in the reassuring atmosphere of his own office. When Rojak had voiced his opinion of Theodore Karras' quarters, Doyle had not felt its full force. From the viewpoint of Newburg's dilapidated police station, Karras had not seemed underprivileged. But from the viewpoint of this downtown professional building, nothing could be more tawdry than a grimy venetian blind.

Dr. White had his own interpretation of poverty.

"And I fail to see why you are taking up my time because of some crime in another part of the city," he concluded.

"I haven't singled you out, Doctor. I'm talking to all seven of you."

"But why are you bothering us when you should be investigating Karras' associates? A man like that could have been up to *anything*. He probably had Mafia clients. They're the ones you should be talking to."

Lieutenant Doyle sounded like a kindergarten teacher explaining the alphabet. "If Karras had been into the Mafia, he would have been a lot richer. Their lawyers aren't on the other side of town, they're right in this building."

"Then he was involved with low-level criminals," White insisted. "My point is that he didn't have anything to do with people like us."

"I don't see how you can say that. Karras had already filed suit against you. The others were afraid they might be next in line, afraid enough to join you in a general meeting yesterday afternoon. You must have been plenty bothered by him."

"We certainly were!" Dr. White agreed. "The whole situation is an outrage. We were being persecuted and the authorities were standing by, doing absolutely nothing. I was going to demand that the medical association take a very strong position."

Lieutenant Doyle stared across the desk. To his certain knowledge, Howard White was under subpoena by a Congressional committee, he was about to be hauled into a court of law by Wanda Soczewinski and he was being questioned by the police about a murder case. God only knew what other hot water he was in. And still he thought that the only authority that counted was the American Medical Association.

"I don't see what the medical association could do about Theodore Karras."

White blundered on. "Good God, it wasn't Karras we wanted them to pressure, it was Great Lakes." Belatedly, caution reared its head. "You wouldn't understand these technicalities, Lieutenant, but I can tell you it concerns the cost of malpractice insurance. If the company were to raise its rates, then the already high cost of medical care in Newburg would soar. And we all want to avoid that."

"As you say, Doctor, I wouldn't understand about technicalities like that," Doyle said smoothly. "So let's come to something I do understand. Can you tell me where you were yesterday evening from nine until midnight?"

"I suppose that kind of question is typical of our police force," White retorted. "As a matter of fact, I was right here. My accountant will corroborate that I was going to spend the evening assembling my records. For some reason, he wants even more material for this tax audit. Naturally, you're wondering why a doctor of medicine has to spend nights doing clerical work."

"No," said Doyle, rising. "No, that isn't what I was wondering."

It was the end of a long, hard day when Lieutenant Doyle reported to Chief Owen Jones.

"Well, I've seen all seven of them and, no matter how you slice it, they're a weird bunch," he summarized.

The Chief had swiveled sideways so that he was parallel to the desk, with his feet in a drawer, his head tilted to observe the ceiling and his hands cradling a cardboard cup of coffee.

"All doctors are like that," he growled.

"Maybe so. But some of them, somewhere, must have an alibi for last night."

"You mean none of yours do? I know you said Rojak was alone in his apartment and White was alone in his office. But, Jesus Christ, weren't any of them home with their wives?"

"So they say." Doyle shook his head dubiously. "But it doesn't work out that way from where I sit. Dr. Costello was home, all right, but from ten to eleven he was walking the family dog."

The Chief's eyebrows shot up. "It was pouring last night and he claims he walked the dog for a solid hour?"

Doyle spoke in a voice of doom. "Curryville just passed a leash law."

These cryptic words explained the whole situation to Jones. When Newburg's leash law had gone into effect, it had taken weeks for life to return to normal.

"And the others?"

"I had high hopes of Deachman. He went out to a dinner party with his wife. But he got called to the hospital around nine and didn't bother to go back. So the next thing we know about him is that his wife found him at home when she came in around eleven thirty. Then there's the guy who claims he never stirred from his house. Unfortunately, his wife had some kind of ladies' meeting, so he went down to his workshop and wasn't seen from eight to eleven."

"What the hell?" said Jones on a wave of fellow feeling. "That's what *I* do when Marge has the girls over."

"I'm not saying it couldn't be true. I'm just saying that none of them have alibis and they all have guns—nice, clean guns, fully loaded and freshly oiled."

"Ballistics any help?"

Doyle was disgusted. "Not on your life. The bullet passed through Karras' head and into the air-conditioner on the windowsill. The unit was on and the bullet got chewed up. All the lab boys will say is that it was a small caliber."

For a few moments the Chief of Police considered this information. Then, as if reaching a decision, he swung his feet to the ground and turned foursquare to the desk. "I admit the way this murder was timed, the doctors stand out like sore thumbs. But you don't want to lose sight of other possibilities, George. We don't know much about Karras. He could have had wife trouble, he could have been a chaser, he could have been into the loan sharks."

"Sure," Doyle agreed. "I've got a couple of men working on the background. But it doesn't look like it's going to give us much, Owen. Karras was sixty-five and a solid family man until his wife died a year and a half ago. Since then he's been working nights a lot, but otherwise his habits haven't changed. Every couple of weeks he goes to Cincinnati on business and he always stays with his married daughter. During school vacations she brings the grandchildren to Newburg for five or six days. On Sundays, regular as clockwork, he has dinner at his sister's. She and her husband own the Roadcoach Restaurant on Route 25."

"Oh, I didn't realize Karras was Nick Andreades' brother-in-law."

"He was, and Nick says there was no chasing. Just the opposite. The last month or so Karras has been squiring around some Greek widows. He wanted to remarry and have a home life again."

Jones sighed, but accepted the obvious. It was difficult to connect a crime of passion to a sixty-five-year-old widower in search of a congenial widow.

"What about money?" he continued.

"That's a washout, too. Karras' income is fully justified by his practice and he was living well within it. He never moved out of the old neighborhood and he was putting a little something by for the grandchildren."

"Maybe that explains the shakedown," Jones reasoned. "Maybe he wanted something bigger for the grandchildren."

Doyle grinned. "If you talked that way to Karras' secretary, you'd get your eyes scratched out. She says Karras never had any HEW documents until Mrs. Soczewinski brought hers in, and that he was pure as the driven snow. Of course, she's worked for him fifteen years, thinks he was a wonderful man and was crying buckets while I was there."

Owen Jones dismissed character references by devoted secretaries with a wave of the hand. "No reason why he should let her know what he was up to, anyway. But did she say anything about his appointments, either for last night or eight o'clock this morning?"

"No, and the diary didn't list any, either. But she says Karras was casual about logging appointments he made himself. He figured he'd remember them unless they were two weeks in the future."

"So we just have Rojak's word for his appointment—or the whole shakedown story, for that matter."

Lieutenant Doyle was determined to be fair-minded, even about witnesses he disliked. "You have to be reasonable. If Patrick Costello, for instance, went to a meeting last night that ended in his blowing someone's brains out, he sure as hell isn't going to tell us all about it."

"That applies to Rojak, too," Jones pointed out. "He could have gone back this morning because he thought it looked better, or because he left something behind."

"Or because someone else did." Doyle hesitated before continuing his speculation. "I'll tell you something I noticed about Rojak. He thinks the police are beneath him, and he didn't give a damn whether I liked most of his answers. But he went out of his way to justify using that drugstore phone. It's fishy as hell. He would have used the secretary's phone if he'd been willing to take a chance on being overheard. He wanted a nice, soundproof booth. And once he was there, I know he called us. But I'd give a lot to know who else he called."

Owen Jones plucked his lower lip thoughtfully. "We seem to have gotten right back to your doctors," he complained.

"You can't stay away from them. Look, when I said they were a weird bunch, I meant it. Any doctor in Newburg can make eighty thousand a year on the up-and-up. And plenty of them are satisfied with that. I expected to find these seven were extra greedy. But it's deeper than that. I also expected to find that they were embarrassed at being caught. Not on your life! They weren't embarrassed by the publicity, they were mad as hell. And that's before there was any real threat. Every single one of them is convinced he's got a God-given right to anything he wants and nobody should even ask questions." Doyle paused to order his thoughts. He was very serious. "After White let the cat out of the bag, I checked with Great Lakes. With Karras, it wasn't simply going to be a question of a mortifying cross-examination. He could put these bums out of business. And when bone-deep arrogance meets an obstacle like that . . ."

Jones supplied the conclusion for himself as Doyle's voice trailed into silence. "Then you expect bullets to start flying?"

Doyle screwed up his empty coffee cup and dropped it into the wastebasket as punctuation for his final observation.

"Well, it wouldn't surprise the pants off me."

— 8 —

While the police quietly moved around Newburg in civilian clothes and unmarked cars, the Cincinnati papers were not so discreet. Ever since naming the Newburg Seven, the *Inquirer* had followed every twist and turn in the scandal. Quentin Trumbull had been harried for one statement after another, the doctors had been photographed plunging in and out of cars, the subcommittee had been interviewed and Dr. White's testimony had received full coverage. Under these circumstances the murder of Theodore Karras became instant journalistic property. Within twenty-four hours everyone in southern Ohio knew that Karras had been shot down after starting a malpractice suit against Dr. Howard White.

The results of this paper onslaught were immediate. The HEW switchboard was jammed, the White household was in a state of siege, the subcommittee had adjourned for forty-eight hours and the Mayor of Newburg was yelling for his Congressman.

"I told him you'd be there first thing this morning," Janet said as she poured coffee.

A half-hour later Ben discovered that Mayor Wilford Wilhelm, normally a man who loved his work, was seriously perturbed.

"Ha! Congressman Safford," he barked.

Since they had been on first-name terms for years, Ben instinctively looked around. There was not a reporter—or a voter—in sight.

"We had a nice, peaceful town until you and that gang of yours stirred up the wild animals," said the Mayor sternly. At eighty plus, he was slowing down a little, but his voice was still in fine shape.

"What about the strike out at Frawley's?" Ben countered.

"Nobody got killed," said the Mayor, peering over his glasses at Ben.

"No," Ben conceded, without adding anything about rock-throwing, truck-burning or fistfights.

"Nice and peaceful," said Wilhelm firmly. This point established, he unbent. "Just had the Chief on the line. He says they're investigating a lot of leads. Pfa! Owen watches too much TV, that's the trouble."

Civic pride wanted an immediate arrest. But was there one in the works?

"That's why I told Janet to send you down, Ben," said Mayor Wilhelm craftily. "The Chief wants a crack at the dirt your staff has dug up on those doctors."

Under Wilhelm's wise old eyes, Ben was not going to pontificate on the relationship between Congress and local law-enforcement agencies. "All right. I'll give Owen a ring and we'll get together this afternoon."

Suddenly harsh, Wilhelm continued: "And I told him I wouldn't stand for any horsing around. You know how the police pussyfoot with doctors."

Ben did. In towns the size of Newburg, doctors seem to miss all the speeding tickets, even with liquor on their breath.

"I laid it on the line. Told him he can do whatever he pleases when he catches one of them in the Reservoir Motel with a high-school kid—but murder's different."

There is an old morality, as well as a new morality. Having expressed it, the Mayor relaxed. "Glad to get that settled. You shoot us whatever you can. The sooner we clean this up, the better. Hell, I've got a new incinerator to worry about."

Ben still had private doubts. There was almost too much information about the doctors available. What was lacking was information about Theodore Karras.

"Did you know him, Will?" Ben asked.

"Never met him in my life," said the Mayor, echoing Janet Lundgren and Fred. "Heard his name a couple of times."

"How come?" Murder apart, Ben was getting curious about his

dead constituent. How many Newburg lawyers had practiced as long as Karras with such a low profile?

"He had some clients who sued the city," said Wilhelm. "A couple of them got pretty good settlements, too."

This gave Ben a clue. Karras had been active, all right, but in different circles. It occurred to him that the man who knew about those circles was within walking distance. For many reasons, Ed Daly, chairman of the Newburg Democratic Organization, had offices close to the Courthouse, City Hall and the Federal Building.

Daly was reading the *Newburg News* when Ben strolled in.

"Henry wants to go to war to keep the Panama Canal," he said by way of greeting. Henry Hurd was the rock-ribbed Republican editor of the *News*. "It's all your fault, Ben."

Safford didn't see why until Daly spelled it out for him. Armed intervention in Panama was Henry's way of distracting public opinion from domestic events.

"So Henry's waving the flag," he concluded. "He's going to start pushing for us to annex Canada next. How are you, Ben? Stirred up a real mess this time, didn't you?"

Since Daly sounded amused, Ben inferred that the eruption of murder into the Medicaid hearings raised no problems at the polls that Daly could foresee.

"No, the police will eventually get whoever shot poor Theo, and that's that," said Daly. "As for going after local doctors—hell, everybody in Newburg is cheering you on. Except Henry Hurd of course. The only millionaires I advise you to watch your step with are basketball players."

Ben met realism with realism. "I'll try to avoid tangling with any rock singers."

Daly thought about it. "As long as they don't lower the voting age to twelve, you'd be safe. Speaking of teenagers, this employment bill . . ."

Ten minutes of shop talk ensued before Ben got around to asking his question.

"Sure, I knew Karras," said Daly. "And so did you."

A memory for names and faces was part of Congressman Safford's stock in trade. Without hesitation, he contradicted Daly. "Nope. First time I ever saw him was when he served that subpoena under Lou Flecker's nose."

"You sure, Ben?" Daly asked. "Theo was a poll-watcher down in the Third for years."

"What!" Ben was startled. True, his tour of the precincts on election day was a blurred montage. But if Theo Karras had been one of the party faithful . . .

"No," Daly reassured him. "Karras was the International Justice Party. Been big with them for years. I don't think he ever ran himself, but he was secretary, treasurer—you name it. Theo's the one who finally got them on the ballot. You remember that fight—ten, twelve years ago."

While Daly spoke, Ben tried fitting this piece into the picture. A small, one-man office in a rundown part of town, the International Justice crowd—a dwindling band of aging ideologues who had brought their lost causes with them when they arrived from the old country.

"Not the kind of guy you'd expect to try blackmail," Ben observed.

From his perch in Courthouse Square, Ed Daly had seen just about everything. "There's always Robin Hood."

"Robin Hood with a malpractice suit?" Ben wondered. Any quixotic romance in Theo Karras had been well hidden. "Speaking of robbing the rich to give to the poor, are you getting any feedback on the Curry River Flood Control Project?"

"Jobs," said Ed Daly, packing a lot into one word.

Ben left with plenty to ponder. Any politician worth his salt is a juggler, and even the best jugglers miss a trick now and then. The Curry River Flood Control Project was too big to fumble.

Lost in thought, Ben found that force of habit had led him to drop in at Phil's Coffee Shop. Phil was leaning over the counter, studying the *Newburg News*. For a customer he would have straightened. For Ben he stayed comfortable. "Hi, Ben. I see you got a big treat in store for you."

Ed Daly's appreciation of "Pound Panama!" had let him skimp another front-page feature: "PERRIN TO TESTIFY."

"What's this?" said Ben, unceremoniously appropriating the paper.

"Too cheap to spend a quarter, huh?" said Phil equably.

Ignoring him, Ben brought himself up to date. Chairman L. Lamar Flecker (D., Ala.), bowing to demands of the Newburg Medical Association, was allowing its president to read a statement to the Medicaid subcommittee when it resumed hearings.

Phil craned his neck. There were no customers within earshot.

"Perrin's a horse's ass," he said cheerfully.

"He has to be if he's going to stand up in public and defend Medicaid swindling," said Ben.

"You know these doctors. They think they've got a right to—"

Phil broke off in midsentence as two customers entered and headed for a booth. Summoning the smile of a host, he waited until they were settled before offering two menus.

"Morning, ladies. We've got some of the cinnamon coffee cake you like today."

The older, a woman around fifty almost obscured by a mound of shopping parcels, settled for this suggestion. Her companion, a pretty girl in her twenties, wanted blueberry cheesecake with her coffee. After they had been served, Phil returned to Ben and identified them.

"The first Mrs. Deachman," he said in a whisper that spoke volumes, "and the daughter."

Ben's eyebrows rose. "I suppose that means there's a second Mrs. Deachman."

Phil's hands sawed an hourglass from the surrounding air. "A real dish," he murmured. "Poor old Deachman never had a chance once Nesta Malone decided being a doctor's wife beat working."

Mulling over this exchange when he was back in his car, Ben wondered if the doctors yet realized the full consequences of being in the public spotlight. Arnold Deachman no doubt thought he had lived down his divorce. But today Phil could not see his ex-wife without remembering the circumstances—and passing them on. Ben was willing to bet that all over Newburg similar memories were reviving. If any of the White children had ever been busted in a drug raid, today's *Inquirer* would bring back the details for some people. If any of the doctors had a wife who had been dried out in a sanitarium or a son whose forged checks had been covered, it would all be part of dinner-table conversation tonight.

Except, of course, where there were more important things to worry about, like the Hackett farm, into which Ben pulled at the end of forty minutes.

Elroy Hackett shooed Alma and her hospitality away. "We've got business," he said sternly, leading Ben into his office.

Out near Murren there were farms with hex signs on the barns and colonial plows over the mantel. Elroy ran a real farm. He had a minicomputer on his desk and facts at his fingertips. He was also state chairman of the Farm Bureau.

". . . reducing the soil-conservation allotments. But hell, Ben, they shove this dam down our throats and we're losing ten thousand acres. And God knows what those damned fools will do to the water table."

Only Elsie Hollenbach had a lower opinion of the Army Corps of Engineers.

Ben listened. With Elroy, he didn't have to explain about pressure from Columbus, from Washington, from Newburg. Neither did he have to say he would do his damnedest. Acres and farmers were important to him, too.

"So you cogitate about it," said Hackett, his austere old face crinkling into a smile. "Now let's go see what that woman's up to."

Alma was ready for them in the kitchen with lunch and a little gentle gossip.

". . . Loomis' oldest boy—you remember him, Ben—he's getting married. And the Archibald farm is up for sale."

Both the lunch and information from an old friend were appreciated. Ben knew how to reciprocate.

"I suppose you've been reading all about the doctors," he said.

"Never would have believed it," she said. "And murdering this lawyer, too."

"Well, they're not sure they've gone as far as that," said Ben.

"From what it says in the paper, it sure sounds that way to me," she retorted.

"Now, Alma, you know you can't believe what you read in the paper," said Elroy weightily.

On this familiar theme Ben took his departure, gathering one more straw in the wind as Elroy accompanied him to the car.

"No, we haven't had a doctor out this way for twenty years. So, if I'm going to travel, I'm not going to settle for second best. Went up to Mayo for my gallbladder."

By two o'clock Ben was back in Newburg, satisfied that his morning had been well spent. He was not the only one who had been busy.

"I've packed your things, Arnie. Do you want to take some books with you?" Nesta Deachman closed the overnight case and looked at her husband, who was striding restlessly around their bedroom.

"Don't bother," he said absently. "Anything I need, Friend or one of the nurses can run out and get."

A shadow touched Nesta's lovely eyes. It was wonderful to see Arnie so collected. But there was such a thing as being too collected. "That's true. But, Arnie, you're supposed to be going into the nursing home for complete rest and relaxation, don't forget. It wouldn't look right for you to be asking the staff to run a lot of little errands for you."

"You think of everything, don't you, Nesta?"

"I'm sure Graham Friend will tell you the same thing," she persisted. "After all, our story is that this is an emergency. You're on the verge of collapse. . . ."

Seeing that he was not going to respond, she went on, "So I'll just put in something for you to read. Of course, I'll be coming by every day—"

"If Graham Friend thinks I should have visitors," he interrupted sardonically. Graham Friend would do exactly what Dr. Deachman told him, as they both knew.

This levity took her aback. "Oh, Arnie, don't," she said reproachfully.

"Just a joke," he said without apology.

"Well, this is no time for joking!"

Still pacing back and forth, he said over his shoulder: "Nesta, this would be easier on both of us if you'd stop fussing."

There was a moment's silence. Then, as if their last exchange had not taken place, Nesta said: "Once you're in Riverside, nobody will be able to bother you until the whole situation calms down."

He looked at her keenly. "Maybe *you* should be checking into Riverside instead of me."

This made her whirl away from the suitcase. "Will you please stop talking like that? You're the one the police have been questioning, aren't you?"

"Don't I know it," he retorted. "I've gone through it once and I don't intend to do it twice. We both agree that Riverside is the best idea, under the circumstances. But there's not much point in discussing it endlessly, is there? I think it's about time for us to get going."

In many ways, Nesta decided, it would be a relief to have him out of the house.

"I'm not driving you down," she said. "I thought it would be wiser if we had the ambulance. They'll be here any minute. I'm going along, of course, but I'm going to follow in my car. Then I'll give the subcommittee the good news."

"And be sure you make it good and strong," he ordered.

Before she had time to reply, the front doorbell buzzed a summons. "That's the ambulance," she said, drawing a deep breath. "Come on, Arnie. I'll help you down the stairs."

At the door, the burly ambulance attendant took one look and said what he always said: "Don't worry, ma'am. We'll take good care of him."

"I know you will," she said brightly, nipping Deachman's arm tightly to remind him of his role.

"And you'll be a lot more comfortable in a little while," the driver continued, helping Deachman into the ambulance.

"Yes," said Dr. Arnold Deachman weakly. "Yes, I hope so."

Downtown, meanwhile, Ben Safford was just mounting the steps of the Federal Building when he spied a familiar back.

"Owen!" he called. "I'm right here, and I'm sorry if I'm late."

The Chief of Police explained that he was deliberately early. "I couldn't stand it down at Headquarters anymore, Ben. You can't move without stepping on a reporter. Those Cincinnati papers act as if they don't have any scandals in their own town."

Ben offered the fruit of his own experience. "People are interested in doctors these days. And when you throw in grand larceny and murder, you've got a story that everybody's following."

"The way I look at it, Ben, the murder is my baby and the larceny is yours. I figured maybe we could help each other out."

Prudently Ben delayed his reply as they passed through the usual crowd in the lobby. Not until they were alone in the elevator did he say:

"Don't get your hopes up, Owen. The larceny isn't really my baby in the sense you mean. Sure, HEW has been cranking out some grand totals for us. But our mission is to find out how badly the system is working, not to zero in on particular abuses. I told Wilhelm you were welcome to what we've got. I didn't tell him I think it's useless."

Jones grinned as they emerged from the elevator and started the trek down the corridor. "It would have been a waste of time," he agreed. "When Wilhelm is in one of his moods, there's no point talking sense to him. But maybe I can pick up something from your files just by looking at them from a different point of view."

"Good luck to you," said Ben, leading the way into the temporary quarters of the subcommittee. At first sight they looked deserted, but the rumble of voices from the inner office told him that Lou Flecker had not forgotten his promise to be on hand. "Over here, Owen," he said, forging ahead and then stopping short on the threshhold. Flecker and Tony Martinelli were in conference with an unfamiliar woman.

"Come in! Come in!" Flecker sounded suspiciously happy to be interrupted. "Mrs. Deachman, I don't think you've met Congressman Safford."

At first glance Ben was disappointed. Mrs. Deachman was certainly an attractive woman, but she didn't live up to her billing at Phil's Coffee Shop. Then, as he took in more detail, he realized that she was deliberately underplaying her charms. A severe gray suit with a black handbag was enlivened only by a touch of white at the throat. Her long, dark hair was drawn back into a low knot and she wore almost no make-up.

"I have been explaining to these gentlemen that my husband won't be able to testify," she said to Ben in tones barely above a whisper. "This morning he became very seriously ill."

"I see," Ben replied, committing himself to nothing.

"It seemed right that you should know as soon as possible."

The funereal tempo afforded Ben a sudden insight. Mrs. Deachman had decked herself out in half-mourning so that the subcommittee would recognize the gravity of the situation.

Lou had pushed his chair back from the desk. "I'm glad you dropped by. And we'll certainly take Dr. Deachman's condition into consideration when we prepare our schedule of witnesses."

She paid no attention to the farewell note in his voice. "My husband is not a well man at the best of times. Of course, he's been overworking himself for years. But he simply has no reserves to fight an illness. I can only hope that with rest and care he'll make a good recovery."

"Come now, Mrs. Deachman," Ben said heateningly. "Try to look on the bright side. I'm sure your husband's physician doesn't take such a dark view."

Flecker's voice was completely expressionless. "Apparently Dr. Deachman doesn't *have* a physician. He's making his own diagnosis."

Nesta lowered her eyes. "I can only thank God my husband is a doctor," she said, as if she were agreeing with Flecker. "He recognized the symptoms immediately, so we knew exactly what to do."

The implication was that the Deachmans had rushed to the nearest hospital. Tony Martinelli did not want to see Ben under any false impression, so he said helpfully, "Dr. Deachman thought that the best place for him to take these symptoms was some kind of nursing home."

Mrs. Deachman nodded. "We both know how good the care is."

Lou Flecker had decided that finesse was futile. Rising, he padded across the room and held the door open.

"I know you want to get back to your husband's bedside, so we won't keep you now. But we'll be in touch—about rearranging his appearance."

"I'm afraid that can't be for some time," she said gently, as if denying a request with great reluctance.

Flecker was more than a match for her. "That's too bad," he said with unimpaired amiability, "but at least you can be sure Dr. Deachman will be getting the best attention available. If he doesn't make good progress, we won't hesitate to send in our own doctors."

Nesta ignored the iron fist. "We'll all just have to pray for the best, won't we?" she said, departing with a sad, brave smile.

In stupefied silence, the four men listened to the retreat of her clicking heels, then the latching of the door. The Chief of Police, whose existence Nesta had steadfastly ignored, was the first to recover.

"And which nursing home would that be?" he asked.

Flecker consulted his notes. "Riverside Manor," he reported.

"Stands to reason. Deachman owns seventy-five percent of it. They'll say whatever he tells them to."

Ben was racking his memory trying to separate the seven doctors. "Let me get this straight. Was Deachman next in line to testify?"

"Sure thing." The whole scenario was clear as a bell to Flecker. "He probably wasn't crazy about the idea to begin with. But then look what happens. White testifies, White gets socked with a lawsuit. So Deachman decides he wants out. This morning he ducks into this tame nursing home and tells them to lock the gates. His wife's part is to do a snow job on us about overwork and heart attacks."

Tony Martinelli shook his head in disgust. "Well, he sure picked the right dame. That one expects the whole world to dance to her tune." He turned to the Chief of Police. "Say, Trumbull told us none of the doctors had an alibi. How come Mrs. Deachman didn't swear she was by hubby's side every minute? It would be just her style."

"She would have if she could have gotten away with it," Jones agreed. "But Deachman was called to the hospital from a dinner party. So the best she could do is claim that by the time she got home he was already there. Not that all the other wives aren't the same. White's wife started to tell my boys he was in all evening before she realized that the maid had seen him leave. And I hear one of the others tried persuading her bridge group to alibi the husband."

"Do you realize what you're saying?" Tony groaned. "If they do everything alike, then all seven of them will bolt into quarantine and we'll be stuck in this two-bit town for weeks." As his words floated on the air, as Lou Flecker stared at him reproachfully, he realized the famous Martinelli tact had slipped. "Sorry about that, Ben," he muttered.

While Ben flapped a forgiving hand, Flecker did some constructive thinking. "You know, we could turn this to our advantage. I don't much like holding these hearings in the middle of a police investigation, particularly when we can't count on a smooth schedule. If Elsie and Val are willing to go along, I say let's go back to Washington and let these doctors stew in their sickbeds for a week or two."

"Yeah. We can always boot them out when we want them." Martinelli's eyes gleamed with enthusiasm, at the prospect either of escape or of cracking the whip.

Owen Jones decided that his remarks had been misconstrued. "Now look, don't get me wrong. What I meant is that all doctors—and their wives—think there are special rules for MD's. But they're different types and they react differently. Deachman, in case you haven't guessed, is the kind who thinks that if he pretends a problem doesn't exist, it will simply go away. Now, Rojak, he's the tough one. He'll give you a standup fight because he's convinced that, with the AMA and enough money on his side, he can tell the world to shove it."

"Well, that would certainly make a change from Howard White," said Flecker skeptically. "All *he* told us was that doctors should be rich and happy, and any legislation on the subject is un-American."

Jones shrugged. "I guess White reacts to pressure by taking it out on someone smaller than he is. The boys tell me he tried to raise hell with Wanda Soczewinski for daring to sue him."

"I thought she was just a pawn." Ben was genuinely puzzled. "Did White think she might be Karras' partner in the shakedown?"

"Hell, no! She's not much more than a kid. White just wanted to hit out at somebody who wouldn't hit back."

The Chief of Police continued, but he had lost some of his audience. Ben Safford was suddenly aware of his own remissness. Too much attention had been lavished on HEW, on the Newburg Seven, on Theodore Karras, while one participant had been overlooked. In the meantime Wanda Soczewinski had been brow-beaten by her doctor, interrogated by the police and left without a lawyer.

Under the circumstances, she might welcome a call from her Congressman.

9

It had been in the back of his mind for some time, but never insistently enough to surface into action. He only knew that Wanda had two small children and a husband with multiple sclerosis.

Janet always claimed that Ben was a coward about this sort of thing, and, on the whole, she was right. Human suffering never left him untouched. That was the reason he had gone into politics. He was willing to work day and night to make the country everything it should be, to see there was enough food and work and decency for everyone.

Where he fell down was on the personal level. Easy sympathy did not flow naturally from Ben. At best, he was tongue-tied. At worst, he wanted to haul off and punch someone, which was not always the best way to convey compassion.

But if he was a coward, he was also a man of conscience. Squaring his shoulders, he set out for South Newburg, where Mrs. Soczewinski lived.

It was one of the bungalows on Marengo Avenue, a long street narrowed to one lane by cars parked on both sides. Ben, looking for 1432, pulled up behind a large green station wagon blocking progress. There was a passenger in the car but no driver. On the sidewalk, a stout woman stood talking to a young girl. Sighting Ben's car, the matron pantomimed her intention to move on, said a final word to the girl and bustled back to the driver's seat.

"Take your time," Ben bawled out the window.

The station wagon proceeded, and Ben followed, noting out of the corner of his eye that the girl was waving vigorously. When he walked back from his parking place, she was just opening the door of 1432.

"Yes? I'm Mrs. Soczewinski," she said.

Ben introduced himself and started to explain his mission when she broke in.

"I know you! I voted for you—and so did Tommy. Oh he'll be so mad he missed you!"

"You don't look old enough to vote," said Ben truthfully.

"Come on in," she said with a glowing smile. "The place is a mess. . . ."

There was a crib in one corner of the minute living room. In another, there was a wheelchair. It was clean as a whistle.

"Maybe if you don't mind the kitchen," she suggested with a look over her shoulder. "The kids are in the backyard."

In the kitchen there was a rack of drying dishes on the sink, some potted plants on the windowsill and crumbs on the table, which Wanda Soczewinski whisked away.

"Mrs. Soczewinski," Ben began.

"That's Tommy's mother," she said with a pert smile. "Why don't you call me Wanda? And can I get you a cup of coffee, Mr. Safford? There's some left. Oh, I can't get over it. A Congressman—right here! Wait until I tell Tommy."

While she spoke, Ben revised his preconceived notions. Wanda Soczewinski was a tiny thing, barely five feet tall. And she was so thin that her face was all eyes. But despite the boyish cap of blond hair, she was not the little girl Ben had taken her for on the sidewalk.

"Oh, was that you?" she exclaimed. "That was Mrs. Williams from the Ladies' Guild. They take Tommy out once a week." With a sudden wary look at him, she asked, "You know . . . my husband . . . ?"

Not trusting himself with words, Ben nodded and she seemed to breathe a sigh of relief. "You see, we don't have a car. And it's hard on Tommy, never getting out. So Mrs. Williams or one of the others takes him around to different places like the zoo or the arboretum. Tommy really appreciates it."

She could have been defying him to see any poignancy in the situation. Ben, better with facts than emotions, said, "I didn't know whether Tommy was able—to go out, I mean."

Putting down a cup of coffee for him, she settled herself opposite and told him about multiple sclerosis, the cruel wasting disease that afflicts young adults. In the process, she told him a lot about herself. Wanda Soczewinski had learned the terrible part about *no known cause* and *no known cure* by rote. But she was not a lecturer; her eloquence sprang from the heart.

". . . important to understand that his mind's the same as it always was," she said earnestly. "And Tommy's brilliant. So it means a whole lot for him to get out of the house—"

A sudden uproar outside made her jump to her feet. Barks, children shouting . . . and Wanda was gone. Ben went over to the window to look out. There was a pandemonium of activity, all swirling around an aged beagle.

When Wanda reappeared, she had a pint-sized replica tucked under an arm.

"This is Robin," she said, flopping Robin onto her lap like a rag doll.

Robin, sex unknown to Ben, stared at him unnervingly, tears forgotten at the fearsome sight. Ben smiled tentatively.

"Robin won't leave doggie alone," said Wanda.

The little face crumpled slightly, and, fearing the worst, Ben burst into speech. "Have you ever heard about Wheels for Shut-Ins?" he asked.

Wanda shook her head and Robin stared.

"Maybe they could help you out," Ben continued, trying to recall the details of one of Janet's many good works. "Zoos and arboretums are okay, but I know Wheels organizes outings to baseball games and things like that. Of course, I don't know if Tommy likes—"

"That would be wonderful," she broke in, unconsciously hugging Robin. "Tommy's nuts about sports."

"I'll tell my sister to get in touch with you," Ben said, withdrawing his pocket diary to jot a reminder. Looking up, he caught Wanda and Robin watching him with fascination. Robin was transfixed by the pencil.

"That would be wonderful," Wanda said again.

Ben kept on writing. He didn't always say the right thing, but sometimes he avoided the wrong one. He knew better than to ask when Wanda ever got out. It would turn out that she didn't like to leave Robin and Robin's brother with strangers. Or that Tommy needed her. Or something else.

"The reason I dropped by was this trouble with Dr. White," he began, only to be silenced by a warning look.

"Do you think you can play with Bully without pulling his tail?" she said, rising to place Robin on her chubby legs.

Robin gave assurances of some sort, cast a last longing look at Ben's pencil, then let Wanda lead her to the kitchen door.

"Now you be a good girl!" her mother yelled before turning back to Ben. "They pick up more than you think," she said solemnly.

It was not the murder of Theo Karras that was unfit for Robin's ears.

". . . couldn't make head or tail of it when it came in the mail. But there was a note explaining that all this stuff showed what Dr. White was telling the government," she said, color mounting in her cheeks.

Dr. White had charged three hysterectomies and one abortion to the Medicaid account of Mrs. Wanda Soczewinski.

"It made me see red," she confided.

"I don't blame you," Ben replied.

"It wasn't as if—" Whatever she was going to say, she thought better of. "Anyway, the note explained it all. Because, you see, the only thing wrong with me when I went to Dr. White was anemia. That was all. So the note said I should take everything to Mr. Karras. Tommy and I, we talked it over for a couple of days. I wasn't sure, but Tommy was so mad . . ."

Everything Wanda said was straightforward. Out of the blue, a packet of Medicaid documents had arrived at 1432 Marengo with a typed note explaining Dr. White's money-making scheme and directing the Soczewinskis to Attorney Karras.

"Did you know Karras before all this?" Ben asked.

"No," she said, quickly defensive. "That's what the police keep asking. But I never met him before in my life." Misinterpreting his silence, she cried, "My father-in-law knew him, but we didn't."

"I didn't mean to upset you," Ben apologized. "I was just wondering if Karras himself sent you—"

Half exasperated, half alarmed, she interrupted: "I know! That's what Lieutenant Doyle said too. But I told him how Mr. Karras was real surprised when I turned up. I could tell. Then, when he started reading the stuff I brought, he began talking to himself. You know, the way people do when they don't believe what they're seeing? Then he began figuring out how much money Dr. White made—and started swearing."

Anxiously, she studied him. "You think we're in on it together," she said flatly. "Just like Dr. White."

"What?" Ben exclaimed.

Dr. Howard White had not hesitated to accuse Wanda of every crime in the book. There were jails for people like her, he had told her in a tirade that included recriminations, threats and, apparently, obscene language.

Ben was shaken, and when he recovered he found he had been speaking his thoughts aloud.

Wanda was not shocked. "That's what Tommy said, too. Anyway, I had a few things to say to Dr. White myself. But he wasn't the least bit ashamed of what he'd done—in fact, he claimed it was none of my business. That's when I stopped hesitating about going on with the suit. That—" here she smiled—"that and the money. Mr. Karras said we might collect one hundred thousand dollars."

For the first time her voice trembled. In this family, what would a sum like that mean?

Gently, Ben asked.

"We'd get off welfare," she said simply. Then, hurriedly: "Oh, I don't want you to think I'm not grateful. . . ."

This was the point at which Ben Safford wanted to start swinging, preferably at Dr. Howard White, his tanned wife or his tanned children.

She was going on. "We'd get ourselves a car. They have them with special equipment for Tommy. That would make a big difference. Then, well, you know how expensive kids are."

"Yes," said Ben harshly.

It was not as inadequate as it sounded. Wanda was emboldened to air a private worry.

"Do you think . . . I mean, now that Mr. Karras is dead . . . ?"

There was nothing wrong with Ben Safford's ears. "Don't worry about it. Your suit goes on, Karras or no Karras. And you're going to get a whopping big settlement, too. I'll get hold of a good lawyer for you. And if that doesn't work out, I'll represent you myself. I've got a law degree I've never used."

She laughed aloud at his vehemence, but sobered immediately.

"That's terrible, isn't it, after what happened to Mr. Karras. He was awfully nice to me. You know, he came here to the house to talk things over with Tommy."

She was no child, as Ben had already discovered. "You know the doctors claim that Karras was blackmailing them," he said.

"That's not true," she said with calm certainty. "Not Mr. Karras."

Again, this told Ben something about Theo Karras, and more about Wanda. She was midway between what she had been and what she had to be. Once Tommy had been a tower of strength for her. Once she had been overawed by policemen, by lawyers, by Dr. Whites. Now this was a luxury she could no longer afford. For the life she faced, Wanda had to rely on her own hands and heart and brain.

"I'm willing to bet you're right about Karras," said Ben slowly.

"Excuse me, I'd better check Robin," she said, jumping up and darting to the door.

Ben rebuked himself. There were too many problems in this house to leave Wanda much margin for outside puzzles.

"Behaving like an angel," she said, on returning.

It would be heartless to ask if there was anything he could do to help her. "I've got to get back," said Ben, rising. "I'm sorry I missed Tommy. If it's convenient for you, I'll drop in tonight after dinner. I'd like to talk things over with him."

She looked at him as if he were a sleeping baby Soczewinski.

"Also, these rules and regulations can be pretty confusing. I want to be certain you're taking advantage of all the assistance you're entitled to. I'm going to ask—"

"Oh, thank you," she said. "But down at Social Security they've been just wonderful. Mrs. Gregorian spent hours with the books. Would you believe we get forty dollars extra every two months because Robin has an allergy? Mrs. Gregorian says we're entitled to every penny we can get. And, boy, do we need it!"

"Right!" said Ben.

She grinned up at him. "You know, there are a whole lot of good people in this world."

Congressman Safford made himself say it. "There sure are."

— 10 —

Forty hours later Theodore Karras was laid to rest next to his late wife. The attendance—consisting mainly of family, local residents from South Newburg and members of the International Justice Party from a tri-state area—did not suggest that the funeral had any significance over at the other end of town. Nonetheless it was a signal for movement on several fronts. Six doctors cautiously emerged from their houses, while the seventh testily told his nurse to take that bed table away and put his tray on the balcony. A whole clutch of reporters checked out of the Sunset Motel and began the drive back to Cincinnati. Val Oakes, Elsie Hollenbach and Tony Martinelli caught the breakfast flight to Washington. Even Lou Flecker, held up by administrative detail, was able to make the eleven o'clock plane.

"Thanks for the lift, Ben," he said in parting. "I know you'll keep an eye on the situation here."

Ben promised that if anything happened Lou would be the first to know. "Not that I expect any developments over the weekend. And I'll be at the House on Tuesday."

As he strolled back through the terminal, he realized that others were returning to normal as well. A cheerful party was marching toward the corridor which led to the private-aircraft area. There was not much doubt about their destination, as the roly-poly man in the group was encased in a raccoon coat and carrying an Ohio State pennant. But what caught Ben's attention was Nesta Deachman prancing along on the arm of a familiar young man. Today her black hair was flying loose over her shoulders and she was wearing a white fisherman's sweater with tan suede jeans tucked into glossy boots. There was red on her lips, blue on her eyelids and long gold earrings glittering as she turned her head in vivacious chatter. Ben grinned to himself. He had a strong suspicion that this was the real Mrs. Deachman, as opposed to the subdued creature in the Federal Building, bowed down by premature widowhood.

"So much for sitting at a hospital bedside," he muttered under his breath.

Even Nesta felt some explanation was required.

"I still don't think it looks right," she said, leaning across Jim Rojak to address the Whites. "But Arnie's feeling so much better that he's taking charge again. He says we've got to start living life normally. So here I am."

"Great," they said perfunctorily.

Rojak, on the other hand, looked at her oddly. Nesta was a strange combination of conventionality and extravagance. He could see that she was ready to have a wonderful time. But simultaneously she was worried about appearances. He had absolutely no doubt that she had balked at coming until Deachman insisted.

They were setting off on one of Jim Rojak's famous parties. In the middle of the summer, long before his world started coming apart at the seams, he had marked the date on which Ohio State (his own alma mater) played Notre Dame, which Howard White had attended. It seemed like the ideal occasion for airborne hospitality, but the closer the day came, the less likely it appeared that the outing would materialize. With flashbulbs popping wherever he went, even Howard White realized that he should be seen on errands of mercy, not pleasure jaunts. But then, within forty-eight hours, the storm-clouds had begun rolling away. The police were at a standstill, Wanda Soczewinski's lawsuit was becalmed and, as an additional fillip, the subcommittee had folded its tents and returned to Washington.

Rojak, who was a gambler by nature, knew that it was now or never. Gone were thoughts of a modest afternoon expedition. It was going to be a tailgate party at the airport, seats on the fifty-yard line, then on to a suite in Chicago and a night on the town.

Rojak had planned a show of strength. But he had found himself saddled with an embarrassment. What had thrown a crimp into his plans was the guest list. Originally, it had included the Deachmans as well as Dr. and Mrs. White and Rojak's companion of the moment. When Deachman went into hiding, Rojak had begun thinking about alterations. But then Deachman phoned from Riverside Manor and talked and talked and talked. As a result, Rojak found himself squiring Nesta while the Costellos filled the rest of the six-seat Cessna.

So Rojak was not expecting to have a marvelous time. Still, there was enough festivity in the air to pass muster. Nesta was reveling in a young escort and the prospect of her first college football game. She was providing almost as much satisfaction for Connie White, who intended to store up all of Nesta's gaucheries and relay them to Margaret Deachman. Howard White, temporarily liberated from the cares of Newburg, could almost forget they existed. The Costellos, long envious of the good times provided by Jim Rojak, were in seventh heaven. Patrick Costello had spotted the straw basket from the Curryville Petit Gourmet the minute he entered the plane. Round-eyed, he ticked off smoked salmon, caviar, goose-liver pâté. This, he decided, was the way to live. The discovery that her high heels and fur stole were all wrong had not noticeably dampened Ethel Costello's spirits. The real test was still ahead and she had every confidence that the suitcase at her feet contained the perfect outfit for dinner and dancing.

As for Rojak himself, he knew perfectly well that his troubles had not evaporated, but he had always believed in seizing the moment. The ritual of take-off with its emphasis on his commanding position, the open admiration of the Costellos, Howard White's fatuous comparison between air and marine navigation all acted on him like a tonic.

"Next stop, South Bend!" he sang out as they leveled off and began cruising.

If anything further was needed to make spirits soar, the tailgate hour provided it. The weather in South Bend was well-nigh perfect, with a few fluffy clouds impelled across a clear blue sky by a spanking breeze. The Petit Gourmet had excelled itself, ably assisted by the Newburg Liquor Mart. And, best of all, they were in full view of every other private aircraft debouching passengers for the big game.

"Boy, will you take a look at that," marveled Costello as a sleek jet began to unload ten or twelve couples.

He was soon set right.

"It's just some corporation entertaining customers," sniffed Howard White. "When you get right down to it, everyone there works for someone else."

He was just slightly off target, as they learned when one of the new arrivals hailed Rojak as a classmate. A Cleveland bank was hosting some local businessmen. Any doubts about the superiority of the Newburg contingent's position were laid to rest by the deference which greeted Rojak's lordly offer of caviar sandwiches and Bloody Marys.

In rapid succession there arrived a retail chain rewarding its most successful managers, an embryo sports syndicate wooing participants and a manufacturing company from Akron with a full load of purchasing agents. Not until Connie and Ethel were packing up the debris did another single-engine plane arrive.

"Hi, Jim," said the pilot as he strolled past.

"Hi, Pete!"

They were two sovereigns.

Rojak's explanation came as no surprise to his guests. "Pete's an orthodontist in Toledo. I didn't know him at school, but we run into each other a lot these days."

Inside the stadium they had sacred rituals to help them prove what a good time they were having. Pat Costello and Connie White produced a mock-fierce rivalry requiring agonized groans or ecstatic yells at every movement of the ball.

"Call that passing?" scoffed Connie as the ball sailed into the hands of a receiver surrounded by the entire Notre Dame defense.

Then, arriving from nowhere, two Ohio State giants cleared a hole in the forest, and the receiver, with an agile swivel, evaded a pair of clutching hands and began to snake-dance toward freedom.

"C'mon, twinkletoes!" Costello roared.

When Ohio State scored on the next rush, he exploded into an orgy of pennant-waving, back-thumping and exultant screaming.

Rojak and White were less partisan. Busy exchanging courtesies with nearby spectators, greetings with passing classmates and college reminiscences with each other, they only occasionally rose to their feet for an obligatory war cry. Ethel Costello, profoundly grateful not to be chilled to the bone, broiled to a crisp or soaked by a downpour, assumed the Mona Lisa smile she reserved for sports events and refreshed herself too frequently from the flask Jim Rojak had provided.

Nesta Deachman needed no stimulants. She was drinking in the whole spectacle—the gyrations of the cheerleaders, the marching bands at half-time, the students unfurling signs in front of the television cameras. She enjoyed eating hot dogs, recognizing the Governor of Ohio and mastering the intricacies of point-spread betting.

"Then if Notre Dame makes this touchdown," she said toward the end of the final quarter, "you owe me seventy-five dollars, Pat."

Ethel Costello had a bookkeeper's mind. "That's in addition to the fifty you'll get from Jim," she pointed out, more in a spirit of accuracy than reproach.

Nesta was hunched forward, her chin cupped in a hand, her gaze intent on the field. Her tongue flicked out to remove a dab of mustard before she replied. "I can use it all," she said dreamily.

Two minutes later both Notre Dame and Nesta had won. As the same goal was putting money into Howard's pocket, even Connie White was pleased.

Only one event marred the afternoon. As they were making their way to the exit, a classmate of Rojak, with more brandy than sense in him, yelled a greeting over intervening heads and struggled toward them.

"Jim, old buddy! How're ya doing? I see you're getting your name spread all over the papers."

Evasion was impossible. They were hemmed in as effectively as if they had police guards.

"Say, Jim, we've got a room for the class of '65 and we're going to have a ball. Bring your friends and tell us all the dirt about Newburg."

There was a glint in Rojak's eye. "Sorry, Gene, we'd like to stop by your little get-together, but we've got a suite at the Ritz waiting for us. And I don't do my drinking until after I've finished flying my plane." He paused to flick a playful fist at Gene's shoulder. "Good to run into you, though. I hope they're treating you all right at that high school where you teach."

After that, Gene was only too glad to let them escape to the exit and, ultimately, to Chicago. At the Ritz there was no need to fear tactless references to events in Ohio. This was partly due to the high standards of the hotel, partly to their palatial accommodations and mostly to the fact that nobody cared. They were all used to being big frogs in a small pond and normally they resented the anonymity of large cities. Today, however, they reveled in it.

In the cocktail lounge they were conscious of being one of the most attractive groups present. Even Pat Costello, shorn of football regalia, was revealed as a portly figure of distinction. In the most expensive restaurant on Michigan Boulevard, they all emerged as knowledgeable gourmets, with Jim Rojak and Howard White more than upholding the honor of Newburg in their wine selections. And the discotheque which climaxed the evening was an unalloyed triumph. They could switch partners often enough to avoid boredom.

"Nesta certainly seems to appreciate the good time you're showing us, Jim," purred Connie White.

Rojak was amused. Several rounds earlier Nesta, in a burst of enthusiasm, had lightly clasped his knee, and way out on the dance floor Connie's eyelids had blinked open and closed like a camera shutter. And like a camera she had recorded the moment for all time.

"I'll tell her you said so," he promised.

Whatever he passed on to Nesta, her reaction was enough to draw Pat Costello's attention.

"Jim doesn't seem to have the magic touch," he observed to Howard White as they made their way back to the table. "Nesta looks mad as fire."

White was not surprised that Rojak's gently shaking head should induce Nesta to lift her chin in defiance. "Well, he's saying no, and pretty ladies don't like that."

He could have added that they don't sit still for it.

"I wonder where Nesta and Howard have gone off to," Ethel Costello said idly later in the evening. "I haven't seen them in ages."

Rojak had no doubt that they were innocently occupied somewhere, but that Nesta would delay any return until Connie had noticed their absence. "They may have found another room," he said vaguely. "This one is getting pretty crowded."

Ethel was placidity itself. "That must be it."

In a wave of approval Rojak urged food, drink or another dance on her. Already regretting his mischief-making, he was finding it restful to spend some time with a woman oblivious to the undercurrents between the other two.

Fortunately, Connie and Pat had barely seated themselves when Nesta returned, leading Howard by the hand.

"It's so stuffy down here that we went upstairs for some air, and the time flew by," she twinkled. "I simply had to drag Howard back. I hope we haven't held you up."

But Connie was far too old a hand to show displeasure. Like a veteran tennis player, she might not be as fast on her feet as the youngsters, but she had mastered tactics that Nesta was still developing.

"What a good idea!" she said warmly.

On this happy note they returned to the Ritz, capped the weekend with a leisurely Sunday brunch, then finally piled into the Cessna for the trip home.

Like every weekend, this one had its period of anticlimax when thoughts began to leapfrog to the week ahead. But there was a geographic dimension to the process as well. Every sweep of the minute hand brought the plane's passengers closer not only to Monday but also to Newburg, where their problems lay in wait. What would have been unthinkable on Saturday morning was brute reality by Sunday evening: they had been granted a breathing space, not a permanent remission.

Nesta Deachman didn't see it that way.

"What are you all so down in the dumps for?" she demanded, breaking the silence that had prevailed since Rojak announced they were in radio contact with Newburg Airport. "It isn't as if we have anything to worry about."

"Are you crazy?" White's voice was so high it threatened to crack. "I sometimes think we're just as badly off as we were at the beginning of this mess."

Nesta inspected him in the deepening gloom of the plane's interior. Doing the hustle with him was fun, but Nesta cherished no illusions about Dr. Howard White, or any of the Newburg Seven.

"Howard," she said impatiently, "that woman doesn't have a lawyer for her suit anymore, the subcommittee has left town and nobody's stealing files from HEW. How can you say that things are just as bad as ever?"

Pat Costello's ebullience had been deflating for over an hour. "God knows what the police have been up to while we've been out of town," he said dolefully. "And the subcommittee has simply adjourned, Nesta. They may come back any day."

She found it impossible to take him seriously. "Well, they may come back," she said mockingly, "but they're not going to trouble Arnie. *He's* still sick."

The triumph in her voice grated on Rojak. "That's just fine. Do you expect *me* to stand up and cheer? Remember, I'm the one who'll get called in Arnie's place."

"But, Jim," she protested, "you yourself have been saying that the subcommittee is no reason to get uptight."

He sighed with exaggerated patience. "That was before we were all part of a murder case, Nesta baby. Now there's plenty to worry about."

Anger began roughening her style. "Then why the hell don't you do something about it? The trouble with all of you—and I'll include Arnie, too—is that you spend too much time talking and not enough doing. No wonder these creeps think they can kick us around."

It would have been wiser to leave her unanswered, but White couldn't let the subject rest.

"Exactly what do you suggest?"

She had plenty to suggest. "For openers, isn't there some way to get to Safford? You're doctors, you know other doctors. Maybe he's had a nervous breakdown, like the one who ran with McGovern. Or —he's a bachelor, isn't he? Can't you find out if he's gay?"

This ruthlessness left White speechless. Jim Rojak took over. "Look, Nesta, this isn't TV and we're not private eyes. Besides, just forget about Safford and the subcommittee. Our real problem is malpractice insurance. Great Lakes is running scared because of this lawsuit against Howard—"

"Good God, that suit's over and done with!" she cut in.

"Wake up!" he replied harshly. "Somebody got rid of Karras, but they didn't get rid of every lawyer in Newburg. Sooner or later, one of them is bound to pick up this Soczewinski woman. I'm sorry for Howard, but Great Lakes has already half-swallowed one suit. If there's a second, Larry Fournier will go up in smoke."

"Then get to Fournier some way," she said fiercely.

"You mean, prove *he's* gay, too? So that Great Lakes will roll over and play dead out of sheer embarrassment? Listen, I'm worried about the same thing Fournier is. I'm afraid there's somebody out there trying to get us."

"Well, why don't you try to find out who it is?" she asked with perfumed venom.

"My, my!" said Connie White with a silvery laugh. "You two could be married to each other, the way you argue."

"Bitch!" said Nesta lightly under her breath.

But Connie had performed a useful function in diverting Nesta long enough to let Rojak lower the temperature of the discussion. "I know it looks as if you're taking all the lumps, Howard," he said. "But if there's only one lawsuit, and if we all stand together, I'm sure we can make Great Lakes play it our way."

"That's one hundred percent right," Costello chimed in loyally. "Hell, they've been making a mint out of us for years and this is the first time they've had to shell out."

Nesta, meanwhile, had begun assembling her possessions as the lights of Newburg Airport appeared ahead.

Connie White thought she saw an opportunity to score a point. "They're right, you know. If we all stick together, everything will come out all right in the end."

For the first time in memory, Nesta spoke to her as one woman to another. *"We?* Who are you trying to kid, Connie? You've got your problems and I've got mine. And you can run right back to dear Margaret and tell her that from me!"

But by the following morning all the Deachmans had something else to occupy them. Jim Rojak's worst forebodings came true with a vengeance. A second malpractice suit was filed.

This time the defendant was Dr. Arnold Deachman.

II

It was just as well for her peace of mind that Nesta was not present during the electrifying half-hour after the arrival of the summons at Riverside Manor Nursing Home. Arnold Deachman outdid himself in an emotional spectacular that began with shock, escalated rapidly into rage at the entire world, then distilled itself into wild threats against his adversaries. What he wanted was someone to join him in these sentiments with perfect, unfeigned sincerity. With the best will in the world, Nesta would have had a hard time playing this role.

But, fortunately, sitting at his bedside was just the woman to fill the bill. Penelope Deachman Taggert was twenty-four years old, a wife, mother and chatelaine of a substantial household, but she was still the little girl who had been raised by a mother saying: "Your father is a wonderful man, dear." Even after the great apostasy Margaret Deachman had merely shifted to: "Your father was simply putty in that woman's hands." To Penny, Arnold Deachman was an indulgent father, a doting grandfather, a bounteous provider, whose furies—never directed at her—were the natural response to a world that was just too unfair.

At first her uncritical sympathy poured over Deachman's wounds like balm.

"The nerve of it! Imagine a malpractice suit—against you, of all people!" she exclaimed as indignantly as he could wish.

"They'll pay for this," he stormed. "I've taken care of trouble-makers before. They won't get away with it."

"I should think not!"

The wild glare in his eye began to fade as he modulated into self-pity. "I don't even remember who this Atkins is."

"That just shows," she chimed in as if making a tremendous debating point.

"Whoever he is, he has big ideas. He's asking for three hundred thousand dollars."

Penny gasped. She lived a life in which houses, cars and charge accounts simply appeared, and would have been stupefied if anybody had ever calculated the total expenditures of the Taggert family. In all honesty, she was convinced they led a simple life. Why, she even had to go to Daddy when they decided to park Trigger with his grandmother and spend their vacation in Greece.

But numbers had never been able to claim her attention long. "And to do this when you're sick! They think you won't be able to fight back."

"He's probably a welfare patient," Deachman grunted.

"Well, doesn't he have any consideration?"

Unhappily, the more Deachman returned to rationality, the less useful his daughter was. Partisanship she could provide, but not campaign strategy.

"Of course, in my weakened condition I can't be expected to cope with this," he began significantly. "I could never answer for the consequences."

"You mustn't even think of it." Penny was all eager action. "I'll call your lawyer right now. We can give him the summons and he'll take care of everything."

"You will not!" Deachman came upright in a hurry. "I'm not going to be saddled with the bills for this ridiculous suit. This is the insurance company's problem. That's what they're paid for."

His daughter was willing but bewildered. "Then do you want me to call *them?*"

"God, no! That will just bring them down on me. This has to be handled carefully, and Nesta's the one to do it. God knows I've taken care of her well enough—"

"You certainly have," Penny said too quickly. The news of the forthcoming mink coat had already been relayed by Connie White.

The smooth rhythm of Deachman's fault-finding was interrupted.

Normally, he would have gone on to an examination of Nesta's flaws, but he was reminded that this was one issue upon which he and his daughter were not as one.

"Nesta is a very competent woman," he said, giving credit where credit was due. "She kept that subcommittee out of my hair, and now she'll make Great Lakes understand that I refuse to be involved. So *she's* the one for you to get hold of."

"If I can," Penny retorted. "Maybe she's not back from her big weekend. If you ask me, it's a bit much, traipsing off to a football game while you're in the hospital."

"Nobody *has* asked you, young lady. That was my idea, in case you're interested. Nesta wasn't really enthusiastic." His lips twisted maliciously. "And, for that matter, neither was Jim Rojak. He probably didn't like not being able to take one of those stewardesses of his, thought it cramped his style having my wife along. But I wasn't having that bunch think we have any more to hide than they do. And why should Rojak have fun and games right now? He's in this just as much as we are. Does he think he's entitled to a free ride while Howard and I take all the knocks? It's high time he pulled some of the weight. He's great on talk, but when it comes to action all he does is . . ."

"All he does is what?" Penny pressed when her father showed signs of running down.

But Deachman preferred not to go into detail during his appeals for sympathy. He leaned back and pulled the blankets around him. "Get Nesta," he repeated. "She'll take care of this. I'm far too unwell to be disturbed."

"Oh, I know, Daddy. You must feel simply terrible."

At Great Lakes they felt even worse when they heard the news.

"Do you realize how much these jokers in Newburg can cost my division?" Larry Fournier stormed at his staff.

The division accountant made the mistake of answering. "They could put us in the red."

"I thought they shot the guy who was in back of this," someone else said hastily.

"Well, they didn't do a good enough job."

The news flashed through the medical circles of Newburg within hours.

"Naturally, I think it's terrible, but I have never seen why Howard should have to carry the whole brunt on his shoulders," said Connie White.

Margaret Deachman continued to relay Penny's tidings.

"So Nesta is going to deal with the insurance company." Connie emitted a ladylike snort. "Well, her tactics should be interesting. Did I tell you about the cleavage she was showing in Chicago . . . ?"

In the Community Medical Building, Pat Costello took advantage of his newfound intimacy with Jim Rojak to descend one floor for a consultation.

"We're next!" he wailed. "What are we going to do?"

Unlike most of his colleagues, Rojak had been thinking. "Now's the time for Giles Perrin to earn his keep. To hell with little statements to the subcommittee. The AMA has got to lay it on the line to Great Lakes. They negotiated the policy and they have to insist that all doctors be treated the same. Great Lakes can't single out scapegoats."

"Absolutely," said Costello fervently.

Little as the AMA approved, the HEW office was also part of Newburg's medical circle. Particularly when it came to subpoenas for billings.

Quentin Trumbull cradled the telephone receiver with a thump, then turned challengingly to his audience of one.

"I've had it up to here," he announced, guillotining his own throat. "You know what Fournier was asking? He wants HEW to join Great Lakes in a formal protest to the bar association. He thinks their ethics committee should discipline any lawyer who has the nerve to sue him!"

Charlene Gregorian gave a brief chortle of laughter, then sobered. "He must be hysterical."

"Of course he is. Great Lakes thought they were out of the woods when Karras was murdered. They'd make a modest settlement with his client and the trouble would be over. Now, out of the blue comes this second suit, and they realize that Karras had a partner who's sitting on the HEW files."

Charlene Gregorian gave it as her opinion that Lawrence Fournier had relaxed too soon.

"Well, he's paying for it now. Did I tell you that Deachman is the target this time? But what I'd really like to know is the basis of this second suit. That's why I asked you to check out the Kenneth Atkins file."

Charlene stared at him. "You mean that Fournier doesn't know? Why didn't he ask Deachman?"

Until now Trumbull's face had been a rigid mask of disapproval, but at this question the frown began to melt. "Fournier didn't talk with Deachman. It was *Mrs.* Deachman who called." A full-scale grin appeared. "Haven't you heard the latest dirt? Deachman is hiding out in his own nursing home, pretending to have heart trouble, so he won't have to testify before the subcommittee. I suppose when the summons came he decided it wouldn't help his public image to come busting out and take charge himself."

"And so his wife is pinch-hitting for him."

Trumbull was still amused. "If you ask me, half of Larry Fournier's trouble comes from dealing with Mrs. Deachman. Apparently she's putting on an act as the admiring wife of a wonderful husband. Larry couldn't let loose at her with all the shots that Deachman has coming. So he bit down hard and just made sure it really was another malpractice action. He's flying in tomorrow to learn the grisly details."

"Well, I can do better by you than that. It stands out from the file like a sore thumb. This time it's appendectomies."

"What could be wrong with that?" Trumbull demanded. "Only a couple of days ago Congressman Martinelli was recommending it as damn near foolproof."

"Yes," Charlene agreed temperately, "but not three of them on the same patient."

"They never learn, do they?" Trumbull muttered. "At least that should make it simple to tell if the references to our files are accurate. You want to take a look?"

Charlene Gregorian accepted the subpoena he pushed across the desk, flipped to the list of documents demanded and began to compare it with her own notes. It didn't take long for her to render a verdict.

"Correct in every detail," she announced cheerfully.

"I didn't really expect anything else. And if Kenneth Atkins is a Social Security case, I suppose he'd be sympathetic to a jury. Is he over sixty-five?"

"No, he's blind," said Charlene absently. She was still studying the subpoena.

"Boy, that's another one that Fournier won't dare take into a courtroom. You have to hand it to Karras. When he set this thing up, he sure knew how to pick his files."

Charlene might not have heard him. "You've been concentrating on the wrong names in this thing, Quen," she charged, tapping the subpoena like a school teacher.

"What do you mean? There are only two names. It's *Atkins* v. *Deachman*."

"There also happens to be an attorney of record."

Trumbull snorted. "What difference does it make who he is? We already know it's some two-bit lawyer who went in on this with Karras. It hardly matters . . ." His voice trailed away as he realized that Charlene was authoritatively shaking her head. "No?" he asked weakly.

"No, it's not some two-bit lawyer. For God's sake, Quen, this is Michael Isham of—" She broke off to lower her voice impressively. "Of Briggs, Briggs and Isham."

Momentarily, Trumbull goggled. Then he gave a long, low whistle.

No small American city can boast the kind of giant law mill that exists in New York and Washington. In the hinterland most attorneys practice either alone or in partnerships of three or four men. But if the city houses a respectable amount of industry, if its banks and brokers and insurance offices provide financial services for a wide enough area, if there has been money around long enough to generate complicated estates, then there will be one law firm that towers above the rest in size, respectability and influence.

In Newburg that firm was Briggs, Briggs and Isham. Their letterhead listed eleven lawyers. Their offices needed a full floor of the bank building to accommodate legal file clerks, a law librarian and four paraprofessionals.

"And," said Charlene Gregorian with a snicker, "Duncan Briggs is president of the Newburg Bar Association. Someone might mention that to Larry Fournier before he organizes a march on the ethics committee."

But Trumbull was busy calculating the effect of this new element on his own position. "This changes everything," he remarked, scratching his head with the eraser end of a pencil.

"I don't see why. Ken Atkins' case is self-evident without a first-class lawyer."

"I'm not looking at it from Atkins' point of view. I'm looking at it from HEW's point of view. With Karras, we could assume that he filed the first suit as a show of force. Then he would have put the word out that he could be bought off. In view of what's at stake, the other six doctors would have coughed up and that would have been the end of it. HEW and the subcommittee would have stayed on top of the Medicaid situation without any of these end-runs."

"On top of the situation!" Charlene repeated derisively. "When HEW and the subcommittee were helpless to do anything? And don't talk to me about legislation in five years' time. I mean these particular seven doctors. Besides, I've never believed Theo Karras was on the take. You didn't know him, but he was one of those old-fashioned socialists still worrying about the Pullman strike."

Quentin Trumbull was not a man who shifted gears readily. "Then maybe he thought shaking down Rojak and the others was a primitive form of justice."

"You're missing the point. No matter what he felt about the doctors, he would never have double-crossed a Wanda Soczewinski or a Ken Atkins."

"What difference does it make?" Trumbull asked grumpily. "Karras isn't around anymore. And instead of returning to the old rules, we've got another outsider lobbing grenades onto the field."

Charlene raised her eyes to the ceiling in a parody of exasperation. "Oh, Quen," she reproached him. "Use your head. The minute Karras was murdered, the old rules went up in smoke. There are a lot of outsiders circling around us now, and, in case you haven't noticed, most of them are wearing police uniforms."

"Well, yes, there's that." Trumbull forced himself to consider this aspect. "I realize that if we end up with a murder trial against one of those goddamned doctors, that's going to raise even more Cain than a string of malpractice suits. But all of that's in the future. I'm worried about what I should be doing now. And there's no way to decide without knowing what Michael Isham plans."

"We could try asking him."

"Sure!" Trumbull bleated sarcastically. "And a fat chance we have for a nice informal huddle with anybody in that firm. They'll just tell us to buzz off."

"Oh, not with us." Charlene, her head bent studiously over her corner of the desk, was doodling furiously on a scratch pad.

Quentin Trumbull was not a native of Newburg. He had been deputy director in the Cincinnati HEW office before his promotion. But in three years he had learned a good deal about Newburg and even more about Charlene Gregorian. She was a walking encyclopedia about her hometown. She knew the names and the faces, she knew the current deals in the making and the past scandals that had been forgotten. And whenever she contemplated releasing a nugget of information, she doodled her way to a decision.

"Then with who?" he said softly.

"It's possible, just barely possible, that Isham won't say no to an off-the-record chat with Congressman Safford."

Past photographs from the *Newburg News* rose to haunt Trumbull. "But Wesley Briggs is on the Republican County Committee," he protested.

"All the Briggs are Republicans. But Michael Isham is a big contributor to the Democratic Party." Suddenly Charlene raised her face, revealing the wide smile that etched a dimple in her chin. "Briggs, Briggs and Isham has always played both sides of the street."

It was not just in politics that Briggs, Briggs and Isham covered the field. They offered a wide range of personal styles. Duncan Briggs conveyed an air of such mummified permanence that it was worth money in the bank. Wesley Briggs was a pragmatic man of affairs—conservative by inclination, but willing to accept benefits from the right kind of government intervention. Michael Isham, who did the trial work, was the firm's rough-and-ready extrovert. He preferred the courtroom to the boardroom, frankly admitting that he enjoyed the opportunity for showmanship and combativeness.

"Hi, Ben!" he shouted from three tables away as he barreled through the lunchtime crowd in Corrigan's. "Sorry to be late. But I got held up at a hearing in Curryville."

Ben waved a welcome. Isham was one of his favorites among the party faithful. He could always be relied on to take two tickets to the fifty- and hundred-dollar-a-plate dinners. More important, any table that held Mike and Fanny Isham was so entertaining that it was worth—almost—the price of admission.

"There is no courthouse in Curryville," Ben pointed out as his guest finally thumped his burly form into a chair.

"This was a hearing before their Land Use Board." Isham leaned forward to pluck a breadstick from Ben's plate and, elbows on the table, began to chomp contentedly. There was a glint in his eye that told its own story. "And have I put the cat among the canaries!"

Ben considered what he knew of Curryville. Until fifteen years ago it had been a sleepy little community. Then a new road had brought it within commuting distance of Newburg and the town fathers had seen an opportunity to broaden the tax base. Discreet developments of expensive homes on substantial lots had been approved. Zoning variances had been granted for two private schools. The main shopping strip had been so artfully preserved that it was a jewel of old-time perfection.

"Somehow it doesn't seem like the right environment for you, Mike."

Isham's spirits were dancing. "I'm representing the developer. We're applying for permission to put up low-income housing."

Ben had a strong suspicion that there was worse to come. "And they don't like it?" he asked warily.

"Today was only the first round. I explained to them that, according to Federal statistics, they owe the world 453 units of low-income housing and we're only planning for 218. They should be thanking me."

In spite of a football build, a mop of wiry dark hair, and bushy black eyebrows, Michael Isham contrived to look virtuous. Ben, however, had caught the significant word.

"Did you say *Federal* statistics?"

"That's right, Ben."

"Then they'll be on *my* neck. Thanks for the warning."

Isham waved graciously. "Any time," he said before turning to order a vodka martini.

Ben waited patiently for the drinks before introducing his main theme. "I can do without a lot of crazies from Curryville in my office right now. I have my hands full with these Medicaid hearings."

"I figured that was what you wanted to see me about."

"Naturally, I wouldn't ask you to disclose the contents of a confidential conversation between you and your client."

"Naturally."

Calmly Ben continued, "I wouldn't even ask you how you got your client's files from HEW."

"You'd better not," said Isham genially.

"Because I don't care. But, Mike, we're trying to run some Medicaid hearings in this town. And if you're going to drive all of our star witnesses underground, I'd like to know about it. It's going to mean some replanning for us."

Isham twirled the stem of his glass as he considered his reply. When he looked up, he was serious. "I just don't know yet, Ben. For the record, I'd like to point out that I haven't driven anybody underground yet. Old man Deachman was in his foxhole long before I had him served. I expect the others are already digging theirs. For what it's worth, I'm willing to let you know once I make up my own mind. At the moment I'm just contemplating one malpractice suit. But I'll tell you something, Ben. This kind of case could grow on me."

Ben was too pleased to have won this much of a concession to press for more. "And you've got a sure thing. They tell me this is another perfect plaintiff."

"It's easy enough to say that. Hell, I said it myself before I got to know Ken Atkins. But there's such a thing as being too cynical. You know, Atkins is only twenty-four. There he is, a big, athletic guy who's always led a physical life. And two years ago he's blinded when his car goes off the road. His big problem now is that he's stir-crazy. He's got nothing to do, nothing to think about. Well, I intend to change all that. I admit that I like twisting the tail of insurance companies, just for the exercise. But, believe me, Great Lakes is going to change Ken Atkins' life. They're going to support his family while he goes to school, they're going to train him for a profession, if necessary they're going to set him up."

Ben laid down the menu and stared at his companion. "This is a new tune for you, Mike."

"What the hell, Ben? Most of us spend our lives not getting much done. I'll bet it's the same with you as it is with me. I may get a niggling change in the interpretation of the antitrust laws into the casebooks. Oh, I'm not saying that there isn't satisfaction to be derived from that. There's the satisfaction of having done a good, professional job, even of having seen right prevail. But it hasn't changed anybody's life. And I've come to the conclusion that there isn't much pleasure in the middle-sized jobs."

"Like the ones I spend my time on?" Ben asked politely.

Michael Isham was too intent to notice the jab. "That's right. Real satisfaction comes from the big jobs—like devoting your life to outlawing child labor—or from the little jobs that make a big difference to one human being, that are damn near life transforming."

Ben was so silent that Isham had to prod him. "Don't you agree?"

"Oh, I agree. I can spend days working on a fairly important amendment to some legislation and it doesn't give me the same bang as helping one constituent who's gotten into a tangle with the Veterans Administration. But I wasn't thinking about me. Look, Mike, how would you like to transform two lives?"

"What?"

"I've been trying to think of the right lawyer for her since Friday. It's a girl called Mrs. Wanda Soczewinski. . . ."

12

Nero believed in bread and circuses, and so has every government since. The skimpier the loaf, the grander the pageantry. Washington, D.C., is no exception. At inconvenient intervals, Congressmen and civil servants with better things to do are asked to drop everything and participate in spectacles.

Ben Safford knew his duty, and, having promised to be on the South Lawn of the White House at three o'clock on Tuesday afternoon, he was there. But he was seething at the futility of the whole performance. If Newburg was anything to judge by, soybean prices and OSHA rules were not driven from anyone's mind by flapping flags and Presidential cavalcades. Ben did not know exactly what could make Elroy Hackett forget the Curry River Flood Control Project; he doubted if it was within the capacity of the Federal government to lay it on.

Greeting the Prime Minister of Canada sure as hell did not fit the bill.

"I suppose they'll get over it in time," he said with desperate fair-mindedness to Tony Martinelli. "All the others have."

New administrations were always ceremony-happy. It was part of the human condition. Nor were Chief Executives the worst offenders. It was the White House staff, the new Cabinet members, the most recent regulatory and diplomatic appointees—all pleased as punch to be young, powerful and in the public eye. They were going to change the world overnight and they wanted everybody to see them do it.

Normally, Ben was tolerant of this failing. But there was another force, besides Elroy Hackett, beyond the control of the Federal government. That was the weather. Over the weekend, when these proceedings were being planned, there had been fleecy clouds and blue skies in Washington as well as South Bend, Indiana. The master of protocol had extended himself—an honor guard to be inspected, the Marine band to play, speeches to be delivered. Unfortunately, Mother Nature had produced a steady drizzle, not bad enough to cancel outdoor activities but sufficient to delay flights, to drip from hat brims into collars, to turn the South Lawn into a soggy morass.

"It may be too late by then," croaked Tony, who was sadly watching his black patent-leather shoes sink deeper and deeper into the mire. "Do you think the Canadians will ever get here?"

They were already half an hour late.

"It's just low visibility delaying them, not a typhoon," Ben pointed out before continuing on a more positive note. "And once they get the welcome ceremony out of the way, there's a reception inside. Say what you want about the White House, at least it's waterproof."

"We'll probably all have pneumonia before we get there," predicted a strangely disembodied voice.

Val Oakes could be heard, but not seen. He was gallantly sheltering Elsie Hollenbach under the grandfather of all umbrellas. From Ben's point of view, the two of them were hidden inside a gleaming black tent.

"I do not wish to raise false hopes," said Elsie suddenly, "but I believe I hear the sirens."

As usual, she was correct. Within seconds the banshee wail was audible to all. The limousine with its escort arrived and, right on the dot, the Presidential couple emerged from the White House and came forward under a sheltering canopy. The Chief Executives shook hands and clasped shoulders, the first ladies embraced, from nowhere a small child appeared with a bouquet of American Beauty roses. Then the company stiffened to attention for the band's rendition of "The Star Spangled Banner" and "O Canada!," the honor guard was reviewed on the double and the last lap of the ceremonies was at hand.

Smiling benignly from his dry podium, the President spoke for eight minutes about the United States' good neighbor to the north. By rights, the Prime Minister should then have used the same amount of time in eulogizing Canada's great neighbor to the south. Had it not been for his nation's peculiar internal problems, no doubt that is what he would have done. But at the eight-minute mark, with terminal phrases rolling off his tongue, he suddenly raised his voice and picked up speed. Those present had time only for a brief premonitory shudder before he plunged into a word-for-word repetition of his speech—in French.

At precisely that moment the drizzle became a torrential downpour.

The discipline of public life kept the ranks from breaking. Huddled in misery, they simply endured as water cascaded off canopies, trombones and raincoats. The Prime Minister, his eyes rolling in apology, discharged his polished Gallic sentences at a faster and faster clip until, after the final benediction, he was swept off to the private quarters. The lesser fry stampeded into the shelter of the public rooms set apart for their entertainment.

With soaked garments out of the way, with the first bourbon down the hatch, the guests reverted to standard operating procedure. Even in ordinary times Washington social events are mere camouflage for the sleepless political instinct to caucus, to cajole, to buttonhole. This emphasis on personal contact, however, becomes intensified in the first year of any administration. Legislative and executive personnel are both busy sending out cautious feelers to discover what manner of beings they are dealing with.

Legislators at least have the advantage of being able to recognize their quarry.

"Look," said Elsie, who could dispose of any number of martinis and still be the first to see what was going on. "Why do you suppose Lou is bringing Joseph Buckley over here?"

"Buckley? He's Secretary of HEW," Val Oakes rumbled accusingly.

"One of the Kennedy leftovers," Tony chimed in. "Always available."

Ben could have made the identification without all this assistance. Joe Buckley had been one of the last Cabinet appointees to climb aboard the Ship of State, and it was barely two months since his picture had been plastered all over front pages and television. In his publicity Buckley had been smiling and relaxed. Today, however, he looked strained and intent. Ben didn't make the mistake of suspecting a crisis in government. Buckley was merely trying to match the right face to the right dossier. That creased forehead, that tight jaw merely signaled the effort not to take Val Oakes for a Democrat from southern Ohio or Ben Safford for a Republican from South Dakota. It was not so long ago that an Under Secretary of Defense had somehow managed to identify Tony Martinelli as the elected representative of the Mormon Church from Salt Lake City.

"And this is Elsie Hollenbach," said Lou after the difficult hurdles had been negotiated.

"Mrs. Hollenbach, of course!" cried Buckley with genuine pleasure.

There were still so few women on the Hill that they stood out. For a man struggling to master over five hundred faces, they were oases in the desert.

Flecker didn't let them stray into small talk. "Joe here has just been telling me about an interesting proposition that was put to him. I thought you'd like to hear about it."

"It only happened this morning," said Buckley, taking up the tale. "The lobbyist for the insurance trade association called. Jackson started off by apologizing for taking up my time on such a small matter. He just wanted to bring to my attention a petty detail in paperwork that had been overlooked."

Val Oakes emerged from his glass suspiciously. "In this town when people describe one of their problems as petty, it usually means that they've got a real tiger by the tail."

"That's the way I figured it." Buckley had shed his unnatural tension and was becoming more buoyant by the moment. "Jackson went on to say that naturally HEW wanted to give the health industry the same protection that the airlines and most manufacturers get."

Now everybody was suspicious.

"All it took to set things straight was a simple change in our application form for Medicaid," Buckley continued. "Just before the signature line, there'd be a new clause establishing limited liability for the provider of any health service. In exchange for this, the applicant would waive all other legal remedies." He paused as if politely assuring himself of his audience's attention.

He could not have been in any doubt, Ben thought. Tony was breathing in and out like a steam engine. Ben, on the other hand, realized he had been holding the same breath for several seconds. And

Val was enveloped by the unnatural calm of a placid elephant who is about to stop being placid.

"The limit that Jackson suggested was five thousand dollars," Buckley ended neatly.

"Jesus Christ!" snarled Tony before he was drowned out by the explosions of his male colleagues.

Elsie of course reacted differently. First she waited for the tumult to subside. Then: "And what was your reply to this outrageous proposal?" she asked with such icy precision that Ben expected the air to crystallize.

"Oh, I told him where he could put his petty detail," Buckley chuckled, then paused in horror at his choice of phrase.

"Splendid!" said Elsie warmly.

The whole exchange passed by Tony, who was still boiling. "I suppose this bastard never mentioned malpractice suits?"

"Hell, he never even mentioned doctors." Buckley was becoming hilarious. "To hear him tell it, we were discussing innocent misfortunes happening to hospitals—a power breakdown, an elevator accident, an ambulance skidding on a rainy night. When I pressed him about medical personnel, he did allow that a nurse might give a patient the wrong diet tray."

Lou Flecker believed in giving new Cabinet Secretaries congratulations whenever possible. In his experience, the occasion seldom arose after the first six months.

"This end-run by the insurance companies could have raised Cain. We're all grateful, Joe, that you quashed it right at the start."

Buckley was modest. "I might not have seen the implications if I'd come to it cold," he admitted. "But this regional director we've got out in Newburg seems to be on his toes. He sent me a memo just last week predicting that the insurance companies would have to try something. And when I called him today after Jackson tried his little game, Trumbull brought me right up to date on everything. Or at least everything that's relevant to HEW. I suppose you could say that we don't have a justifiable interest in the more sensational details."

The wistful note of his conclusion was not lost on his listeners. Joe Buckley yearned for an irresponsible gossip about the murder embedded in Newburg's Medicaid scandal. But, far away in Ohio, Quentin Trumbull was being understandably cautious in his dealings with this unknown quantity now heading up HEW. Ben glanced at his colleagues. Surely a Cabinet Secretary who could fend off marauders like this deserved some encouragement? The way Val Oakes lowered his eyelids was as good as a vigorous nod from another man.

"It just so happens that the Police Chief back home is an old friend of mine," Ben began. "We were talking about the Karras murder the other day and he said . . ."

Five minutes later they were all well away on a tide of discussion and speculation.

"So the timing of the murder wasn't simply a weird coincidence," Buckley marveled. "There really isn't any other motive for the shooting except that malpractice suit?"

"None that the police have been able to come up with," Ben reported. "But you have to remember that the motive varies a little from person to person."

"It sure does." Lou Flecker had every reason to recall how Theo Karras had served his subpoena. "Howard White was the only one Karras had directly attacked."

Elsie Hollenbach was at her crispest. "Come now, we mustn't forget that Dr. Rojak was actually placed at the scene of the crime. Oh, I know it was hours after the murder, but surely that argues some kind of contact."

"And from what your friend Chief Jones tells us," Oakes said, "that Rojak has a reputation for meeting trouble halfway. Maybe he decided not to wait for his subpoena."

"He admits as much," Ben pointed out. "But, according to Rojak, it was bribery, not shooting, he had in mind. Besides, if you ask me, the doctor who did the murder took good care not to be found at the scene of the crime."

"If it was a doctor."

Everybody stared at Tony as if he had gone mad.

"Look, I just thought of this," he defended himself. "If Karras was gunning for all the doctors, who was going to be the big loser?"

As the incredulous silence continued, he became impatient.

"Well, who's having hysterics all over Joe Buckley's phone? The insurance companies, that's who! The doctors were only afraid that something terrible might happen to them. But Larry Fournier knew he was going to lose a bundle. Maybe Karras was shot to put a stop to seven malpractice suits, not only one."

Elsie was the first to recover. "But Tony," she protested, "Lawrence Fournier merely works for Great Lakes. He isn't going to lose anything himself."

"Like hell he isn't! The day his division becomes a money-making machine for people on welfare is the day he's out on his can."

"Personally, I wouldn't put anything past that industry." The telephone call from Jackson had left an indelible mark. Secretary Buckley was now prepared to believe that no outrage was beyond the men who had dreamed up that limited-liability clause. But, like all government officials, he had to reserve most of his attention for the broader issues. "Leaving aside the question of who actually killed Karras, we can all see how the poor guy's actions stirred up a hornet's nest. The doctors thought they were going to steal from HEW with impunity. The insurance companies thought they could cover these jokers without getting dragged into the mess. The AMA thought they could protect any individual member because of their group clout. Suddenly it's a whole new ballgame, and they're all roiling around trying to relieve the pressure. A lot of crazy things are bound to happen, from murder to trying to pull a fast one on me. What I don't understand is why there haven't been headlines from coast to coast. I assume the main facts are common knowledge?"

As Ben Safford reviewed the headlines and the front-page stories that had rocked Newburg during the past two weeks, he came to a surprising conclusion. "Not as much as you might think," he said finally. "Of course, the Cincinnati papers already had a crusade going when the murder broke. They had cast the doctors as villains, so they were satisfied with the surface outline—phony Medicaid bills were filed, Karras was smart enough to use that fact for a malpractice suit, and the minute he did, he was shot. They certainly weren't going to muddy the waters by suggesting Karras was an extortionist. But, for all I know, they never got wind of Rojak's testimony. There sure as hell hasn't been one single word about outsiders having access to HEW files."

Buckley grimaced. "I'd be the first to know if there had. And, as a matter of principle, I suppose our files shouldn't be used in lawsuits." He paused as a wonderful vista opened before him. "Not unless we're doing the suing."

Flecker sternly reminded him of administration policy. "And we're all agreed that wouldn't be in the best interests of the country."

"Of course not," said Buckley, unable to hide his regret. "Although I'd sure enjoy hauling some of these doctors into court. And it makes more sense for the Federal government to put them through the wringer than some unknown blackmailer."

Elsie was still suffering the aftereffects of Tony's wide-ranging suspicions. "Speaking of blackmailers, there's another possible solution to Theodore Karras' murder. Presumably he had a confederate who actually stole the documents from HEW. Maybe the confederate decided it would be more profitable to continue the operation single-handedly."

"No, that won't hold water anymore. I haven't had a chance to bring you up to date on the latest wrinkle." Rapidly Ben told them about the Kenneth Atkins suit and the emergence of high-powered legal talent. "So whoever is feeding evidence to Mike Isham is not out for personal gain."

The committee members naturally were concerned with the impact of this development on their own plans. Tony, who had not forgotten Nesta Deachman's Gray Lady impersonation, predicted that now her husband really would have a heart attack. Flecker began to fuss about the possibility of a new delay in his faltering schedule. Val and Elsie were convinced that wily old Ben must have extracted the provenance of Atkins' medical records from his good friend and political supporter.

Joe Buckley's attention, however, had been riveted by a familiar name. "Michael Isham!" he repeated. "According to Trumbull, he's the one who's turning the screw on Great Lakes."

"That sure was what he had in mind," Ben agreed.

"And now that Jackson hasn't gotten any change from me, I suppose he'll be canvassing the rest of Washington," Buckley predicted darkly. "I guess I'd better start warning some people."

He left them almost immediately to start the good work, and Flecker, watching his jaunty progress across the room, said: "Pleased with himself, isn't he?"

"And who can blame him?" Tony asked. "So far Buckley's been smart enough to take coaching from a regional director and to dodge a bean ball thrown at him by some lobbyist. That's not bad going for a rookie."

To a man, they agreed that they had all seen dumber Cabinet members. But they shared the legislator's ingrained distrust of non-elected officeholders. When Ben remarked that it was still early in the game, Val replied somberly:

"It sure is. Great Lakes may have to take a trouncing from your pal Isham this time, but they're not going to make a habit of it. They've got to do something. The only question is what."

— 13 —

Larry Fournier was way ahead of the subcommittee. When Michael Isham, baring his teeth in a wolflike grin, announced a decided preference for taking his case before a jury, the soul-searching began.

The law department at Great Lakes, far from being helpful, was affronted at the mere suggestion of a courtroom defense.

"We're not miracle workers, you know," they said testily. "Look what Isham has going for him. First, there's the policyholder. Everyone knows he's defrauding the government to the tune of a hundred thousand a year."

By now Fournier was desperate. "Isn't that what we've got jury selection for? Can't you keep out the people who know that?"

"What's prejudicial about it?" they challenged. "All the papers did was print the grand total of his billings. White himself testified before the subcommittee that the amount just showed how hard-working he is. Besides, fraud is the least of your problems. Half of Ohio is convinced that he's a murderer to boot. That's your client. Now take a look at Isham's."

Fournier appreciated another distinction that was being made: Howard White was *your* client, not *our* client. The law department proceeded to elaborate.

"According to our reports, Wanda Soczewinski is young, pretty and worn to the bone trying to make a home for two small children and a dying husband. What's more, White knew all about her circumstances because when she came to him for anemia he insisted on talking with the specialist treating her husband."

"Does she say that?" Fournier demanded. "How do we know it's true?"

They looked at him as if he were six years old. "Because White charged for the consultation. You know, it's not just the plaintiff who can subpoena HEW records. *We've* looked at them, too."

Fournier had never been a last-ditcher by nature, but this seemed to be the time to start. "All right, all right. So White's an SOB and the Soczewinski girl is a saint. That doesn't change the facts. We all know that White couldn't have damaged her because he never operated on her."

"He couldn't have damaged her physically," said a legal precisionist. "But what about psychic damage from defamation?"

"Defamation?"

"Picture how it's going to look to a jury. There's Tommy Soczewinski in a wheelchair, trying to defend his wife with his last ounce of strength. There's Wanda Soczewinski looking young and frail and embarrassed. And there's Isham describing how she's working herself to death taking care of a husband who's been incapable of fathering a child for over two years when along comes White to tell the world—entirely for his own fraudulent purposes—that she has to have an abortion."

This aspect had never occurred to Lawrence Fournier. "Oh, my God!" he cried.

At that moment he abandoned all resistance to Michael Isham's claims in behalf of Mrs. Soczewinski. In his heart of hearts he knew that he was not going to contest the Kenneth Atkins case either. All that was so much spilled milk. Great Lakes could survive two settlements. But was there any end in sight?

There was no point in looking to allies. HEW, in the person of Quentin Trumbull, had flatly refused to endorse Medicaid fraud. The insurance industry, when alerted to the problem, had spurred its lobbyist into action that had failed. The AMA had not only rejected sanctions against embezzling members but had mounted threats of its own.

By the time that Lawrence Fournier was meeting with Michael Isham to exchange one large check for a battery of releases, he had reached a fundamental decision. Potential allies were either hostile or helpless. All the firepower was in the hands of that unknown X who, with such unnerving omniscience, raided HEW files at will, unearthed uniquely deserving plaintiffs, selected ideal lawyers. Maybe it was a signal of submission to X that was needed. Fournier was beginning to think of X as some primitive deity belching thunder and lightning unless propitiated with a sacrificial offering. And he knew just where to find the sacrifice.

He was already making his plans as he handed over the check and rose to say goodbye.

"No hard feelings I hope, Isham," he said producing a weak smile and a limp handshake.

Michael Isham patted the breast pocket where he had placed his haul.

"None in the world," he trumpeted joyfully.

Two hours later the scene was the same, except that Dr. Howard White was occupying Isham's chair.

"Now that you know the size of the settlement Great Lakes has had to make with Mrs. Soczewinski," Fournier continued his introduction, "I'm sure you won't be surprised at our additional actions."

"Go on." White's shoulders were hunched as if prepared for the battering to come.

"We would, of course, be fully justified in seeking full monetary restitution from you."

White flapped an impatient hand. "I'd like to see you try," he grunted. But it was an automatic defiance. He was too intent on the blow that was coming to produce his usual outrage.

"But our directors have decided that under the circumstances they will forgo recovery." Actually the directors were trying to placate the AMA. "The one step they insist on is that your policy with us be canceled immediately."

White had never really believed it could happen to him. In spite of anticipation, in spite of calculation, in spite of financial preparation, he was so shocked he could not speak for several seconds.

"You can't get away with this," he said at last.

"Oh, yes we can."

"You don't understand." White licked suddenly dry lips. "It's not just me you'll be fighting, it's the whole AMA. You can't have thought of that."

There was no sympathy in Fournier's glance. "I have just had a very thorough discussion with the regional AMA outlining Great Lakes' proposed action."

"Well—what did they say?"

"They didn't like it, but what could they do about it?"

White stared in dismay. In his experience, the world always jumped through hoops for the AMA—the drug companies did, the insurance companies did, even Washington did. And now Lawrence Fournier was telling him that Great Lakes didn't give a damn whether the AMA was happy.

"That doesn't make any difference," he said doggedly. "I can still go to court and force you to insure me. Your agreement with the AMA obligates you to offer malpractice coverage to every licensed MD in the area."

Fournier might have been finishing his sentence for him. "Except where there has been fraud on the part of the policyholder."

"But that's in all insurance policies. It's supposed to protect you against people who lie in the application. It doesn't mean me."

"And against people who burn down their property to collect fire insurance or people who sell things and pretend they're stolen. A policy is not an invitation to steal from the company."

White was pleading now. "You call it canceling my coverage, but you know that you might just as well take away my license to practice. You can't do this to me."

Suddenly Fournier was tired of the whole exchange, tired of the stately phrases masking ugly realities. "Why the hell not?" he asked, almost conversationally. "Look, White, it's time you came down from the clouds. You've been robbing the government blind for years. Now, with the Soczewinski settlement, you've managed to rob Great Lakes. And still you think we're under some moral obligation to let you go on doing it. Well, we're not."

White had never heard his activities described so bluntly. It was as if the protective mantle of his profession had already evaporated.

"But it's not going to happen again," he stammered, sounding like a guilty adolescent. "That's all over."

"It could happen again tomorrow," Fournier said brutally. "You weren't just greedy with your rotten little schemes. That wasn't enough for you. You had to be lazy and stupid, too. You don't even know how much dynamite may be sitting in those HEW files. But, let me remind you, there's someone who does. And another Wanda Soczewinski out of your past could walk in here any time."

"Look, you're just trying to pressure me about the settlement, aren't you?" White assumed a ghastly parody of a smile. "Maybe I was over hasty about that. I could see my way to splitting the tab with you and then—"

"Forget it. There isn't going to be any deal. You're too hot to handle."

White was looking at an incomprehensible future. "But what am I going to do?" he asked.

"Look for a job."

There was a brief flash of the old White. "A job?" he gasped before stiffening. "That's out of the question."

"It's what quite a lot of us do." Fournier gave a harsh bark of laughter. "Maybe you could find an insurance company that would hire you."

White glared at him with something very close to hatred. "You don't know what I've done to get where I am and stay where I am. It can't all be wasted. It would be too unfair."

Fournier was not laughing anymore. "We've all made big mistakes," he said grimly, "and I guess we're all seeing the things we've worked for go down the drain."

"I didn't want you to hear it from anyone else, Connie," White told his wife almost humbly.

Connie White shook her head as if that simple action could somehow produce clarity from the tumbling kaleidoscope of her thoughts. Cut down on expenses! Sell the house! Move to another part of the country! It was all too much for her.

"They cut you off—just like that," she repeated dully. "Then it's all over with us."

"Oh, no, it isn't. Things could be even worse." Quickly he added: "You forget, doctors are always in demand."

She ignored his attempt to hearten her. "And I thought you'd taken care of everything," she said.

Sadly he shook his head. "So did I, Connie, so did I."

Patrick Costello was the only doctor who had taken Jim Rojak's reassurances about the future at face value. As soon as he learned the news, he dialed Giles Perrin at the local AMA, convinced there was some mistake.

"Giles, what's this I hear about Howard White? It can't be true that Great Lakes has canceled."

"I'm afraid it is, Pat." Perrin had the perfect voice for grave sympathy. In a pinch he could have substituted for an organ.

"But how can that be? I thought we'd agreed you were going to back him."

Perrin was gently reproachful. "We agreed that the medical association would remind Great Lakes that our agreement calls for coverage of all physicians."

"Then do it!"

"We have." Perrin, mindful that he was addressing one of the Newburg Seven, coughed delicately. "Unfortunately, it seems that there is a clause, a purely technical clause—you know what insurance fine print is like—that exempts the company in cases of fraud."

Perrin's tact was wasted on the raging Costello.

"You call that backing Howard? To hell with their fiddling technicality! Why don't you use some muscle on them? Tell them we'll all pull out of their plan and go someplace else. Remind them how much money they make out of us."

"That was exactly the line I took. I told them that this was no way for Great Lakes to keep us as friends."

"That's more like it. What did they say?"

Perrin choked at the mere recollection. "Fournier said: 'Who needs friends like you?'"

"What!"

For a moment the line buzzed as they both silently contemplated this blasphemy. Then Perrin completed his catalogue of woe. "And when I reminded him of our total premium payments, he laughed and said that Great Lakes would be losing money on us before these malpractice suits are over. He practically invited us to find another insurer. And really, Pat, if half the things he predicted come to pass, I don't know where we can go."

"Never mind about that. What are you doing for Howard?"

"What *can* we do? I've told you what they said to me."

"There must be plenty. After all, we contribute a mint to the AMA for just this sort of situation. Go to the national office. Make *them* do something."

Perrin was now on home ground. "Our contributions are used to lobby the government and educate the public. Well, Great Lakes isn't the government and it isn't the public. All they care about is dollars and cents."

He infused so much disgust into his final statement that a stranger would have found it hard to believe that he spent one day a week at his broker's, reviewing his stock portfolio.

Stubbornly Costello persisted in his assault. "Well, there must be some way to bring pressure to bear. Can't Washington force Great Lakes into line?"

"Apparently it's the other way around. HEW is simply handing out medical records to anyone who drops by with a subpoena. They're not doing a thing to protect us. Of course, I always said that it was a mistake to allow Medicaid to be administered . . ."

Pat Costello had already heard Perrin's speech on the iniquities of Federal intervention and he was not interested in a replay.

"So you mean you're just going to let poor Howard hang there, slowly twisting in the breeze?"

"I don't know what you mean," said Perrin, who did understand and did not care for the Watergate reference.

"Well, you're not doing much to help the poor guy."

"That is simply not so, Pat. I did everything I could. Even after Fournier started taking pot shots at the whole Newburg Medical Association, I hung in there. And I did manage to accomplish something. Great Lakes agreed not to make any attempt at reimbursement for its settlement with Mrs. Soczewinski."

"I thought Howard had already transferred everything into Connie's name."

"I wouldn't know about that," Perrin said loftily. "I merely thought he'd probably need the money."

This transformation of Howard White into overnight indigent startled Costello. "He's still a doctor," he said sharply.

After carefully examining this statement, Perrin accepted its accuracy. "Yes, yes, I suppose you could say that," he agreed slowly. "Of course, he won't be in private practice. And these MD's who go into research or work for companies, it's simply foolish to claim that they're the same as us. I always have maintained . . ."

Costello was not a sensitive man, but the detached nature of this observation sent a chill down his spine. Giles Perrin was making Howard sound like someone encountered a long time ago in a faraway land. How many weeks would it be before he was taking the same tone about Patrick Costello? "Oh, Costello," he would say, dredging up the name from the depths of memory, "yes, I believe I did know him once."

Pat gulped and barely listened to the organ notes still coming down the wire. It was a great mistake, he realized, to have adopted Jim Rojak's faith in the power of professional solidarity.

From now on, it was going to be every man for himself.

— 14 —

When Ben Safford had reluctantly left Newburg to take part in the extravaganza on the South Lawn, he had intended to remain in Washington long enough to record his vote on the farm bill, then return to his fence-mending in Ohio. These plans were scuttled when Lou Flecker, carrying a legal pad filled with scrawled notes, entered Ben's crowded office. He was too preoccupied for greetings.

"I've just been with the Speaker," he announced. "He's very upset about my adjourning the hearings in Newburg."

Three startled faces lifted.

"How can that be?" asked Ben. "We weren't getting anywhere. Did you explain to him that all of our witnesses are getting hit with malpractice suits?"

"That's when they're not getting grilled by the cops as murder suspects," Tony amplified.

Flecker shook his head. "He says it doesn't make any difference. The hearings have got to go on."

"Now, that's not like Gus," Val Oakes said comfortably. "I wonder what's biting him."

A martial voice spoke from the doorway. "Probably this irresponsible behavior by Gerry Ewell." Having said her piece, Elsie stalked into the room, sat bolt upright in a chair and impatiently waved away Ben's mute offer of hospitality.

Senator Gerald Ewell was a Democrat, and, by the rules, a fellow party member had to open the attack.

"What's Wonder Boy done this time?" demanded Tony.

"I was just coming to that." Lou squared his shoulders and resolutely carried on. "It seems that when Ewell was on *Face the Nation* last week he promised immediate action in clearing up the Medicaid mess. Then after Buckley talked to him at the White House yesterday, Ewell held a big press conference. He's proposing a bill that requires all HEW regional offices to isolate cases of fraud and immediately start criminal prosecutions. He wants to throw three or four hundred doctors in jail before year-end."

There was a horrified silence. Every member of Congress realized that the slow, steady seepage toward a national health program was reaching a critical point. There was not a single respectable body of opinion that condoned the current situation. Strange to say, this surface unanimity was the major obstacle to legislation because it blanketed at least a hundred different approaches. A complex process of synthesis was taking place whereby the hundred approaches were being reduced first to fifty, then to twenty and finally to a number small enough to permit conference negotiation.

Into this delicate web Senator Ewell had just thrust his big, heavy foot. He would distract attention from the real issues, force legislators into alliances they would later be stuck with and, incidentally, intensify the already serious shortage of doctors.

"You know," said Val Oakes reflectively, "I think the biggest barrier to running this country may be those nuts on the other side of the Hill."

Historically, relations between the two houses of Congress have always been tortuous. Recent elections have not helped, with too many successful candidates undergoing their political boot training on the Senate floor.

Lou Flecker, who would have enjoyed letting his hair down on this subject, made a misguided attempt to divert the storm, "I suppose we were all young and foolish once."

This piece of imbecility received the treatment it deserved.

"It is true that I was once as young as Gerry Ewell," said Elsie through clenched teeth, "but I have never been as foolish."

"Well, Gus is going to talk to the Majority Leader about it."

Flecker was answered by four heartfelt groans.

"And we all know how much good that will do, with the kind of party discipline they've got over there," he continued hurriedly. "So Gus wants all the medical hearings to be in action nonstop for the next couple of weeks. He figures that if we can't stifle Ewell, then we can drown him out."

"Back to Newburg, uh?" Tony Martinelli was unhappy.

"No, not Newburg," Lou said. "The mandate of the committee has been enlarged. We're staying in Washington and we're looking at the big, broad picture of Medicaid abuse, not just doctors charging for nonexistent treatment. We're going to call the bigwigs from Public Health, from the armed services—from Sweden, if we can get them. And Gus says the more headlines, the better."

Eugene Valingham Oakes had long been acknowledged as the supreme political realist by his colleagues.

"If that's what he really wants, Gus may be making a mistake not sending us back to Newburg," he rumbled. "Say what you want, a nice, juicy murder will get you headlines a lot sooner than some quack nobody's ever heard of."

Offhand, Ben would have agreed with Val—until he met Dr. Patrick Costello two days later.

"Costello? Dr. Patrick Costello?" Ben repeated doubtfully when Madge Anderson announced the visitor. "Say, wasn't he one of the . . . ?"

Madge proffered an old newspaper clipping. "This may refresh your memory."

Ben did not have to read very far. "That's what I thought. He comes after Deachman and Rojak. What do you think he wants? He sure wasn't seeking my company in Newburg."

Madge knew exactly what he meant. She raised an eyebrow in inquiry.

"Yes," he decided. "I'll want you to sit in on this. And bring your book with you."

Patrick Costello was so distracted when he entered that he did not notice Madge seating herself in a corner and poising a pencil. In fact, it took him some time to come to grips with Ben's presence. He began by stumbling over a small table, pushed himself away from it, managed to land successfully in a chair and then peered desperately around the room. After scanning the ceiling, the floor, the drapes, he allowed his glance finally to settle on Ben.

"It's hard to know how to begin," he said and stopped short.

Ben was deliberately formal. "Of course, Dr. Costello, I am aware that you have been subpoenaed to appear before the Subcommittee on Medicaid Abuse, and I assume you received our notice when we temporarily adjourned the hearings in Newburg."

"I know you left Newburg," Costello exclaimed petulantly. "But that hasn't helped things any. I tell you, I can't stand much more of this."

"The subcommittee's departure was largely due to lack of cooperation from the first three witnesses we called," Ben said stiffly.

Patrick Costello gave no indication that he had heard a word. He was continuing his lament.

"It was bad enough at the beginning, when the papers started all that lousy publicity. I can remember our discussing it at the hospital. We all agreed we'd never expected to see doctors smeared that way. Little did we know what was coming." Dr. Costello swiveled his head, inviting the world to share his wonder. "Say, what's she doing?"

"My secretary is taking notes of our conversation."

"Oh, no, she isn't. That way, you'd have me coming and going. We don't need notes to settle this problem."

"All right. Miss Anderson, would you put your book away?" Ben wanted a witness more than he wanted a written record. "Now, what's this problem, Dr. Costello?"

"My God, I want to get off the hook, that's the problem. I'm just as tough as the next guy, but things have gone beyond a joke. Do you know that the cops actually came to the medical building and questioned all of us? Now, how do you think that looks?"

Ben blandly returned his visitor's glare while he decided which question to answer. "No, I hadn't heard that."

"Well, you must have heard that yesterday Great Lakes canceled Howard White's malpractice insurance. For God's sake, if you don't know that, what do you know?" This was such an earth-shaking event in Dr. Costello's world, he never doubted it was receiving national attention.

The news did, in fact, interest Ben. He hoped that Great Lakes' action was the result of a gigantic settlement for Wanda Soczewinski. But at the moment inquiries on the subject would be tactless.

"Dr. Costello, I can see that you're upset at what the police and Great Lakes are doing, but I must remind you that none of this is the subcommittee's fault."

"You're the ones who are trying to put us out of business."

Ben's tone sharpened. "The subcommittee is a lot more interested in encouraging doctors to behave responsibly and honestly than in putting them out of business."

"Oh, I know all about that system. You encourage the rest of the medical profession by making object lessons out of us." He narrowed his blue eyes and assumed a look of childlike cunning. "Well, Patrick G. Costello doesn't intend to be one of the whipping boys. It's not enough that you're yanking our insurance, now you want to throw us in jail. That's enough to scare me, and I'm not ashamed to admit it. I'm getting out from under, and I'm willing to pay for the privilege."

Ben could scarcely believe his ears. "Dr. Costello," he said warningly, "I am one member of a subcommittee that has five members. I am not even the chairman."

Patrick G. Costello was not the man to back down in the face of a little resistance. "Yes, but you're my Congressman, and it's your job to help me."

Ben was beginning to think that he didn't need a witness, he needed little men in white coats. Anybody who was foolish enough to offer a bribe in the face of a clear red light was foolish enough for anything. Across the room, Madge Anderson looked like one of the avenging furies.

In tones as portentous as he could manage, Ben said, "I think you may have been misled by recent political scandals. In spite of what you clearly believe, it is still not common practice to—"

Costello interrupted indignantly. "It's not just politicians, it's everybody. So why can't *I*? I began thinking of it as soon as I saw that Senator on *Face the Nation*."

Behind his left shoulder, Madge was violently semaphoring as she prominently mouthed the same set of syllables over and over again.

"Senator Ewell?" asked Ben, stalling.

"That's the one. I want you to keep him off my neck, and I'm ready to do the usual thing."

Suddenly light dawned. "Dr. Costello, do you mean that you want immunity from prosecution if you testify?"

"Of course that's what I mean," the doctor snapped. "What else could I have in mind?"

"I can't imagine," Ben murmured absently. Who would ever have thought that Gerry Ewell's self-indulgence would bear such useful fruit? "Tell me, have you consulted your lawyer about this?"

Costello's eyes nearly started from his head. "Are you crazy? Look at the trouble that White and Deachman have gotten into with lawyers. I'm not going anywhere near one."

"I see." Ben nodded. It was not his job to explain the difference between lawyers working for you and those working against you. "If the chairman approves, it is possible, just barely possible, that we can provide immunity against Federal prosecution."

Costello folded his arms and struck a Napoleonic pose. "That's what I want, and I won't settle for less. Not one word do you get out of me otherwise. After all, I can always come down with heart trouble, too."

This remark erased the last of Ben's scruples. If the occasion should arise, there was plenty of time for Dr. Patrick Costello to learn that the murder of Theodore Karras was a matter for state prosecution. There was one point, however, that had to be raised.

"You do realize that any immunity granted by the subcommittee will not necessarily be a protection against Great Lakes?"

"Oh, yes, it will. I've thought the whole thing out." Costello hunched forward and explained his strategy. "If HEW can't prosecute me for fraud, there's no reason why I can't take the stand in my own defense and testify that I didn't perform any of those operations I charged for. So Great Lakes wouldn't lose a penny in a malpractice suit."

He beamed broadly, inviting congratulation.

"Always assuming the jury believed you," Ben said.

Costello was affronted. "Good God, why shouldn't they? I'm the doctor. I know whether I performed an operation. Besides," he continued buoyantly, "nobody's going to come after me, not now that I've changed sides. I'm going to be a voluntary, cooperative witness."

Many men have made this promise. Few have fulfilled it as completely as Patrick Costello did in the days that followed.

During the first few hours of the resumed hearings he behaved like any witness with something to hide. He weaseled, he hedged, he palliated, he justified. But when Elsie Hollenbach's turn at the microphone came, a miracle took place. It soon became apparent that, all his life, Costello had been looking for someone who found every tawdry detail of his existence as interesting as he did. In Elsie he recognized a genuine thirst for knowledge, in himself he discovered a genuine desire to instruct. A torrent of names, dates and facts began to pour across the subcommittee table. There were only a few newsmen in the room, but after twenty minutes with Mrs. Hollenbach at the helm they knew they had a front-page story.

"We call it ping-ponging," Costello told her chattily.

"I've never heard that expression before. Could you tell me what it means?" Elsie asked.

"You see, we all have offices in the same building. So when someone on Medicaid comes in to see me, I look him over and say he ought to see the internist across the hall. Then the internist sends him back to see the cardiologist, the cardiologist routes him to the neurologist and so on. By the time he gets to the end of the corridor, instead of just one billing, we've got eight or nine racked up. It really maximizes his visit."

"So it would seem." Elsie was devoid of all human expression.

Under these circumstances, Lou Flecker was far too shrewd to continue rotating the microphone. With silent unanimity the subcommittee delegated its tasks to one member, and the hearings became a dialogue. The success of these tactics was self-evident at four thirty when participants and onlookers spilled out into the waiting arms of television reporters eager to tape a few comments in time for the evening round-up. By six o'clock there were even headier signs of triumph.

"CBS has just asked Gus for permission to televise tomorrow's hearings." Flecker was so overcome he was whispering.

The next day was even better. In front of a packed gallery, Elsie Hollenbach made an incautious remark suggesting that she was now familiar with the depths of medical avarice.

"Oh, that's nothing. If you really want to clean up, you should try nursing homes," replied Costello, who seemed to have convinced himself that Elsie was on the brink of graduating from medical school.

Elsie cocked her head thoughtfully. "Of course, that way you get rid of the civilians, as it were," she reasoned. "You have a population consisting entirely of patients."

"That's only half of it. The big thing is to *own* the nursing home. And don't worry about the cost," he advised her earnestly. "The bank finances most of it. After all, why shouldn't they? It's a sure thing."

"Because the government is the ultimate guarantor?"

"Sure. A lot of people over sixty-five are already on Medicaid. So if a doctor decides a nursing home is a medical necessity, the tab just goes on their bill. And even if they're not on Medicaid when they go in, HEW picks them up when their money runs out. But the monthly fee is only the beginning. There are all the extras—examinations, tests, therapy, psychiatric observation."

Elsie was grim but determined. "And, as the patient's doctor, you have no competition in a nursing home. You decide on what services are necessary."

This was so obvious that Costello merely nodded. "But the real gold mine is prescriptions," he continued enthusiastically. "All you have to do is come to an understanding with a pharmacist. Then he can supply the stuff by the barrel, you okay it and the two of you split the take."

"And they all agree to this arrangement?"

"Well, naturally. Do you realize the mark-up on drugs? Besides," said Costello as if the thought had just occurred to him, "a pharmacist who didn't agree to the split would never get to fill a prescription for one of our nursing homes."

During the afternoon Costello regaled his audience with a further refinement on this scheme. It was possible for physician and pharmacist to set up their own drug house. Then the physician wrote brand prescriptions rather than generic prescriptions and the mark-up was even higher.

"All you have to do is make yourself into a company," Costello confided. "That's the way we handle the nursing homes. In 1972 we set up Rest Vale Homes, Inc. We just had to put in a hundred and twenty thousand, and in 1977, after all expenses, we made . . ."

That evening Gus sent more than congratulations; he sent reinforcements.

"We've got two full-time staff members now," Lou reported upon meeting Ben and Val on their way out to dinner. "They're going to winnow out some more witnesses for us. Gus doesn't want us to lose momentum now we've started rolling."

"That's fine for Gus, but what about poor Elsie?" Ben objected. "She's been on stage for two full days now and she's had about enough."

"It wouldn't be easy for me," said Val, wagging his head solemnly, "and I don't feel things the way she does."

Lou rushed to agree with them. "I know it's hard on Elsie. She's carrying the full load. But what can I do?" He raised his hands help-lessly. "You saw what happened when I tried to spell her this morning. Costello clammed up, and then she had to work twice as hard as if I'd never interfered."

This was so true it needed no discussion. During the past forty-eight hours Lou had tried to introduce every single member of the subcommittee into the dialogue—to no avail.

"Elsie isn't the only one who's been in the spotlight," Ben said op-timistically. "Maybe Costello will start to run down."

These hopes were dashed the next morning. Elsie arrived looking like an aristocrat on her way to the guillotine. Costello, on the other hand, came bouncing in, all boyish anticipation. Back in Newburg he had his own private gold mine and a certain status. In Washington, for the first time, he was tasting the sweets of fame. He could hardly wait to take Tony Martinelli aside and tell him that the headwaiter of a downtown restaurant had addressed him by name.

"And it was the first time I was there," he marveled.

Tony's reply was more a form of gargling than an attempt at human speech.

By eleven o'clock Elsie had decided on desperate measures. In an attempt to stem the flow of Patrick Costello's disclosures, she raised the hitherto banned topic of billing Medicaid for nonexistent services.

"I really don't know why we bothered with that," said Costello, willing to consider the subject philosophically. "After all, there are plenty of surgeons around who'll operate at the drop of a hat. You just shove your patient on to them for gallbladder or something, they give you the regular kick-back and everybody's happy."

"Everybody?" Elsie's control was beginning to weaken. "What about the patient?"

Dr. Costello defended himself. "Mrs. Hollenbach! I always make it a point to use a first-class surgeon."

After that Elsie pulled herself together and doggedly went on doing her duty, while Ben reflected that Wanda Soczewinski could be thankful that Howard White had confined himself to paper crime. He could have used a knife.

When Lou Flecker entered Ben's office six hours later with his daily ration of good news, it took him some time to realize that a mutiny was brewing.

"We've done it!" he said gleefully. *"Meet the Press* has scrubbed

Gerry Ewell for this weekend. They want Elsie in his place. Gus says keep up the good work."

Lou had not expected the room to ring with cheers, but the total lack of response led him to examine his colleagues warily. Elsie Hollenbach was lying back in the most comfortable chair with her eyes closed. Val Oakes was examining the ceiling. Ben was looking for something in a drawer.

It was Tony Martinelli, who had his back to the room while he messed around with a small hotplate, who finally brought himself to reply.

"You want to know what Gus can do with his pep talks?" he asked with menacing calm.

"Oh, come on," Lou protested. "I know this has been a hard week for all of us, but Gus is just trying to get some results, Tony. He didn't invent Costello. Tony, what the hell are you doing over there, anyway?"

"I'm making tea," said Tony defiantly. "That's what Elsie wants and that's what Elsie is getting."

"And what Gus wanted was to have Ewell drowned out," Val said. "We've done it, and now we're through."

It was Ben's turn. "The whole thing is a circus. We're not Congressmen questioning a witness. We're an audience watching some kook act out a fantasy with a mother substitute."

Nervously, Lou cast a glance at the brooding, silent figure in the middle of the room. "If I'd only known you felt so strongly," he began and then could think of no conclusion.

"Here, Elsie," said Tony, tenderly offering a cup. "I think this stuff is dark enough to drink by now."

Given the personalities of the two principals, Tony, in spite of his office, did not resemble a ministering angel. He looked more like a second trying to get a punch-drunk fighter on his feet before the bell rang. What's more, he succeeded.

After an invigorating sip Elsie straightened and fixed a basilisk gaze on Flecker.

"As you know," she intoned somberly, "I am opposed to violence in all its forms on principle. But if I have to face that man for one more session, I shall not be responsible for the consequences."

"Attagirl!"

"But, Elsie! Tony!" Lou pleaded. "I'm on your side."

He had just made the decision. Like every chairman, Flecker spent his life alternately propitiating the party leadership and the members of his committee. Gus had just had three days' priority, and now, Lou realized, it was time to shift his weight to the other end of the seesaw.

"I'll tell you what," he cajoled. "We won't call Costello anymore."

"You'd better not."

"What's more, we won't even go public tomorrow. As a matter of fact, this fits in very well. You know Robarts, this staff man we've got now. Well, he's got a witness he wants us to see in executive session."

There were times, Ben mused, when Lou Flecker came apart under the pressure. "Now wait a minute," he said. "The whole point of our holding these hearings, Lou, is to attract publicity. If Robarts has decided this witness isn't appropriate for public hearings, then there's no point in calling him."

"But that's just it. Robarts refuses to make the decision himself," Lou replied. "He says that either this guy is exactly what we want or else he's too hot for anybody to handle."

— 15 —

"This guy" was Dr. Alexander Urquhart, and it took only ten minutes the next morning for the subcommittee to understand Robarts' quandary. Urquhart's credentials were overpowering. His illustrious career had included the Army Medical Corps, UNRRA, the World Health Organization, the U.S. Public Health and the Rockefeller Institute.

His paper record misled the committee. Of course, they knew that expert witnesses are never really unbiased. That, after all, is why special-interest groups hire economists, scientists and engineers to do the talking. What they are buying is the appearance of being above the battle. To a man, these professionals cultivate a veneer of scholarly detachment.

Compared to his colleagues, Alexander Urquhart might have been a bull in a china shop. He was a large, grizzled man of incredible vigor and passionate conviction. For his appearance on Capitol Hill he had chosen to wear a bright red shirt and a sky-blue tie under a disgraceful jacket. As he argued his case, the scrap of tissue he had applied to his chin after shaving waggled in rhythm to his speech. He freely characterized his opponents as a bunch of corrupt mercenaries or, at best, a pack of mindless idiots.

His platform was as startling as his personality.

"You want to know what to do with the present medical establishment?" he demanded, lowering bushy brows. "Well, I'll tell you. Sweep the whole damn thing away!"

The illustrative gesture accompanying this proposal toppled the carafe on the table. As Robarts rushed forward to mop up the stream of water, Urquhart continued, "You're not going to get anywhere with a lot of mincy-pincy little changes. The rot goes too deep. Now's the time to cut!"

At least three of the subcommittee members flinched at Urquhart's gusto. Only Elsie Hollenbach was unmoved.

"Perhaps you could be more specific, Doctor," she said composedly. "We would be interested in your detailed recommendations."

Urquhart grinned ferociously. "That *was* a specific recommendation."

Lou Flecker looked worried. A playful witness was the last thing the House leadership wanted as an encore to Patrick Costello.

"Come now, Doctor," he said impatiently. "We've been holding hearings for over a month, and we've learned a lot about some pretty nasty corners in modern medicine. But we do realize that there are many fine, dedicated men in the profession."

"So you think you know the worst," Urquhart said. "Oh, I've followed your proceedings in Bangor and Newburg, and I suppose they were all right. Although, if you ask me, you should have been able to have them without getting some poor lawyer gunned down. I even listened to that bastard Costello. Not that any of that even scratches the surface. When are you going to stop horsing around and get down to brass tacks?"

Tony Martinelli was stung. "Horsing around?" he repeated. "We've uncovered rip-offs wherever we've gone. What are you complaining about? That we haven't gone to every town in the country?"

"You're letting some petty thefts blind you to the big picture. Larceny doesn't have anything to do with medical care. Why, in Malaysia I had to protect the antibiotics with armed guards. But that didn't affect the real problem, which was a cholera epidemic."

Only Elsie was on top of the situation. "Granted that fraud does not directly relate to patient treatment, still it is a major defect in our present system." She narrowed her eyes. "Moreover, it diverts Federal funds that could be more usefully employed."

"I suppose you think that it's the crooked doctors who are a menace," Urquhart said. "Well, let me tell you, it's the *good* doctors who are imperiling decent health care!"

There was a moment's silence. Then Ben Safford cautiously ventured into the arena. "Would you care to expand that and explain to me why we couldn't use some more hard-working doctors?" he said, remembering good old Doc Yarborough cruising off Tahiti while sending in bills for long-dead patients.

"Sure." Urquhart was openly enjoying the subcommittee's reaction. "First off, you've got to realize that most doctors don't have the sense of a groundhog. How can they? From the minute they step inside a medical school, they start losing contact with reality. They're supposed to become high-powered specialists, to keep up with all the advances, to master the modern technology. So what happens?"

With a well-honed instinct for timing, he broke off to refresh himself.

"I'll make it easy for you. If you had a serious accident a hundred years ago, they'd cart you off to the nearest shelter. There some woman would run around stanching the blood, yelling for blankets, washing the dirt away. Her techniques may have been primitive, but she was addressing the right problem. She was trying to keep you alive. Now, suppose you got smashed up on the throughway in 1972 before my shock program."

Urquhart beamed at them as he prepared to reel off supporting evidence.

"They'd take you to a hospital. Someone would draw specimens for tests. The orthopedic man would want a lot of X-rays. The burns man would decide what skin grafts you'd need. The neural surgeon and the kidney specialist would get in on the act. In the meantime you would die. My shock program is the modern equivalent of that housewife who had enough sense to put first things first."

Elsie Hollenbach was beginning to take his measure. "As a matter of fact, the subcommittee is familiar with your shock program and the quite remarkable results it achieved," she said. "But we can scarcely scrap an entire system because it has failed in a special instance. We are concerned with medical procedures over a broad range of applications."

Urquhart's smile became even wider. "So it's general applications you're interested in. What about birth and death? Is that general enough for you?" he added with genial contempt.

Four of the subcommittee members looked as if they suspected a trap. The fifth stretched and, for the first time, assumed an air of wakefulness.

"I like the sound of that," Val Oakes said. "But where are you going with it?"

"Nowhere unless we agree on certain fundamentals. I proceed on the assumption that a human being is born, lives a certain number of years and then dies."

Oakes nodded approvingly. "That's what the Good Book says. Threescore and ten."

"Fine! You're already way ahead of most doctors," Urquhart encouraged him. "Take birth, for instance. In nine cases out of ten delivery is normal. But, Jesus Christ, have you seen what's going on in the maternity wings these days? The standard procedures are designed for the one-in-a-thousand genuine emergency. It costs a hell of a lot, it wastes resources and, above all, it's turning women off. Before we know it, they'll be having their babies at home, where they're unprotected against the one overwhelming danger, infection."

Lou Flecker always made an effort to see both sides of the question. "I can see how it's wasteful, but why should the women complain?"

"Horse water! How would you like it if you got a small cut and some nitwit shoved you into intensive care?" Satisfied that he had quelled all signs of revolt, Urquhart went on, "The minute you get inside a hospital, everybody acts as if you're sick. But if what you're doing is natural, you're *not* sick. A mother delivering a baby isn't sick. And if you really want to get down to the crunch, an eighty-six-year-old man who's dying isn't sick. But try telling that to most doctors. Medicine doesn't have any business waging war against death. It should be concentrating on providing maximum function and maximum comfort throughout a normal life span. And I'm telling you that when an establishment has lost its marbles about birth, about death and about any accident you have in between, then it's ready to be junked."

Val Oakes was not only staying awake, he was bandying words with an expert witness. Dr. Alexander Urquhart was the only person in the room who did not recognize the compliment.

"Now, that all sounds pretty God-awful, Doc," Oakes said. "Got any suggestions for improving the situation?"

"Ah, ha! What do you think I came up here for? There's no mystery in providing decent health care, not if you've got the guts to ram your program through." His gaze roamed the table, seeking those qualities. "Mrs. Hollenbach, the first thing you have to do is take the administration out of the hands of the doctors. They don't know anything about running large institutions and they can't handle financial problems. It's like expecting Picasso to run the Metropolitan Museum of Art."

Elsie was competently taking notes. "Of course, doctors are often notoriously bad executives," she agreed.

"If that were only the worst of it." Urquhart fanned out three large-knuckled fingers. "First, they run hospitals for their own convenience instead of the patient's. That's why you have unnecessarily radical surgery. It's not that they're all crooks, but it's a lot easier to overdo rather than exercise judgment. Second, they're patsies for the drug companies, handing out estrogens and tranquilizers like peanuts. Finally, they're indifferent to the policy implications of what they do. Look at any city with old people on Medicaid. Somewhere you'll find an operating theater where a whole team of surgeons is putting a pacemaker into a ninety-two-year-old who's going to die the next week of kidney failure."

Tony Martinelli nodded. "The action always follows the money," he said sagely.

"Well, it shouldn't do so by accident," snapped Urquhart. "Nobody in his right mind would allocate scarce medical resources to the dying instead of the living."

"Naturally, we realize there's a shortage of doctors, but—" Lou Flecker began.

"Of course there's a shortage. And there will be as long as you people let the AMA walk all over you." Urquhart was still ruffled. "We need to triple the number of MD's. And not with a lot of dermatologists and plastic surgeons. What this country needs is an army of GP's."

"Medical students don't want to be GP's!"

Urquhart was beginning to flail again. Silently Robarts rose and removed the carafe to a side table.

"To hell with that! There are probably a lot of boys at West Point who don't like their first assignment. You should establish a dozen medical schools, support the kids through their training and then make them spend five years doing what the country needs. Apart from relieving the shortage, you'd get some ballast into the medical profession that way."

Privately Ben thought you were more likely to get a doctors' strike, but he understood that to get information from Dr. Urquhart, you had to play by his rules. "And just what do you mean by ballast?" he asked.

"In the old days when doctors were GP's they had some common sense," said Urquhart, who had never spent a single day in general practice. "That kind of experience wouldn't be a bad idea for young doctors today."

"Maybe not," Flecker conceded, "but the Army can send officers where it wants because it pays their salaries. How are these young doctors going to be taken care of?"

Urquhart bared white teeth. "Exactly the same way. The sooner these kids are weaned from the fee-for-service system, the better."

Elsie Hollenbach drew herself up. "I fail to see that. Doctors have traditionally charged on the basis of services performed."

"Why the hell should they? If your house is ablaze, the fire department comes and puts it out without sending you a bill based on the size of the fire or the amount of work they had to do. If you hear burglars breaking into the house, you call the police without haggling about how much it's going to cost you. Those are public services designed to protect human life. So is medicine. Why should doctors be handled the same way as electricians and plumbers?"

Elsie was caught on the horns of a dilemma. She regarded fee-for-service as the hallmark of the professional. Urquhart had just reminded her of its use on a lower level.

"But surely there is a reason," she argued. "Fire and police protection has to be institutionalized. But doctors—and plumbers, if you like—are individuals. Would the taxpayer be willing to salary individuals whose major effort in any time period may be for someone else's benefit?"

Urquhart raised his bushy eyebrows. "That's what they do with their Congressmen," he retorted. "Honest to God, I don't know what ails you people on the Hill. You set up Medicaid so that the more services a doctor performs, the more money he gets. Hasn't it crossed your minds that the mess you uncovered in Newburg would never have occurred if the doctors had been salaried? Doesn't that recommend a change to you at all?"

"It depends on the changes," said Flecker. "You're coming up with the kind of overhaul I'd expect from the Baader-Meinhof gang."

"You haven't heard the half of it," Urquhart promised.

Three hours later Ben Safford reeled back to his office, his head ringing. Lou Flecker, after announcing he would defer consideration of Dr. Urquhart's future role, had scuttled off to the seats of the mighty. Elsie and Val had disappeared, arm in arm. Only Tony trailed in Ben's wake.

Madge Anderson needed only one look to realize that refreshments should come before questions. She waited until they had collapsed with glasses in hand before asking:

"Well, what was Dick Robarts' mystery witness like?"

"He's a wild man," said Tony uncompromisingly.

Ben expanded on this simple judgment. "Oh, he's a real expert, there's no doubt about that. But he hits his audience like a train going downhill without brakes. Anything in his way is just going to get smashed to smithereens."

In some ways Madge was as much a politician as her employer. "Yes, but is he for or against a national health plan?" she asked with lively interest.

"Oh, he's very much for," Ben reassured her.

"And with allies like him, who needs enemies?" Tony added.

Madge was backed against the desk, her chin resting thoughtfully on one fist. "You mean you're not going to call him in open session, even though he's an expert and he's on your side?"

"How can we? The guy doesn't know how to behave." Tony looked confidently toward Ben for support. When it was not forthcoming, he sat upright, a perplexed frown forming.

Ben was studying the contents of his glass. At last he raised his eyes. "What makes you think he can't persuade the American public, Tony? He hasn't done a bad job on the committee."

"The committee!" Madge had every right to be dumfounded. The last people likely to be influenced by expert testimony are those to whom it is addressed. The subcommittee included many political views. Ben and Tony were the standard-bearers for thoroughgoing reforms. Elsie, representing her affluent suburb, was concerned with skyrocketing medical costs. Val and Lou were the two fiscal conservatives.

Until today it had been assumed that this spectrum would remain unchanged throughout the hearings.

"Dr. Urquhart," said Ben, almost strangling over the name, "has persuaded Val and Elsie to consider a major government role in health care."

At first Madge gaped. Then she tried to look on the bright side. "Well, you were hoping to persuade Mr. Oakes to modify some of his opinions."

"Val hasn't modified his opinions. He's had a religious conversion," Tony sputtered. "A week ago he wouldn't even listen to a national insurance program. Now he's ready to draft doctors, put the Public Health people in charge of all inoculations, establish Federal licensing, Federal medical schools and Federal panel practices."

Ben joined in the chorus: "Val says Urquhart is the first person who's come up with a coherent program."

"What's more, he's carrying Elsie along with him."

Nobody could have worked on the Hill for more than one week without grasping the implications of this statement. And Madge had been there for five years.

"But that means the Republicans on the committee are running away with the whole ballgame," she gasped.

The silence that followed was mute agreement. Then Ben became philosophical.

"Well, that's the way we reopened relations with mainland China. Maybe it has to be the Republicans who pass a national health program."

Tony, who had been sweating blood in the cause for three terms, was so indignant he was stuttering.

"Who cares about China?" he demanded. "How the hell am I supposed to explain this to my constituents?"

16

Closed sessions were taking place elsewhere. In Newburg, Ohio, for example, there were private discussions going on all over town.

At the Riverside Manor Nursing Home, where Dr. Arnold Deachman was still recuperating, Graham Friend, the manager, sat listening.

". . . put through the call and it turned out to be some damned reporter from the *Chicago Tribune* asking about Costello," Deachman complained. "People don't come here to be disturbed by nuisance calls, Friend. You tell your switchboard that."

Friend nodded wearily.

"And I don't want people just dropping in whenever they please. The desk should check with me before they let anybody in to see me —and I mean anybody."

"I'll make a note of it," said Friend absently.

"See that you do," Deachman told him sharply.

The nursing staff classified Dr. Deachman as a difficult patient— demanding, ungrateful and self-pitying. Graham Friend knew better. Deachman in bathrobe and pajamas was no different from Deachman reviewing the books.

"How long are you planning to stay here at Riverside?" he asked.

Deachman, sitting in a comfortable chair near the window, gripped the armrests. "What the hell kind of question is that? I'm staying here until my doctor decides it's safe for me to go home."

Graham Friend was professionally unctuous. His capable head nurse ran the nursing home while he soothed, sympathized and deferred. For fifteen fat years Friend had offered Newburg families everything a first-class undertaker provides, this side of the grave. To the doctor who made all this possible he was prudently obsequious.

But Friend knew that Arnold Deachman's lawyer was a more frequent visitor than Deachman's doctor. He knew every word of Patrick Costello's performance in Washington, too. And he was scared enough to be himself.

"I know you've got problems, Deachman," he said with a new inflection. "But right now I think you're making one big mistake drawing attention to Riverside."

While Deachman gasped, he continued, "You'd better talk to that lawyer of yours about our arrangement here. That's what *I'm* doing."

"Why . . . why . . ."

But before Deachman could pull himself together, they were interrupted.

"Oh, Arnold. Out of bed? Do you think that's wise?"

Nesta hesitated on the threshhold. She was carrying an armful of packages. "Oh, hello, Graham. Do you think Arnold should be out of bed?"

Graham Friend was all too willing to slip back into his traditional role. "Well, now, I'm not the doctor, you know."

"Never mind about that," Deachman growled. "You'll be interested to hear, Nesta, that Friend thinks I'm bad publicity for Riverside just now. He's going to his lawyer to review our arrangements."

Nesta paid no attention to the querulous tone in her husband's voice. Instead she cocked her head, inspecting Graham Friend thoughtfully. The brilliant blue eyes were very cold.

"Who needs a lawyer? You're simply on the payroll here, Graham. You can leave any time." She paused before delivering her final thrust. "Or we can throw you out."

"Now, wait a minute. I have a proprietary interest—"

But she wouldn't let him finish. "Ten percent!" she said scornfully. "That's just to give you a bonus when you do your job properly. Have you forgotten that I know all the figures? You made a damn good thing out of us last year. If you don't watch your step, there won't be a *next* year."

As if the conversation were finished, she turned away from him and busied herself unwrapping books, depositing a new pair of slippers, tidying away some dried flower petals.

Friend stared at her back for a moment, then shifted his attention to her husband. But Deachman had recovered his assurance during the counterattack.

"You'll remember those points I raised, won't you, Friend?" he demanded.

Graham Friend knew when he was beaten. "I most certainly will," he said, withdrawing.

Nesta dropped her pretense of aloofness the moment the door closed. "Little rat," she muttered.

"He's just the first. They've all heard about Howard White by now. They've all read what Pat Costello is saying. And you know what's going to happen next, don't you? Great Lakes will pull *my* insurance. God knows I've done my best, but it's all been wasted effort." He was deliberately whipping himself into one of his unreasoning, unrestrained rages. "Everything was supposed to be over by now. Karras was just some cheap lawyer on the south side trying a shakedown, you all said. He was supposed to have a hundred enemies. The police would go haring off in some other direction and there wouldn't be any more lawsuits. Instead, look what's going on."

With a sickening lurch in the pit of her stomach, Nesta realized that he was now in that frenzied stage where he would lash out at her.

"It's all your fault," he suddenly charged, just as she had known that he would. "Look what I've done for you. Look what—"

Clapping a gloved hand over his mouth, she spoke urgently, pleadingly, *"Don't* say it, Arnie. Try to get a grip on yourself. You don't know who may be listening. Do you want to ruin your whole life?" Her voice was almost hypnotic. "Think of me for a change. Haven't I been a good wife? Haven't I been trying to help you?"

He thrust her hand away, but the moment of crisis was over. Almost sullenly he agreed with her. "Oh, you mean well. But it's money, money, all the time with you, Nesta. If it isn't a diamond bracelet, it's a mink coat. And I gave in to you. That's the real trouble. I should have put my foot down. None of this would have happened if I had."

She knew it was untrue, but she was all too ready to encourage this new line of thought. "That's all over, Arnie. We'll be more economical now."

"You'll have to handle everything," he insisted. "I'm a sick man, I can't take any more. I don't want to hear about lawsuits or malpractice or Howard White . . . or anything."

Out in Curryville, Dr. White was not reciprocating.

"I suppose they'll sue Deachman once he comes out of hiding," he said with satisfaction. "Then Great Lakes will pull *his* insurance too. And as for that little bastard, Costello—"

He and Connie were barricaded in his den, the only small room in their whole house. They sat as they had been sitting every day since Great Lakes had canceled. Unlike her husband, Connie could still face the children, the housekeeper, the delivery men and the neighbors. But, since she was loyal and supportive, they were huddled together.

"I don't care about Deachman and Costello," she said warmly. "I care about us."

"Then they'll go after Jim Rojak. I've never liked him," said White. "He's too damned smart for his own good."

They had spent long hours on nondialogue like this. By now White was corroded with bitterness. Connie still thought there must be a way out.

"Howie, I understand you can't practice in Newburg anymore. But what about moving to someplace new—someplace like Hawaii? It would be hard on the kids and I'd hate to pull up roots, but—"

Bluntly he told her again what his lawyer had told him: no malpractice insurance in any one of the fifty states.

Connie bit her lip. Then: "But isn't there any way you can practice without insurance?"

"I could join the Army," he said sourly. "Or I could take a job with one of the oil companies and go to some hellhole in Arabia. Or I could become a medical missionary."

"Oh," she said, deflated. She knew that medical missionaries, even oil-company doctors, do not run to yachts, expensive colleges and ocean frontage on Cape Cod. She took a deep breath and forged ahead. "Howie, tell me: how soon are we going to have to sell the house?"

"Soon," he said in anguish.

Straightening her shoulders, she said: "Well, you know how

Phyllis is always saying that I'm really a born salesman. Maybe
now's the time for me to ask her for a job in the real-estate firm."

"Oh, God," he moaned, burying his head in his hands.

She rubbed his neck. "Don't, Howie. Don't."

Raising his head, he peered at her blearily. "God damn them all to
hell. That cheap little shyster. And that little slut of a Polack."

Mrs. Wanda Soczewinski looked around Charlene Gregorian's
office with wide eyes. Usually the door was open and the throbbing
life outside spilled in. Usually Mrs. Gregorian was yelling at somebody in the anteroom or answering the telephone while she looked
up all the rules and regulations for someone. But today the phone
was quiet by request. The door was shut. Mrs. Gregorian, her plump
features crinkled into monkeylike concentration, was giving Wanda
her undivided attention.

Wanda herself was bathed in the golden radiance of utter happi-
ness. Otherwise, she would have been uncomfortable. But right then
nothing could touch her.

"Two hundred and fifty thousand dollars," she breathed. "Mrs.
Gregorian, we're never going to have to go on welfare again."

In the old days Charlene Gregorian would have been whooping
with joy, rushing around getting the secretaries to congratulate
Wanda, breaking out coffee and cookies. Now she said quietly, "You
bet your sweet life you won't. Here, Wanda, you've got to sign this."

True, she looked immensely pleased. But it was an inner glow, not
fireworks.

As Wanda Soczewinski carefully wrote, Mrs. Gregorian studied
her benevolently, then said, "How's Tommy?"

With sunrise in her eyes, Wanda looked up. "He's down at
Lundgren Ford—to see about getting a car that's all specially fitted
out for a wheelchair."

"You're not going on a spending spree with all that loot, are you?"
said Charlene with a fair assumption of severity. She didn't have to
heed Wanda's earnest protestation. Michael Isham had already been
busy. The Soczewinskis were going to live on a modest income from
an annuity tied up by the sharpest lawyer in Newburg. Wanda and
Tommy were in no danger of spending sprees—or of fast talkers
who had wonderful ways for them to invest their money.

". . . kind of sorry for Dr. White because it's so much money,"
Wanda was saying, to Charlene's unconcealed horror. But she went

on, "But Mr. Isham explained how it was the insurance company, not the doctor. And besides, he shouldn't have said those things about me."

"I wonder if he realizes that now," said Charlene, to herself rather than Wanda. "Well, that's his problem and good luck to him. Wanda, I'm awfully happy about this."

"I know you are, Mrs. Gregorian," said Wanda fervently. "You've been so good I don't know how I can thank you. I don't know what I would have done."

"That's what we're here for," said Mrs. Gregorian gruffly. "Now, Wanda, I've got a favor to ask you."

Unresentfully she watched the girl's struggle with sudden wariness. Wanda's life was a triumph and a tragedy. The goodness, the love, the gratitude were real; the innocence was gone forever.

"Anything you want, Mrs. Gregorian," said Wanda Soczewinski steadily.

More touched than she would admit, Charlene said, "I'd like you and Tommy to let me set up a press conference for you."

When Wanda looked blankly at her, Charlene said, "You see, we get so much flak about welfare, Wanda. I'd like to let everybody know that people do go off it."

"We-ell, it's okay for me," said Wanda honestly, "but I'll have to ask Tommy."

"Why don't I drop by tonight to ask, if that's all right?" said Charlene cunningly.

She had lit another candle. "Oh, that's wonderful," Wanda exclaimed. "He loves talking to you. And I suppose it *is* a good idea to let people know how much we want to stand on our own feet."

Charlene Gregorian smiled blandly. She was using Wanda, but in a good cause. It wasn't going to be a media blitz, just a *Newburg News* feature. But before a lot of local sympathy built up for poor Dr. Howard White and his poor wife and his poor kids, Charlene Gregorian intended to remind the taxpayers about Wanda Soczewinski, former welfare mother. Tommy, she knew, would see what she was up to. But Tommy would be with her one hundred percent.

If they were reading about Pat Costello or Wanda Soczewinski at the Newburg Country Club, there was no sign of it. When Dr. James Rojak pulled into the parking lot, when he left his name at the switchboard, when he changed clothes in the locker room, he was met with exactly the same degree of cordiality that his visits always evoked. In many ways the club and Jim Rojak were made for each other. He might be contemptuous of the decorous Saturday-night entertainment, but he appreciated the excellent athletic facilities. He was a familiar figure on the tennis courts for eight months of the year and inside on the squash court during the other four. And when Rojak did something, he liked to do it well.

"That wasn't bad at all, Jim," said the tennis pro as they left the court after their hour together. "You're handling the follow-through on your volley a lot better."

"I've been working on it," Rojak admitted.

After approval came disapproval. "But if you don't do something about your base-line game, some chump is going to steal the tournament from you. You can't rush the net all the time."

This was another facet of the club that Rojak enjoyed. Like the flight room at the airport, like a sports-car rally, it gave him the illusion of participating as an insider in a totally different life—and a suitably virile one. The tournament they were discussing was simply the club's annual event, but Wayne Milton analyzed technique and strategy as if he were coaching Rojak for Forest Hills. And Jim Rojak, who knew perfectly well that he could not pilot a Boeing 707 or tune up his own engine, was willing to abet the illusion.

"Got time for a drink, Wayne?" he suggested.

Milton consulted his watch. Here it was he who was the busy professional, and Rojak who was the patient.

"Glad to. I don't have to be back on the court for forty-five minutes."

Five minutes in the bar proved why Rojak, in his turn, was an ornament to the club. He made a habit of ordering lavishly, always choosing the top of the line whether it was whiskey or beer. He tipped everybody in sight. Unlike the brokers and real-estate agents, he was never guilty of touting for business. His conversation, rigorously confined to his hobbies, suggested not only that he was a man of leisure but that the other members were, too. And when his profession did obtrude—as it did now—it added immeasurably to the tone of the place to have the PA system request Dr. James Rojak to call Dr. Stephen Oldenberg.

"Don't have to leave, I hope?" said Wayne Milton when Jim returned to his seat.

"No, no. Just some test results." Rojak stuffed his notes into his pocket and returned to pleasure. "Now, about my backhand."

Milton was earnest. "You could improve it a lot in the next two weeks if you put in the time."

Rojak looked unconvinced. "Putting in time isn't going to change my nature."

"Oh, you're always going to play an aggressive game," the pro said in laughing agreement. "You'll still get nine out of ten of your points from your serve and the net. All I'm trying to do is stop you losing points at the base line."

Rojak produced his diary in token of surrender. "All right, we'll try it your way. Why don't I have an hour with you this Thursday, then on Saturday and Tuesday? And I'll tell you what: if this scheme of yours seems to be working, I'm ready to put some real work into it, come spring. Then maybe I could blast out of these club games and get into some of the real amateur competition. Aren't there some sanctioned matches for the state playoffs?"

One of Rojak's many gifts was the ability to pick up a conversation at the same point where he had left it. This time he was forced to break off when Wesley Briggs paused at their table for a greeting. But after affable inquiries about a Briggs hunting trip in Michigan, he returned to his point.

"What do you think?"

"Well . . . I guess . . . that is, I mean to say it might work out."

It did not take a musician's ear to detect Milton's embarrassment. Another man might have ignored it. But that had never been the Rojak way.

"What's the matter, Wayne? You think my game's as good as it's ever going to get?"

"God, no! That's not it," Milton answered far too readily. Then, reminding himself that they were on his turf and Rojak was forcing the issue, he met the problem head on. "You see, Jim, the word's going around that you're next in line for one of those malpractice suits."

"So?" The challenge was unmistakable. "What effect is that supposed to have on my game?"

"I just didn't expect you to be making plans that far ahead," the pro answered sturdily. "If you want to know, we haven't seen a sign of the Whites or the Deachmans for over two weeks here."

All of Rojak's arrogance was to the fore. "You don't surprise me. They're probably shivering in their houses, waiting for the roof to fall in. But this is the last place I'd stay away from, it gives me a real sense of security. And hiding isn't the way I play the game, remember? I'm not hanging around the back court waiting to get clobbered. I'm going right in to make things happen my way."

The pro had long since realized that he was paid to help members straighten out their tennis, not their lives. He regularly disengaged himself from conversations about marital discord, sexual frustration, financial failure. The first step was to finish his beer.

"That's fine for tennis, Jim," he said after a mighty swallow. "Let's hope it works as well with this."

"Don't worry about me, Wayne. There are a lot of things worse than losing malpractice insurance, and I aim to avoid them all. You may not know it, but you're looking at a survivor."

The glass grounded with a thump. "I can tell that. And now I've got to get back to the courts." Milton was already on his feet. "Can you make it four o'clock on Thursday?"

"As far as I know. I'll give you a ring if anything turns up." Rojak's smile glinted defiantly. "But why should it? I'm not worried about a thing."

— 17 —

Nobody was tracking the activities of the Newburg Seven more carefully than the Newburg police.

They had followed Patrick Costello's testimony word by word, they had known about Howard White's cancellation within the hour, they had even had a little talk with Graham Friend about Dr. Arnold Deachman's profits from Riverside Manor.

"The whole thing gets crazier and crazier," Lieutenant George Doyle summarized for the benefit of Chief Owen Jones.

"You're not claiming those doctors don't have plenty to cover up, are you?" Jones asked. "If half of what Costello says is true, most of them should be up the river."

"Hell, yes. There's plenty of dirt to sweep under the rug. But I don't see how shooting Karras has helped anybody."

"It sure didn't do White much good. I hear he's closing his practice."

Doyle shook his head in baffled irritation. "And I haven't told you the latest on Theodore Karras. That makes less sense than the rest of it put together."

Momentarily Jones hoped that some interesting anomaly in the victim's private life might have emerged. "I told you to do more digging there," he congratulated himself.

"We dig any further, Owen, and we'll come out in China. I know more about Karras now than I do about my own wife. I've talked with his relatives, his neighbors, his clients, his oldest friends and everybody he routinely bumped into on his daily round. I've even had a session with the boys at the precinct house in his district."

"I thought Karras wasn't a criminal lawyer."

"He wasn't," Doyle replied. "But he was in the habit of obliging the people in his neighborhood. If somebody's kid got picked up on a first offense or somebody's husband got thrown in the drunk tank, Karras would roll around to do what he could. So he was no stranger to the precinct. When you get right down to it, it's surprising the number of fixes we can get on Karras. He was practically a regular at the Federal Building. In the old days they saw a lot of him in Immigration and Naturalization. Lately he's been spending more of his time at all the welfare offices. Only yesterday I was asking about him at HEW."

"Well, we already knew he had an inside contact at HEW. That must be how he latched on to the ammunition for his malpractice suits."

"But this time I was asking about Karras as a man. And everywhere you go, it's the same story. He was old-fashioned, he was small-time, he was a nut about social justice. But he was honest as the day is long. He was enough of an oddball, they all agree, to hanker after the idea of playing Santa Claus. He would have enjoyed dreaming up a scheme to defraud the insurance companies in order to benefit people like Wanda Soczewinski or Kenneth Atkins. But as for his taking a bribe from some doctor to double-cross his clients— no way!"

Chief Jones had good reason to distrust the judgment of ordinary Newburg citizens. Every time an embezzler at the bank was arrested, every time a lawyer was disbarred, his old friends were shocked and incredulous.

"Is that what the boys at the precinct say?" he asked skeptically.

Doyle let the words drop like individual stones. "That's what they say."

Jones produced a complicated sound—part grunt, part groan, part snarl. "All right, *their* word I'll take. But you can't just go around knocking perfectly good theories on the head, George. You've got to—"

Fortunately, the phone saved Doyle. The call wasn't long, but it diverted the Police Chief.

"Sure, send her in," he was saying. "George is right here with me. We'll both talk to her."

As he hung up, he looked inquiringly at his lieutenant. "Somebody called Charlene Gregorian wants to talk to whoever was at HEW yesterday. You know who she is?"

"Sure. I've never met her, but I've heard all about her. She's a bigwig at Social Security. You know the one I mean. She cleared things up for Duane's father."

Owen Jones was more than willing to be cordial to a lady who had helped the father of a policeman, but he never got the chance. Charlene took charge of the discussion while he was still drawing a chair forward.

"Somebody was with Quen Trumbull yesterday asking a lot of questions about Theo Karras," she said accusingly.

Doyle misunderstood. "I'm sorry I missed you, Mrs. Gregorian. I guess that was a real mistake. After all, Trumbull hasn't been at the agency for all the years you have."

"Never mind about that," Charlene flicked back. "It's not who you were talking to, it's the questions you were asking. Quen says that you've got some harebrained idea about Theo being an extortionist."

George Doyle suppressed a sigh. Not only was everybody he visited prepared to endorse Theodore Karras' character, now they were storming the police station with their testimonials.

"That's not quite fair," he said, using every ounce of control. "When a man is murdered, we have to look at all the possibilities. We've kept as much as possible out of the papers. But you know the HEW set-up, you must realize how it looks to an outsider. Karras had found some way to penetrate the HEW files and get the raw material for a bunch of malpractice suits. He was getting in touch with the doctors to put the pressure on. Of course, that doesn't necessarily mean he was out to line his own pockets. Maybe he was just trying to jack up the ante for his clients by getting the opposition nervous. But we have to be realistic: somebody blew his brains out because of what he was doing."

Charlene was aghast.

"There's another side to all this. We haven't forgotten that," Doyle pressed home his advantage. "Maybe Karras was honest and he had a partner who wasn't. But in that case you'd expect the shakedown attempts to continue."

"And this is the way you try to solve a murder!" It was an indictment, not a question.

Like all policemen, Owen Jones regularly modified his tone to suit the circumstances. If Doyle was going to be warm and sympathetic, then Jones automatically became harsh. "We have to work with what we've got. We still don't know how Karras arranged for Kenneth Atkins' file to surface. If we can't figure it out now, it's a cinch the murderer didn't foresee it."

"But Theo didn't bribe anybody at HEW. He never had any files until Wanda Soczewinski brought hers to him."

"Mrs. Gregorian, you knew Karras and we didn't. We respect your opinion, but there's no way anybody can know what he had and how he got it."

"Of course I know! I'm the one who rifled the Medicaid files. I'm the one who sent Wanda to Theo Karras!"

Both policemen froze into immobility and stared at their visitor. Charlene stared right back, her cheeks flushed with determination, her jaw cocked defiantly.

When Doyle at last found his voice, he spoke softly and slowly, as if to displace a minimum amount of air.

"Let me see if I've got this straight. You claim that you and Karras were in this together?"

Charlene shook her head so vigorously that the frosted blond curls bobbed like corks. "There's no claiming about it, and Theo Karras didn't have the slightest idea what I was doing. I sent that file to Wanda Soczewinski and told her to take it to Theo. Then I repeated the operation with Kenneth Atkins and his file, but that time with Mike Isham."

"You got any proof on all this?" Owen Jones challenged.

"Well, that's a fine approach." Charlene was bristling with indignation. "I come here to straighten you out, and you're so hellbent on making Theo Karras out to be a blackmailer that you're not even interested in the truth. There's proof lying all over the place. For heaven's sake, I'm the one who did all the original work on those files, I'm the one who knows them backward and forward. The other five files I was going to send out are sitting in my apartment, so is the typewriter I used for notes to Wanda and Kenneth Atkins. My fingerprints are probably somewhere if you could be bothered to check."

"We've been interested in the truth all along," Chief Jones said gruffly. "What about you? How come you just got around to straightening us out?"

"That's because you're so proud of keeping everything out of the papers. All you've managed to do is mislead people. I knew Wanda would tell you what happened. That should have been enough. How was I to guess that you'd go tearing off in the opposite direction— until Quen Trumbull told me about the questions you were asking?"

"So you're just doing your duty in a murder investigation?"

"No." Charlene was looking at her motive for the first time. "I never thought twice about that. But I'm not going to have you smearing Theo Karras. God knows he had his faults. He could be completely unreasonable, and he liked seeing conspiracies around every corner. But the idea of extortion would simply never have crossed his mind."

"All right, all right!" This time the irritation was coming from Doyle. He had emerged from his bemusement, impatient to move the conversation along. "You're saying that Karras never had any file except the one relating to Dr. Howard White."

"Exactly." Charlene was relieved to see that the Newburg Police Department was finally taking it in. "The only reason he had that one was that I knew Wanda would be too timid to go to one of the flossy downtown offices. But she lived in the same neighborhood as Theo and she'd seen him around all her life."

Owen Jones belatedly saw where Doyle's reasoning would lead. He wanted to explore the possibilities, but not in front of an outsider. "Well, I'm glad you finally came in, Mrs. Gregorian," he said, placing his palms flat on the desk and hoisting himself upright. "I hope you realize that we may not be able to keep your activities to ourselves. As soon as we start checking out your story, somebody at HEW may get wise and—"

"That doesn't make any difference." In her attempt to be casual, Charlene was curt. "I told Quen Trumbull all about it before I came down here. That was only right."

Jones shrugged. "So long as you know what to expect. And if we find all this proof you've mentioned, we'll accept your story. But I'll be damned if I understand your reasons for starting this whole circus."

"You must have been crazy!" In spite of himself, Ben Safford could come up with no other explanation.

Michael Isham squeezed Charlene's elbow reassuringly. "Don't mind Ben," he advised her. "He's had a long, hard day."

Ben glared at the attorney even though his statement was undeniably true. The morning had been spent in Washington on the nagging question of natural-gas prices. The longer the debate continued, the more irreconcilable opposing viewpoints became. Then he had embarked on a jolting flight to Newburg and an endless taxi ride to Curryville, where he appeared as featured speaker to the Southern Ohio Soybean Conference. There followed more taxis, more handshakes and another speech (this time to the Future Veterinarians of America). By the time he trudged up to the Lundgren front door, it was nine o'clock and he was dreaming of a hot tub and a rum toddy. Instead he was met in the front hall by his sister Janet fiercely whispering that she had her most tiresome in-laws in the living room and would he please make himself respectable at once.

Under most circumstances Mike Isham's arrival without the courtesy of a preceding phone call and with a wilting client tucked in his arm would have met a cool welcome. But half an hour listening to Martha Kirkland slander every living member of the Lundgren family had worked its familiar magic.

"Come in! Come in!" he had sung out joyfully. "We can talk privately over in *my* wing."

But somehow they had never got farther than Janet's kitchen. Partly this was because Charlene's blurted confession had halted Ben in his tracks. Partly it was because Mike had cast languishing glances at the electric percolator, which was just issuing its final thumps on the counter. Now, ten minutes later, they were established in the breakfast corner.

Ben had not revised his opinion. "Crazy as a coot," he repeated.

"I'm sorry for the trouble I'm causing Quen Trumbull. I'm sorry for using Theo and Mike." Charlene was pinkly defensive. "But I'm still not sorry that I did it."

"Good girl!"

Ben ignored this contribution from Mike Isham. "It's not as if you were some minor file clerk. You're a responsible Federal official."

"That's just the trouble. If I were a clerk, I might be innocent enough to think something would be done to those seven doctors. But I knew damn well they'd sail through the whole scandal and come out as if nothing had ever happened."

It was Ben's turn to be defensive. "I suppose it looks as if we're lying down on the job. Or, worse, that we just don't care."

"No, no," Charlene said swiftly. "It's not your fault or those other Congressmen's. Your job is to come up with a better health system, not to punish a few crooks. But you've got to remember that I personally know the people whose misery was enriching those doctors. I couldn't help contrasting the burning shame that Wanda Soczewinski felt at being on welfare with the total lack of shame with which Dr. Howard White used her Medicaid number every time he wanted a bigger boat."

Ben was finding it harder and harder to maintain a keen edge on his indignation. "I can see why you were mad," he admitted. "It's the next step that baffles me."

"At first, when I noticed that Wanda's file was the perfect material for a malpractice suit, it was just an academic observation." Charlene sounded almost nostalgic. "I told myself that if only the money were to come out of White's hide, I'd start something. But what was the point if an insurance company was going to protect him? I was really very stupid. It took me almost a week to realize that the insurance company wasn't going to sit down under that kind of loss. As soon as they saw what Medicaid fraud was costing *them,* they'd put a stop to it. If they didn't do it for one suit, they'd certainly do it for a whole series. And suddenly the whole ball of wax gelled. With a simple set of photostats I could get seven deserving people off welfare for life, I could give those seven crooks a kick in the groin they'd never forget and I could probably scare every other doctor in Newburg into being honest for at least a year."

Mike Isham beamed. "Beautiful, just beautiful," he murmured.

"I'm not denying that your motives were good. Hell, they were wonderful," Ben said in desperation. "But what about you? You've spent your whole life in Social Security. You'll lose your job. You may even lose your pension. And you're not a young woman."

"I thought about that. I knew it was a risk." Charlene was very dignified. "But my two girls have finished college. I decided I could always take care of myself. And then, when I went to see Mike to apologize, he said . . ." She trailed away in her first show of confusion. "You'd better explain that part, Mike."

Isham braced the fingertips of his right hand against those of the left and became every inch a counselor at law. "You may be leaping to conclusions, Congressman Safford," he said formally. "On what possible grounds could Mrs. Gregorian be discharged?"

"For God's sake, Mike! She raided confidential Federal files, she disseminated their contents to the public."

Isham's smile had thinned down to narrow legal specifications.

"Any classification of 'confidential' implies that there are certain parties to whom distribution is proper. Are you aware that every document mailed by Mrs. Gregorian was simply a duplicate of information already forwarded to the same recipient?"

Ben knew more about Medicaid's budget than its method of payment. "Then why were her mailings such a bombshell?"

"Because the way HEW mails the information out, nobody can make head or tail of it," Charlene said bluntly. "I pruned."

Isham waved a magisterial hand. "Let *them* say that, honey, not you. And it doesn't change the legal position. Wanda Soczewinski already had everything you sent her. That makes her an appropriate person for distribution in the eyes of the Federal government. In addition, she has a statutory right-to-know that would have enabled her to get those documents. And, finally, Charlene did not disseminate anything to the public. It was Soczewinski and Atkins who chose to do that. When Charlene came to me with this story, I had no hesitation in offering myself as her advocate in the unlikely event that anyone at HEW contemplated action against her."

"Unlikely, is it?" Ben did not know whether to be outraged or hopeful.

"It sure is," said Mike, returning to normal. "How do you think the Cincinnati papers are going to play it when I tell them that it was their investigative reporting that inspired Mrs. Gregorian's conduct?"

"You son of a B," Ben muttered in admiration. The message was clear as a bell. In the first place, any attempt to specify a charge against Charlene would stir muddy waters. Second, Michael Isham was expert at turning muddy waters into a strong current running in his client's favor. Third, with one phone call Mike was going to turn Charlene into a public heroine. "Under the circumstances, it probably *is* unlikely that HEW will make trouble. It's a cinch this Congressman will resist any such attempt."

Isham threw his head back with a bull-like roar of laughter, "I knew you'd see it our way, Ben."

Charlene, who had been anxiously watching first one man, then the other, gave a sigh of relief. "Then you really think I won't be fired? It sounds like a miracle."

"Hell, it's only simple justice. They ought to give you the Medal of Honor."

Ben decided somebody had to introduce a sobering note. "The

question is, how many miracles do you need, Charlene? You may be out of the woods with HEW. But what are the police going to say about all this?"

"Oh, the police!" In Charlene's universe the men in blue came a long way behind HEW as upholders of social decency and compassion. "All they care about is that murder of theirs."

At that very moment Owen Jones and George Doyle were confirming Charlene's opinion of them.

"Okay, the squad car we sent says everything is in Mrs. Gregorian's apartment, just the way she said." The Police Chief was still disgruntled. "So we accept the lady's story as the truth. Where does that leave us?"

Doyle had been champing at the bit for hours. "The only file that Karras ever saw was the one that girl Wanda brought to him. He had no reason to expect to see any others. Nine chances out of ten, he thought Wanda had managed to get it out of HEW herself. Which means that Theodore Karras had no reason to see any doctor except Howard White."

"And in spite of that," said Jones, "we have Jim Rojak telling us that Karras called him out of the blue to try a shakedown."

"He was very careful to say that Karras didn't mention a shakedown specifically."

"What difference does that make? Rojak was lying through his teeth. Karras didn't call him and Karras wasn't blackmailing anybody."

Doyle was more cautious. "Rojak may not have known that."

"Holy Christ, George! We just proved he's lying."

"Sure he is. But don't forget the background. When Karras slapped that malpractice suit on White, he really shook up the whole bunch. All seven of them had a meeting that day, and they assumed he was out for what he could get."

"Why should they assume that?" Jones asked, genuinely puzzled. "Lawyers start suits every day without planning on extortion."

Doyle wondered if he could explain. "You haven't met these doctors, Owen. They're as crooked as corkscrews. Take Rojak. You should have seen him in Karras' shabby little office. He takes it for granted anybody that poor would do anything for a buck. Which means that if anybody tried to sell him a story about Karras' corruption, he'd swallow it, hook, line and sinker."

Jones rubbed his knuckles thoughtfully along his jaw. "If you've got something in mind, George, come on out with it."

"Try this on for size. White goes down to Karras' office to buy him off. Karras won't play, they quarrel and White kills him. God knows why. Maybe in his excitement White gives Karras more ammunition. Anyway, White beats it, and when he's back home, he realizes he left something behind. He considers his buddies and he decides that Rojak is the he-man in the crowd. So he calls him, but he dresses up the story. He says Karras was the one who called, Karras was planning to fleece all seven of them, but he, White, has saved the day. In return for all this self-sacrifice he wants Rojak to go down the next morning and pick up his glove, his lighter or whatever it was. It's as safe as houses. If the body has already been discovered, Rojak simply walks away. If Rojak has to make the discovery himself, the body has been cold for hours."

"If it's that safe," Jones objected, "why doesn't White do it himself?"

"He's afraid of being recognized. That isn't a deserted street by evening. Say White parked in front of the newsstand or the drugstore. He doesn't want to stir anyone's memory." Doyle was growing enthusiastic. "And it explains one thing that's always bothered me. The reason Rojak went to the drugstore to phone in the murder was so that he could call White and tell him everything had worked out."

"I like it," Jones said slowly. "But you realize we don't have nearly enough to bring White in and question him."

"Hell, no! All we've got on White is logic. But we've caught Rojak in a couple of lies. That's plenty to start leaning on *him*."

Jones had not met Rojak, but he had heard enough to be dubious. A man who is not embarrassed by being exposed as an arrant thief has a thick skin.

"It's not going to bother him to be trapped in a couple of lies."

But Doyle was riding a crest of confidence. "It is if he thinks it opens him to serious suspicion of murder. Then he'll sink anyone else faster than you can spit. Believe me, when push comes to shove, Dr. James Rojak is looking out for number one!"

— 18 —

Within twenty-four hours the predictions of both Lieutenant Doyle and Michael Isham came to pass. When Dr. James Rojak was ordered to present himself at Police Headquarters the next day, he seemed to be expecting the summons.

"All right, then. Five-thirty." There was a pause, followed by a sound that could have been a sigh. "And don't get your handcuffs ready. I can clear myself without any trouble."

His lack of surprise might have been due to the fact that Charlene Gregorian's story was spread all over the front pages in Cincinnati, in Dayton, even in Chicago. The press corps had unanimously hailed her as a heroine.

At the Community Medical Building in Newburg, of course, she was viewed differently. There, only a thin veneer of normalcy remained. Patients still sat waiting, receptionists still granted appointments, doctors still appeared fleetingly. But, just below the surface, the Community Medical Building was riddled with dissension, fear and recrimination. This deterioration was amply evidenced by the early arrivals for a council of war.

Dr. Howard White chose to enter by the main entrance and the public elevator. Using the private entrance would have shielded him, but he had decided that this was a gesture that had to be made. Nowadays his life consisted almost entirely of gestures. The substance had evaporated the day he became Great Lakes' sacrificial lamb. White nodded a greeting to his nurse, trying to ignore the fact that there were no patients in his waiting room. The whole rabbit warren of interconnecting cubicles was empty except for himself and Mrs. Blair, Miss Anstruther and the typist.

"You'll be glad to hear that we're holding a meeting this afternoon to discuss action," he announced with an eerie feeling that his voice was echoing through catacombs.

Mrs. Blair and Miss Anstruther had the inscrutable eyes of registered nurses. For the first time in many years White wished he could tell what they were thinking. Unconsciously he pressed for some kind of response. "Now that this woman at Social Security has come into the open—"

"Charlene Gregorian, Doctor," supplied Miss Anstruther acidly.

White did not know how to take this. "Charlene Gregorian," he repeated. "This announcement of hers has changed the entire picture. She actually admits using confidential medical records in a deliberate attempt to destroy me and other doctors. Obviously, there must be laws against that sort of conduct. And redress, too. . . ."

Groping for words with the right resonance, White did not notice their lack of attention until Mrs. Blair, after an exchange of glances with Miss Anstruther, said: "Doctor, since you're giving up all your appointments, you obviously don't need nurses anymore. Irene and I—and Leslie, too—have to start making plans." She saw his incomprehension and became more specific. "We have to start looking for new jobs."

While Howard White watched his world crumble, Arnold Deachman and Nesta were still fighting for theirs on the floor above.

"Yes, I'm feeling better, but I'm not up to seeing any patients," said Deachman to his junior associate, Dr. Garcia. There were still customers in these offices, although the receptionist reported some cancellations. "Mrs. Deachman and I have come in this afternoon for an important meeting. I don't have to tell you, Garcia, now that we know what's behind these so-called malpractice suits, we've got a real weapon."

Dr. Garcia's perfunctory interest drew a hostile glance from Nesta, who was restlessly lighting a cigarette. Charlene Gregorian's bombshell had blasted Deachman out of Riverside Manor Nursing Home, itching for a counterattack. But Nesta, who did not share his confidence, was assailed by apprehension. Usually she enjoyed sweeping into Arnold's office with a brilliant smile for the nurses and secretaries who had once been her co-workers. Today it had been an ordeal.

"Arnie says that we've been stymied until now because we didn't know who was doing this," she said, hoping for agreement. "But now it's a different ballgame."

Garcia merely nodded in silence. It was Deachman who grew enthusiastic. "Mrs. Deachman is sitting in with us because she has been dealing with Great Lakes while I was convalescing," he said weightily. "Not that there's any doubt about what line we should take with them. We have a right to demand that they stop this Gregorian woman in her tracks."

Nesta was wondering how long her husband could ignore Garcia's mask of impassivity when there was an interruption.

Jim Rojak, jaunty in a sports jacket, stuck his head in the door. "Somebody told me you'd left your sickbed to come down here and fight the good fight. How are you, Arnie? Nesta?"

Garcia muttered something about a patient and fled. Rojak looked after him appraisingly. "Poor guy thinks we're contagious," he said, apparently without ill will. "He should try going upstairs. Howie White is roaming around there pretending to be his usual cheerful self. I saw Eddie Cohen duck into the ladies' room to avoid him."

In the old days Nesta had claimed that a little of Rojak's insouciance would be a big improvement in her husband's colleagues. Today she was singing a different tune.

"Howard?" she gasped. "You mean someone was stupid enough to invite *him?* What in the world can he hope to gain by sitting in? He's already lost his insurance."

"He wants to get it back," Rojak told her bluntly.

Her jaw set. "At our expense. His being here could hurt the rest of us." She turned to her husband. "Can't you do something about it, Arnie?"

"I'm not sure that would be wise, although I agree that his presence may be an embarrassment," said Deachman. "Howard would have been wiser to stay away and rely on us to protect his interests."

Nesta was getting jolts from every direction. "Are you crazy, Arnie? We're going to have our work cut out protecting ourselves. Howard is already sunk. Of course it's too bad and all that, but it's not our fault he was at the head of the list."

All of Deachman's old pomposity seemed to have revived. "I refuse to concede that any one of us is sunk. And I shall certainly advocate that we stand by each other. We are all policyholders of Great Lakes. And now they have proof that these trumped-up charges are nothing but a cheap piece of malice, it is their clear duty to hold us harmless. Without regard to the fact that Howard White was number one on that list or—" he took a deep breath to go on—"or that I am number two."

Jim Rojak knew all about these numbers. "Arnie, do you really think this powwow is going to do any good?" he said with undisguised contempt.

Deachman flushed at his tone. "I wouldn't be here if I didn't."

"You and our buddy Pat Costello!" Rojak commented sardonically.

For a moment Deachman forgot his commitment to unity. "Costello!" he said indignantly. "Do you mean to say he has the gall to show his face—after what he did in Washington?"

"He's in the same mess we all are," said Rojak, dropping all pretense of amusement or detachment. "Isn't that what you just said?"

Arnold Deachman stared at him unblinkingly. "When we meet with the lawyers and Fournier at four o'clock—" his Rolex showed it was half past three—"I fully expect to find differences that will have to be ironed out."

"You certainly will if you go on insisting that we try to carry Howard White," Nesta burst out bitterly. "He's nothing but a dead weight now."

"Every man for himself, is that it, Nesta?" Rojak asked.

She refused to be intimidated. "Naturally, we have to look out for ourselves. And you don't have to act as if I'm pushing Howard White off the raft. The way I see it, he doesn't have a chance and it would just be silly to saddle ourselves with him when *we* still do."

"Oh, yeah?" said Rojak evenly. But he was looking at her husband.

Deachman set his lips stubbornly.

With a short laugh Rojak pushed himself off the corner of the desk. "What I need now is a good heart-to-heart with Howie White. I'll see you upstairs at four." And he strode out unceremoniously.

Nesta stared after him in bewilderment. "What was all that about?" she asked.

Deachman glared at her. "Can't you even put two and two together?" he demanded harshly. "My God, it was spread all over the front page."

"But that was all about the Gregorian woman and how she stole files from HEW," Nesta protested. "What are you suddenly so uptight for? You said that was a good thing, knowing who she was."

"A good thing for us and a bad thing for Jim Rojak," he instructed her flatly. "There are still murder charges pending. Or have you forgotten?"

She paled under her make-up. "But what does that have to do with us?" she stammered.

"It's what it has to do with Rojak that's important. He claimed Karras was trying to blackmail him, and we all accepted that. Then this woman comes along and blows his story sky high. Karras had no material with which to blackmail any doctor after Howard. Now that makes me start thinking." His death's-head grin made Nesta shrink. "And naturally it has the same effect on the police. They want to know why he really went to Karras' office."

"My God, Arnie, that's a terrible thing to suggest."

He lost all patience. "It's a lot better than what you've been doing. Here Rojak has just been ordered down to Police Headquarters, he's on the hot spot of his life, and you're prattling about how it's every man for himself, how we should stop standing by each other, how we should throw stragglers to the wolves. You can imagine how that all sounded to him. God only knows how much damage you've done, even though I tried to undo it."

She clasped a hand to her cheek. "Oh, no!" she cried. "But I didn't mean Jim, I was talking about Howard White."

"I think it was your general philosophy he was interested in," Deachman said with savage irony. "Why couldn't you take your cue from me? When you consider all that I have at stake—"

"You!" she snapped, getting to her feet with an energy that shook him out of his pose. "Why do you always think of yourself?"

"What are you doing?"

She was at the door. "I'm going to find Jim and tell him it's going to be all right."

"Nesta, for God's sake!"

But, whipped by emotion, she would not listen to him. "You've enjoyed this, haven't you, Arnie? Sitting there watching everybody at cross-purposes and feeling superior. You're the kind who cuts his nose off to spite his face. Have you considered how much this could cost? Don't you know there are other ways to handle people besides laughing at their misery?"

Deaf to his protest, she swept out.

Deachman sank back in his chair, clenching and unclenching his fists. Then, heavily, like a stricken old man, he forced himself to his feet.

—— 19 ——

The top floor of the Community Medical Building was a private lounge where doctors and their guests could drink and relax over a picturesque view of the Curry River. Traffic in and out was light most mornings, picked up as the day wore on, then peaked between five and six. Today, at four o'clock doctors were lining up for admission. So were lawyers and a delegation from Great Lakes Insurance Company.

Nesta Deachman, out of breath, hurried around the corner to join them. "Is Arnold here yet?" she demanded anxiously. "He's not in his office."

Somebody had seen him going inside earlier.

"Oh, that's a relief," she gasped. "He really shouldn't exert himself too much."

But even as she spoke, the line pressed forward with the mute impatience of all crowds. Nesta was too preoccupied to notice how many new faces had been added to the cast.

This was not lost on Jim Rojak. Hands in pockets, he surveyed the room. Arnold Deachman, pale and stone-faced, sat in an easy chair by the window, watching Nesta thread her way toward him. In the corner, at one of the tables, Pat Costello was alone but smiling hopefully. Howard White trailed in, ready to buttonhole any colleague he could. But also present were at least twenty Newburg doctors who had not, thus far, been part of a published list.

"What are you up to?" Rojak demanded of Lawrence Fournier, who was waiting for the group to settle. "I thought this was a business meeting. Calling a pep rally is a waste of everybody's time—including mine."

Fournier did not answer him directly. Instead, raising his voice commandingly, he addressed the room: "I think we're about ready to get started." When the buzz of individual conversations obediently died, he continued: "Dr. Rojak has just asked me to explain why we have enlarged the participation in this meeting."

"I think my client, Dr. Deachman, should have been consulted first," said a voice from the rear.

But before Fournier could reply, someone across the room yodeled: "Deachman's consulting days are over."

Arnold Deachman shrank at the taunt and the laughter it evoked.

His lawyer would have persevered if Howard White had not taken it upon himself to make peace. "We won't make any progress squabbling among ourselves. I vote to get down to work—that is to say, deciding how to neutralize this Gregorian woman."

He waited for applause. But most doctors were keeping their distance from White. With unkind frankness Jim Rojak said, "I don't think you've got a vote anymore, Howie. Me neither, if that's any consolation to you."

At this, lawyers and doctors began talking at once, their voices rising in anger, so that Fournier had to shout. "Quiet!" he bellowed.

Surprise, more than anything else, achieved the desired effect. Despite all that had happened, most Newburg doctors still did not grasp how the balance of power had shifted against them.

There was, however, one holdout. "Fournier, I demand to know why you asked me here. *I* haven't been accused of Medicaid fraud. *I* haven't lost my malpractice insurance. *I* haven't been subpoenaed by a Congressional committee!"

"You were asked to join us, Doctor," said Fournier, equalizing with a vengeance, "because of your substantial Medicaid billings."

The chill that settled over the room satisfied him. At last the full implications of Charlene Gregorian's campaign were beginning to sink in.

"I'll ask our lawyer, Mr. Vail, to outline the current situation to you," he continued.

Vail, rising, presented the doctors with a succinct evaluation of Charlene's potential for further trouble.

"That's fine, Dave," said Fournier hastily when Vail showed a tendency to linger over Mrs. Gregorian's ingenuity. "So you see, gentlemen—and ladies—we have a real crisis before us."

He pronounced this death sentence, and waited. There was not a sound in the room. Then Nesta turned to her husband. "Arnie, why doesn't Phil say something? That's why you brought your lawyer—"

"Because there's nothing he can say," Deachman said bleakly.

A doctor in the front row was badly shaken. "But there's got to be some way we can reason with her so she won't just go on mowing us down, one after another."

Fournier had been expecting this. "That is exactly what Great Lakes hopes to do," he said. "Mr. Michael Isham, who is representing Mrs. Gregorian's interests, is due here in one hour—at which time we will try to persuade Mrs. Gregorian to drop these highly publicized tactics. Perhaps she can be convinced . . . er, that the sensationalism of her suits against Dr. White and Dr. Deachman has been sufficient for her purposes."

"Who are you trying to kid?" asked Jim Rojak. "You got us together to say you're throwing all seven of us to the wolves, didn't you? Not just Howie and Arnie."

Fournier was stung. "We are trying to contain the damage. If this Gregorian woman stops hitting the headlines, it will be better for the medical profession—and for Great Lakes."

"You mean maybe she'll agree to sit on her other Medicaid files if you yank our malpractice insurance," Rojak said rudely.

Vail interjected himself: "We still don't know what Mrs. Gregorian's demands will be."

Rojak laughed in his face. "Oh, don't we? Come on! We're not kids. That woman is out to get us, and we know it as well as you do. The only question is how many it will take to satisfy her. Well, I'm putting an end to the pressure."

"But, Jim," somebody objected, "that's just guesswork. All that's actually happened is two lawsuits against—"

"Crap!" he shot back. "We've had a man murdered. We've got a woman who can blow us all sky high—and I don't mean just the seven of us. Well, you can sit around playing games, but I'm going to protect my own interests. And I'm going to start right now at Police Headquarters."

"Now, wait," Fournier began.

But with an insulting shrug Rojak ignored him, striding toward the door.

His departure was almost unnoticed in the babble triggered by his cold predictions.

"What was that? You mean they may yank *my* malpractice?"

"How can Great Lakes cancel if we're not sued?"

"Listen, Mueller, do something!"

With an effort Fournier tore his attention away from the door through which Rojak had vanished. "All right, let's all keep cool," he said abrasively. "Dr. Rojak is overreacting. Until we know what Mrs. Gregorian's demands are, we don't know what steps Great Lakes will be forced to take. At that time we will inform you—and your attorneys—so that you can take any appropriate individual legal action you may want."

This unconciliating speech brought a howl of protest from all sides. Urgently, Vail tugged at Fournier's sleeve. "Larry, for God's sake," he said, "don't get them all steamed up again. We want some cooperation."

But the damage was done. Cooperation was now out of the question. Some doctors had followed Jim Rojak's example and stormed out. Others were consulting their lawyers in frantic undertones. The Deachmans sat still, as did Howard White.

Patrick Costello had formed a temporary alliance with fellow sufferers and was on his feet, hurling questions at Fournier.

"Goddam bunch of dummies," said Fournier without bothering to lower his voice.

Vail was getting alarmed. In twenty-five minutes the serious business of the day would begin with the arrival of Michael Isham. Between now and then Great Lakes needed a calm, collected Lawrence Fournier and some semblance of order.

"Larry," he said, recklessly assuming responsibility, "why don't you go take a walk? Let me sweet-talk this mob for a while and clear them out before Isham gets here."

He did not add that the original game plan, which had called for a disciplined delegation of doctors, was now blown.

To his relief, Fournier responded with a rueful smile. "Boy, Rojak really balled it up, didn't he?"

Vail nodded sympathetically.

Fournier looked at the scene before him. Then: "Okay, I'll fade for twenty minutes while you pick up the pieces. We'll have to play Isham by ear."

Vail was too experienced to show relief. "Okay, we play it by ear."

But Michael Isham, when he did arrive, had an innovation of his own. Instead of confronting the doctors alone, he had recruited an ally.

Accompanying him was the Honorable Benton Safford, Member of Congress.

"Look, it'll be money in the bank," Isham had argued. "I know just how Great Lakes will play this. Fournier's going to have some doctors who don't cook their books. And he'll try to break my heart showing me how much harm Mrs. Gregorian can do to them."

"Ye-es?" Ben had replied without enthusiasm.

"So I turn up with the awful authority of the Federal government and it's a new horserace. We remind everybody that we're not talking about Dr. Joe Blow. We're talking about a major reform of the American medical system. That'll jolt Great Lakes—and they'll be willing to cancel everybody that Charlene even suspects of chiseling."

"I'm the muscle man?" Ben had suggested.

"That's right!"

As a result of this conversation, Ben found himself accompanying Isham into the enemy camp. As it happened, he had never before visited the Community Medical Building, and he was under no illusions about how welcome he would be. Assuming the gravity he usually reserved for Presidential visits to the House of Representatives, he stalked in beside Isham, prepared to remind the doctors and Great Lakes of bigger forces in the world.

They never got as far as the lounge. Their crowded elevator stopped without incident at the second and third floors. But on four the doors opened to reveal a near-riot. A milling crowd filled the corridor, including many of the men Ben had expected to see upstairs. More compelling, however, was the woman in a white coat who was sagging against a doorway, screaming mechanically.

"Ai-ee!"

Without conscious thought, Ben pushed the hold button. As he did, Dr. Howard White appeared from nowhere, strode forward and slapped the hysterical woman.

With a ragged sob, she stared at him, then buried her face in her hands, moaning, "He's been killed! They've murdered him!"

The occupants of the elevator surged forward into the maelstrom of confused questions, aimless movements, feverish excitement. Ben, with Isham beside him, did not pause, but straight-armed his way through the human barrier to walk into a waiting room.

In the office beyond, Dr. James Rojak lay in a pool of vomit at the foot of the desk.

It did not take a doctor to see that he was dead.

20

When a patrol car radioed in the first news of Dr. James Rojak's death, Owen Jones responded with model efficiency. He issued careful orders to the patrol car, he dispatched a second unit to the scene and he then spent twenty minutes assembling his field team. By the time they arrived at the Community Medical Building, the situation was not only under control, it was developing along the right lines.

"I've got those doctors all penned up, just the way you wanted, Chief," the officer in charge reported. "And we got identification from everyone who left the building."

"Good," said Jones, preparing to pass on.

"But there's one more thing. I've got Steve Cella in with one of the nurses. She's giving him an earful."

"I told you not to start questioning anybody until I got here." Jones ran a tight enough ship to expect a good reason for this disobedience.

His subordinate grinned. "With her, it wasn't a question of starting. We would have had a hard time shutting her up. And so long as she was flowing, I thought we better keep her going until you could hear her yourself."

Jones nodded. Talking jags were notoriously unpredictable. Once the witness ran down—or was prematurely halted—the original impulse might not be recaptured.

"She really have anything to say?"

"Does she ever! You better take a look-see, Chief. They're in Room 207."

Jones signaled to George Doyle and the two of them broke off from the main party already on its way to the elevator. One flight of stairs and a short walk down the corridor brought them to a door which had been left ajar. They could see that 207 in its normal use was the waiting room of a pediatrician. The bright primary colors, the piles of comic books and wooden toys, the occasional piece of diminutive furniture all hinted at patients under the age of eight.

But the two people sitting on the sofa were oblivious to their surroundings. Officer Cella was perfect for his role. He was a grizzled veteran exuding fatherly wisdom and sympathy. At the moment he was saying: "It's no wonder you were upset, Mrs. Blair. He had no right to talk to you that way."

Mrs. Blair no longer had the inscrutable eyes of the registered nurse. Her cap had been flung off and her cheeks were flushed with color. She was formidably angry.

"Who does he think he is? I wouldn't take that from him even if he was still going to be paying my salary."

"No indeed." Having brought the conversation to the right point, Cella now decided to notice his superior. "Ah, here's Chief Jones. He'll want to thank you personally. It's because of Mrs. Blair's prompt action that we got here early enough to keep the scene from being trampled, Chief."

Cautiously Jones and Doyle moved forward with expressions of gratitude.

"When Mrs. Blair saw Dr. Rojak's body all contorted with the hypodermic lying right there, she went and called the police," Cella continued easily. "Now, you wouldn't think anyone would say that was wrong, would you?"

Jones murmured his agreement.

"But I'm sorry to say that Dr. White seems to have lost his head."

"He behaved like a madman," Mrs. Blair grated. "He claimed I was being paid to make trouble for him, he accused me of being in league with that Mrs. Gregorian and he threatened to blacklist me all over the country. Then he ordered me to call the police back and tell them it was a false alarm."

Cella shook his head. "As if it wasn't too late for that."

"It was too late right from the beginning. Imagine the nerve of it!

He and Dr. Deachman were going to move the body, sign the death certificate and say it was a natural death."

"Oh, they were, were they?" growled Jones.

Retelling her story had relieved Mrs. Blair's emotions enough so that she now discarded the handkerchief she had been twisting and tearing as if it were some portion of Dr. Howard White's anatomy.

"They acted as if they were in control just because it happened in the medical building," she said on a calmer note. "Even though Nancy Diehl was making enough noise to bring people from all over."

"Nancy Diehl is the young technician who found the body," Cella explained in an aside.

"And she screamed the house down. Why, I saw Congressman Safford and Mr. Fournier crowding around the doorway. They certainly weren't going to join in any funny business. Particularly with Nancy yelling that it couldn't have been Dr. Rojak's allergy shot that killed him, that there must have been something else in the hypo."

"Silly, that's what Dr. White was," Cella concluded. "Just plain silly."

Along with her cap and her handkerchief, Mrs. Blair had abandoned the last shreds of professional decorum.

"He wasn't silly," she spat. "He was scared shitless."

The homicide squad was hard at work when Jones and Doyle arrived in Dr. Rojak's inner office. George Doyle took one look and whistled.

"This is some death to try and pass off as a heart attack."

Already chalk marks starkly outlined the body, the vomit, the hypodermic that lay with the other objects swept from the desk. A photographer was recording the overturned chair and the scars gouged along the side of the desk as if by flailing heels. A man crouched over the corpse, and a fingerprint specialist was awaiting his permission to approach. Dr. James Rojak still lay cramped in the tight arc of his final agony.

"It wouldn't have looked like this if White and Deachman had had their way," Chief Jones argued. "Rojak would have been laid out looking as peaceful as a baby, the hypodermic would have disappeared, the rug would be at the cleaner's. Do we have the story on the hypodermic yet?"

The photographer was the one who answered. "It's simple enough. Rojak was giving himself a series of allergy shots. That Nancy Diehl, the one who did all the blubbering, she says his nurse regularly put out the hypodermic and the ampule on his desk so he wouldn't forget."

Owen Jones' eyebrows rose. "I think I get the picture. There's a needle and some dope lying on the victim's desk for an unspecified period of time. Then he comes back to his office, shoots the stuff into himself and dies. What a set-up! That means we have a million unanswered questions. How long was the hypo there, who was on duty in this suite, was Rojak anyplace nearby, how many people knew about this allergy treatment of his? George, suppose you get the boys started on this. In the meantime I want some cooperation from the Coroner's office."

The man crouched by the body looked up alertly.

"Now, Pete," Jones continued, almost pleading, "just for once, will you forget you're a perfectionist? I know you're going to tell me that you've got to do a post-mortem and send the organs and the hypo for analysis before you can be sure of anything. So I'm not asking you to be sure, I'm not asking you to put anything in writing. I just want a starting point. Did Rojak die because of what was in that hypodermic? And if so, what was it?" His voice became a coaxing whisper. "Just an educated guess, that's all I'm asking."

Pete rose to reveal a wide grin. "It sure as hell wasn't an allergy shot. As for the educated guess, you can probably make one yourself —when you see what's in the wastebasket."

He led the way to the other side of the desk, which had been untouched by the havoc of Rojak's last convulsions. Pointing downward, he indicated an expensive, heavy, leather bucket. It was empty except for one crumpled sheet of paper and two small objects lost in the dark shadow.

Chief Jones peered into the depths. "Aren't those the little cartons for hypodermic ampules?" he asked.

"They sure are. And wait till you see what they contained." Pete was openly chortling. Normally, the Coroner's office does its detecting in the laboratory, not at the scene of the crime. "Say, Dave, shine your light in there, will you?"

Now, without disturbing the contents of the basket, the Chief could read the lettering. "Sodium pentothal," he breathed softly. "And is that compatible with the medical evidence so far?"

"Entirely compatible," Pete said. "If he shot that stuff directly into his bloodstream, he'd have been dead inside of seconds."

Owen Jones was plucking and releasing his lower lip. "There's one thing I don't understand. Rojak was thrashing around in here, knocking things over, falling on the floor and, if he couldn't manage to scream, he was at least groaning. How come nobody heard him?"

Pete was still enjoying his victory. "I thought of that one myself. In the first place, you've got to realize that the victim's movements would have been involuntary. He would have been strangling and vomiting and cramping. There wouldn't have been any rational activity like trying to reach the intercom. As for the rest, I'll let Dave tell it."

"I'd better begin by giving you Rojak's schedule today, Chief," Dave began as he flipped through several pages of his notebook. "His last patient was at three o'clock. He'd scrapped everything else to leave the afternoon free. First, he was attending this big meeting with the other doctors and their insurance company. Then he was going to do some errands before his appointment with you at Headquarters. So at three thirty he told his nurse and receptionist they could have the rest of the day off. They were out of there within five minutes. Well, you can see for yourself how these suites are arranged. There's a room between Rojak's office and the hall, and the soundproofing in this building seems pretty good. He would have made plenty of noise, but there was nobody to hear him."

The Police Chief was seeing a good many things. Methodically he attacked them, one by one.

"All right, that means after three thirty there was no one on duty in this suite. And Rojak himself was tied up most of the time in a meeting. Do we know if his nurse put out his allergy shot before she left?"

"Yes, it was the last thing she did before leaving. I got her on the phone at her house." Dave decided to amplify this. "She said she even interrupted Rojak while he was talking to Dr. White to remind him of his shot."

Firmly, Jones refused to be distracted. "Let that go for a minute. Did you ask her if she told anybody that Rojak was letting her and the other girl go? That the suite would be empty all afternoon?"

"She didn't have to. Rojak was out in the corridor in front of a whole lot of people when he told her to close down the office. He made a big production out of it, said it was the last time he'd waste a whole afternoon on ancient history. He was even beefing because he had to detour out to the country club and rearrange his appointment with the tennis pro. Deachman and Costello agreed that it was a fine state of affairs when the police hassled a doctor that way," Dave concluded sardonically.

The Police Chief was too intent on the picture that was forming to appreciate sarcasm. "It's a beautiful set-up, isn't it?" he murmured. "First, everyone can figure out that Mrs. Gregorian's testimony has shot Rojak's story full of holes. Then Rojak himself tells the world that the police have stopped treating him with kid gloves and have ordered him down to the station. In addition, they all know that his offices are going to be vacant. And finally, as the cream in the coffee, there's a loaded hypo on his desk that Rojak is going to inject into himself without a second thought. Boy, if I'd wanted to shut him up before he blabbed, I couldn't have asked for anything better."

Doyle, who had finished giving low-voiced instructions to two of his men, was modifying his earlier views. "No wonder they were trying to pass it off as a natural death. It was worth big risks for the six of them if there was any chance of avoiding this stinking mess. They must be sweating it out right now."

"Let them stew a little longer." Jones knew all about the softening process. "I want all the ammunition I can get before I talk to them. So far, we just know what Rojak was willing to say in public. Do we have anyone to tell us what went on in the lounge?"

"We've got that insurance guy, the one from Great Lakes," Dave offered. "He was in on the whole conference. I think Mike Isham and Congressman Safford came in after it ended."

"And they're still here?"

"Yeah, all three of them offered to stay. They're having coffee together down the hall."

Jones returned to more immediate problems. "All right, I'll see if they can tell me anything. In the meantime I want you to work on the source of the sodium pentothal. I know damn well we're going to find out that this building is full of it and that every doctor has access to it. Nonetheless, pin down exactly where it came from. And while you're at it, you can . . ."

Chief Jones joined the kaffeeklatsch five minutes later.

"I know you're all busy men and I appreciate your waiting here for me. Of course, we could have sent men to your offices, but this saves a lot of time, and just when it may make all the difference."

Ben Safford and Larry Fournier gravely replied that they were anxious to do all they could to assist the authorities.

Mike Isham chose a different approach. "Wild horses couldn't have dragged me away," he said with a gleam of white teeth. "My God, Owen, who would have thought a lousy little Medicaid fraud would pack so much dynamite?"

Ben had the grace to be shamed by Isham's frankness. He too, had been motivated more by curiosity than by civic virtue. "Anything we can do, Owen," he offered in vague expiation.

With the niceties out of the way, Jones became all policeman. "I want to know what went on at this meeting Rojak attended." He looked at Fournier. "Unless you figure it's confidential for some reason."

Larry Fournier was all too ready to talk. Because he had spent the last hour going over the scene in his own mind, he was able to deliver an almost verbatim transcript of what had been said upstairs.

When he finished, Jones expressed disappointment. "Then, except for Rojak describing his police appointment—to anyone who didn't already know about it—you just chewed over the insurance problem. The doctors thought Mrs. Gregorian's confession gave them a way out, and you told them it didn't."

Fournier nodded, Ben Safford had an objection. "Wait a minute. There's more to it than that. From what Larry says, Rojak was the only one who included Theodore Karras' murder in the scenario, wasn't he?"

Mike Isham, who had been subjecting Fournier's narrative to step-by-step dissection, agreed with him. "You're right, Ben. Rojak saw a bigger problem than the rest of them. But for some reason he was confident he could handle it. And apparently he was going to begin the process down at Police Headquarters."

"You may be right." Larry Fournier was only partly convinced. "The one thing I am sure of is that he was confident to the point of arrogance."

Ben thought back to his encounter with Jim Rojak in the Federal Building. "Are you sure that wasn't just his style? Maybe it was all an act. Underneath he could have been as scared as everyone else."

"Maybe," said Fournier. "But he sure told all of us he was going to protect his interests."

"All of you?" Chief Jones narrowed his eyes as he saw the possibilities. "Or was Rojak talking to someone in particular?"

21

While Owen Jones was considering possibilities, his detectives were busy establishing facts. Armed with their findings, Jones entered the doctors' lounge half an hour later.

He wasted no time on preliminaries.

"Good afternoon. I hear some of you did your best to keep us from investigating Dr. Rojak's death. I want to know why."

Howard White rushed into speech. "I suppose you've been talking to Mrs. Blair. It's true that I took her to task for her hasty and ill-advised action in calling you. As a nurse, she should have remembered that is a decision for the attending physician."

"Maybe she didn't see any room for doubt," Jones suggested blandly.

"There is always room for professional judgment. Regardless of how simple the situation may look, there can be factors requiring skilled interpretation by a licensed medical doctor."

White had begun on the defensive, his words tumbling out, his eyes constantly gauging Jones' reaction. But the familiar phrases— *attending physician, professional judgment, licensed medical doctor* —soon worked their customary magic. By the time he paused for breath, he had regained much of his old confidence.

"Still claiming Rojak died of natural causes?" inquired Jones, curious to see how far White would go.

"Perhaps not natural in the strictest sense of the word," White conceded. "But still no occasion for a police investigation."

"You mean it was an accident?" Jones made no attempt to hide his incredulity. "Rojak mistook sodium pentothal for his allergy shot?"

White took a deep breath. "Surely that would be the kindest way to label Jim's death. Of course you can fault Dr. Deachman and myself for failing to follow the letter of the law. But can you really blame us?" All the organ stops were out now. "We were Jim's friends and we have a duty to that friendship. Would society be any better off if we were willing to smear a dead colleague, to distress his family, to destroy his memory?"

"So you're pushing suicide." It was a statement, not a question. Chief Jones had expected this gambit and had prepared himself to deal with it. But at the moment he was less interested in rebuttal than in Howard White's emergence as group spokesman. According to Larry Fournier, just two short hours ago White had been treated as little better than a hanger-on. Now the entire room was yielding him the floor. "Do the rest of you feel the same way?"

Nobody volunteered a remark.

"What about you, Dr. Deachman?" Jones pressed. "You seem to have pitched right in with Dr. White."

Arnold Deachman was lying on a couch while Nesta sat at his side, her eyes fixed on him with painful anxiety. He turned to face the Chief of Police, grunting as he shifted.

"Don't say anything, Arnie," his wife pleaded. "You know you shouldn't try and talk. Remember what it can do to you." She turned on Jones. "Can't you see that my husband isn't well?"

Jones examined the couple. They both looked terrible. Nesta was pale and her make-up was blotched with tear streaks. Her breast heaved as if she were fighting to control herself. Arnold's reaction was quite different. His face was gray and haggard and he was abnormally inert, confining his movements to the bare minimum. There was no doubt he had received a shock, but his breathing was regular, and his eyes focused clearly.

"Your husband has already refused medical attention once," Jones said for the record, "but the offer is still open. We can have the police surgeon here in a couple of minutes."

"He doesn't need medical attention," she retorted, her voice beginning to rise. "He needs rest and quiet. He should be back at the nursing home."

"Mrs. Deachman, there are six doctors in this room, counting your husband. Why are you the one writing prescriptions?" Jones recognized incipient hysteria and hoped to make use of it.

"I know Arnie, I know what's best for him." She caught her breath on a sob, and Dr. Deachman intervened.

"It's all right, Nesta, I can handle it," he said, his gaze still fixed on Jones. "What you say is true. I'm not ashamed of helping Howard White keep Jim's suicide from becoming public. Why should we have to go on suffering for what Jim did, with more headlines and more publicity? It's all over now, thank God. We can put it behind us and forget it ever happened."

The immense weariness in Deachman's voice made it easy to believe that he honestly wanted to put the past behind and never think of it again. That was about all Jones did believe.

"You really are a bunch of prizes, aren't you?" he said, deliberately challenging. "First you want to shovel Rojak out of here and pass him off as a heart attack. Then, when Mrs. Blair gums that one up for you, you shift over to suicide for no good reason."

There was a spontaneous roar of protest and, for the first time, the doctors in the corner associated themselves with White and Deachman.

"What do you mean, no good reason?" Patrick Costello demanded, his round eyes bulging with indignation. "We all read about the Gregorian woman, and she blew holes in Jim's story about that murder."

"Sure, but was he bright enough to realize that?" said Jones, affecting skepticism. "He sounded pretty cool when we told him he'd have to come down to the station for further questioning."

They were all eager to correct him. Four or five voices were raised simultaneously. Jim Rojak always pretended to be cool, they said, but he had realized his danger, all right. In fact, he had specifically said so at their meeting.

"He put it even stronger than that. He said now the crunch had come, he was going to end the pressure. At the time I didn't realize he meant suicide," Costello babbled. "But it's clear now that's what he had in mind."

"No," protested a surgeon. "I'll bet it swept over him when he was about to take his allergy shot. Just seeing the hypodermic may have put the idea in Jim's head."

Jones was pleased with his tactics. Already he had extracted general agreement that Rojak's plans were common knowledge. Cautiously he inched down his list.

"What's all this about an allergy?" he asked innocently.

Obligingly they told him. Everyone knew about Jim's shots. He had tried converting the whole building to his new regimen.

"And even if he forgot about it, it didn't make any difference," the surgeon said, "because his nurse always put the stuff out for him."

It was too good to last. Jones was not surprised when his next question, aimed at the hour and a half during which Rojak's suite was empty, finally aroused suspicion.

"But why are you asking us all these questions?" said Costello, scenting danger.

"Well, there's another possibility besides suicide," Jones said.

"Nonsense!" Howard White exploded. "It's as plain as the nose on your face. Jim murdered Karras and thought he'd gotten away with it. He could afford to relax. Then, out of the blue, this Gregorian woman emerges. Jim must have been desperate from the moment he read her story. Finally you order him down to the station. He knows the end has come. There's nothing more he can do." White had fallen into a funeral cadence—slow, smooth, inexorable. "Finally he goes back to his office. He thinks of what lies ahead—notoriety, disgrace, jail. His eye falls on the hypodermic. He realizes there's an easy way out. The needle's right there and it's almost as if it were meant to be. He injects himself and dies."

Owen Jones' matter-of-fact tone broke the spell. "Having first wiped his fingerprints off the ampule container."

"Fingerprints?" Howard White sounded betrayed.

Systematically the Chief of Police continued to destroy the suicide theory. "What's more, the sodium pentothal didn't come from Rojak's drug supplies. It came from Dr. Barjian's."

"But Mark Barjian is in Europe." It was an involuntary objection from the surgeon.

Jones spelled out chapter and verse for them. "That's right. He's in Edinburgh for six months while his office here is closed. But someone opened the door to his suite with a key, smashed his drug cabinet and stole two ampules of sodium pentothal. No suicide behaved like that, particularly when Rojak's own office was filled with poisons that would have done the job just as well. Now, any of you people want to tell me who had access to Barjian's keys?"

Silence.

"All right. What about master keys? Keys that would open all the doctors' suites?"

There was still no verbal response, but the appalled glances exchanged by the doctors told Jones everything he wanted to know.

"Then I guess we're going to have to do this the hard way," he said menacingly. "Let's start with the order in which you arrived at the meeting and left the meeting."

The next hour proved to be a contest between witnesses and interrogator resulting in a draw. Everyone had had ample opportunity to lay a lethal trap for Jim Rojak. Nobody was cleared; on the other hand, nobody was pinpointed.

"And the keys aren't going to be much of a help, either," Doyle reported later as he and Jones headed for their car. "The whole pack of them has been in this building for over five years. I don't say they're casual about their keys with outsiders. But they go in and out of each other's offices enough so that the maintenance people say there are at least four master keys floating around."

"Just one big, happy family," said Jones. "Until they start knocking each other off. If you ask me, we're not going to get anything more here. They're all too familiar with the ground. We've established that they all had opportunity. And, God knows, we already knew that they all had the same motive."

"I wouldn't go that far, not about the motive," Doyle disagreed.

"For God's sake, George. Rojak *must* have been killed because of what he was going to spill."

Doyle nodded. "Sure. But I was talking about the motive for shooting Karras. It's all very well to say that he looked like a threat to all seven of them. But, by and large, people don't pull out guns until the threat is imminent. If you were the seventh man on that list, a lot of things could happen before Karras got to you."

Jones had no trouble translating this. "What you're really saying, George, is that you still like White as the murderer."

"You can't get away from the fact that Howard White was the one Karras was actually moving against. But I'll give you the fact that Deachman was next in line and, from what you say, Mrs. Deachman was pretty upset back there."

"She was so worried she was ready to flip. But that doesn't necessarily mean that she knows her husband is a killer." They had reached the car. Jones waved his subordinate to the radio as he himself slipped into the driver's seat. Then he continued, "After all, she'd just seen the corpse. Probably it was a shock realizing just how deep a mess Deachman was involved in. Until then it had simply been talk and newspaper—"

Jones broke off because the radio was chattering a message at them. By the time it was over, George Doyle was grinning.

"Still want to go back to Headquarters, Owen? Dave seems to have found something interesting at Rojak's apartment."

But the car was already sweeping into a wide turn away from downtown Newburg.

"No wonder the lady was upset," Jones was saying fifteen minutes later, handing Nesta Deachman's letter to Doyle. "Her lover had just been murdered."

After a swift perusal, Doyle grinned. "He wasn't all that obliging as a lover. According to this, he'd just told her she was good enough to play games with, but he had no intention of getting married."

"He must have sugar-coated it some, because she was willing to go on the same as always. She says she'll meet him at the usual time on Labor Day. That means this letter is over a month old. Say, Dave," the Chief said, "are there any more of these things around?"

It almost needed a shout to reach Dave. Jim Rojak's apartment was actually a condominium that had been expensively remodeled. Most of the downstairs was one huge room, half of it two floors high and half of it topped with a large balcony bedroom reached by a spiral staircase. In the back lurked a kitchen and a second bedroom converted into a study. As Dave loomed up by the railing and then came clattering down the stairs, Doyle allowed his glance to take in the sliding glass doors, the patio, the fireplace, the built-in hi-fi.

"Boy, this place must have cost a fortune," he said.

"Why should that bother Rojak?" Jones asked. "All he had to do was manufacture some fictitious Medicaid billings."

Dave's arrival brought their attention back to Rojak the victim, rather than Rojak the thief.

"No more pink love letters," he announced, "but there are some women's things in the bedroom and bathroom. The other stuff I wanted to show you is back here."

They followed him to the study. Even though it was a severely functional room, it bore signs of the Rojak penchant for spending money. The gun collection was housed in a custom-made cabinet, the desk stood on a handsome Oriental rug and the file cabinets were encased in solid walnut. One manila folder of correspondence was waiting for the Chief's inspection.

"Take a gander," Dave invited. "That line Rojak was shooting about toughing things out in Newburg was nothing but a bluff. He just didn't want anyone to know what he was up to."

The file had been systematically maintained. It began with a neatly clipped advertisement inviting applications for the post of medical director at an oil encampment in Kuwait. At a rapid clip there followed Rojak's application, an exchange about salary in which Rojak demanded all the traffic would bear, then a firm offer of the job. Dr. Rojak's acceptance had been written out yesterday.

"That sure spells it out," Jones sighed. "He knew he was in trouble from the minute Karras was murdered, so he started to open a line of retreat. But as long as there was a chance of riding it out, he wanted to keep his options open. Then when Mrs. Gregorian blew the whistle on him and we made it clear that we were really going to clamp down, he decided he didn't have a future in Newburg anymore and he took the job."

Doyle was willing to go further. "Rojak was no fool. He didn't think an oil company was going to harbor a murder suspect. So he wasn't planning a flit. He thought he could clear himself with us, finger the murderer and then take off for Kuwait."

"Which means it wasn't a simple case of his word against someone else's," Jones pointed out. "If he expected to leave town with our blessing, he had hard evidence."

"And we don't have a clue what it is," moaned Doyle. "Dave, haven't you come up with anything in this place?"

Dave was not sharing the general depression. "I don't know whether it helps, but I do have one last bit for you. It's real offbeat."

Like a magician, he whipped aside the leather-framed desk blotter to reveal an envelope lying beneath.

"There," he exclaimed. "What do you think of that?"

The envelope was empty, but nonetheless it packed a wallop. The letterhead in the upper left-hand corner was that of Theodore S. Karras, Attorney-at-Law. It had been addressed in handwriting to Jim Rojak at his home.

"For Christ sake! You mean Karras was writing to Rojak?" Jones cried in bewilderment. "But the whole point of Mrs. Gregorian's story was that the two of them didn't have anything to do with each other."

Dave beamed broadly. "That's what I thought until I went through the desk. Then I realized that the handwriting is Rojak's."

For a moment there was baffled silence. Then Doyle's mind began clicking on all cylinders. "Wait a minute!" he yelled. "Let me see that postmark." Without apology he snatched the envelope and held it to the desk light, squinting at the smudged figures. What he saw made him too excited for coherence. "I was right all the time! Except that I was wrong."

"You'd better explain that, George," Jones said patiently.

"I always said Rojak's leaving Karras' office to go to the drugstore was phony. But I thought he wanted to call somebody from a sound-proof booth. That wasn't it at all. He needed an excuse to leave the building so he could mail this. The postmark is the day of Karras' murder. He picked up something in that office and wanted to get rid of it before we arrived—in case we searched him. So he raided the secretary's desk for a stamped envelope, addressed it to himself and then mailed it. I'll give you five to one there's a mailbox on that street before you get to the drugstore."

"And then what?"

"He gave it back to White just like I said all along."

They all stared at the envelope as if massive willpower could produce a picture of its original contents.

At last Chief Jones shrugged. "Not necessarily White. It could have been any of the others."

"All right then, Deachman. You say his wife was damn near hysterical. Maybe she knew her husband had just killed her lover."

"I doubt it. She was nervous as hell, but that could be explained easy enough by all this." A wave indicated the whole condominium. "She and Rojak may have been cautious enough for ordinary purposes. But if she's got any sense, she knows a murder investigation uncovers everything. She's probably terrified her husband is going to find out about her love nest."

Doyle was a stubborn man when it came to abandoning a theory. "Why should it bother her so much? A month ago she was ready to dump her husband."

"She was ready to leave a rich old man in order to marry a rich young man." Jones smiled sourly. "Nesta Deachman is an expensive woman and she wants to stay that way. She sure doesn't want to be kicked out in the cold. Mind you, I'm not saying that Deachman may not be our killer. I just don't think that's what's sending his wife up the wall."

"Okay, then we're back to square one." Doyle hunched his shoulders in discontent. "Aside from telling us it was mailed for fifteen cents, this envelope doesn't do us any good at all."

But Jones was shaking his head with new confidence. "I wouldn't say that. If Rojak was planning to walk out from Police Head-quarters—and from Newburg—with a clean bill of health, then he knew there was hard evidence he could put his hands on. And if he could find it, so can we!"

22

The murder of Jim Rojak put Newburg, literally, on the map. CBS, the *Atlanta Constitution* and *Newsweek* all showed the world southern Ohio, with large arrows pinpointing Newburg.

"'. . . where the second body was found,'" Quentin Trumbull read aloud from the Associated Press dispatch.

"'This prosperous community on the banks of the Curry River has been jolted. . . .'"

"That's pretty much what John Chancellor said last night," said Ben Safford. "Janet tells me that ABC is already talking about mass killings and a string of unsolved deaths."

The sensationalism of Newburg's sudden vault into national prominence was not what had prompted Trumbull's SOS. It was the inevitable context. Jim Rojak led back to Theo Karras, to malpractice, to Medicaid fraud—and to HEW.

"They're in a sweat in Washington," he told Safford. "I had three calls this morning before the office opened, including one from the Secretary himself. He wants a full report by noon, with special emphasis on Charlene Gregorian. . . ."

His sentence trailed off suggestively.

Ben knew that the Secretary of HEW was a different quantity to his regional directors than he was to an important Congressman. So Ben tempered his frankness.

"Don't let that worry you too much. Remember, everybody in Washington is publicity-conscious—especially a new administration. HEW is fielding questions from the networks, and the press corps is probably pestering the White House. They want to be prepared."

"Oh, I understand that," Trumbull said uneasily.

"Besides," Ben added, "when you get right down to it, HEW isn't getting the bad publicity. It's Mayor Wilhelm and Owen Jones who are taking the heat."

Although Quentin Trumbull did not look altogether convinced, this was substantially true. Newburg was attracting attention because the news accounts of Jim Rojak's murder were oversimplified, as well as lurid. To most of the media, fear stalked the streets and that was that. Trumbull and HEW were resolutely declining interviews. Arnold Deachman had ducked back into his nursing home, and his fellow doctors, including Howard White and Pat Costello, were lying low. Great Lakes, in the person of Larry Fournier, had simply fled Newburg. Only His Honor and the Chief of Police were available for public comment.

Mayor Wilhelm chatting with Barbara Walters had been a sight for sore eyes. What's more, this overnight notoriety had been less damaging than Ben had expected. Treatment of the Subcommittee on Medicaid Abuse was, he had been happy to see, perfunctory. Charlene Gregorian, when she was discussed, emerged as a public-minded woman.

"And even Owen and Wilhelm look good, compared to the doctors of Newburg," Ben commented with passing satisfaction. He found some poetic justice in headlines screaming:

KILLER MEDIC STRIKES AGAIN

Quentin Trumbull remained unhappy. "You may be right, Ben. But they're still flapping their wings in Washington, and that scares me. What if they decide that they have to make some kind of gesture because of these murders? Charlene could be disciplined—or even summoned before a departmental review board. That could mean dismissal or a reduction in grade. And any disciplinary action would affect her pension rights. My God, the way it sounds, this killer is going to go free. Well, I don't want Charlene to be the whipping boy."

Ben knew, better than Quentin Trumbull did, how the blaze of publicity affects official Washington. The strangest political contortions he had ever seen were the direct fruits of public-opinion polls.

"But I still think you're being overly pessimistic," he said. "Charlene is coming across like an angel of mercy. Still, if it will make you feel any better, I'll put in a good word. . . ."

Trumbull was embarrassingly grateful, and Ben had the grace to feel somewhat ashamed of himself as he left the Federal Building. He did not take Trumbull's bogey seriously, but he was going to use it anyway. What he wanted now was a phone where he could not be overheard.

"Ben said *what?*" demanded Congresswoman Hollenbach an hour later.

"He said that Buckley and HEW are planning to reprimand Charlene Gregorian," said Tony Martinelli without a qualm. Where Ben Safford could bend the truth in a good cause, Tony was ready to dispense with it altogether.

He was rewarded immediately. Elsie, who had dropped into his office on her way someplace else, plunked herself in a chair. More to the point, her draft proposal for a national health-insurance system was placed, temporarily forgotten, on the corner of his desk.

"What is this about Charlene Gregorian?" she said. "I was pleased to see this morning's *Post* had a very strong editorial commending her. Good heavens, she's the one redeeming feature about this dreadful situation in Newburg. Have they lost their minds over at HEW? I thought better of Buckley—I really did!"

Martinelli did not hesitate to malign his fellow Democrat. Gazing out at the Mall, he said: "This second murder has scared him to death."

"Nonsense!" said Elsie.

"No, Buckley's all shaken up. That's got to be it, Elsie. I, personally, don't think the fact that his father and his brother are doctors has a thing to do with it."

If Elsie had not been convulsed with moral outrage, she would have smelled a rat. But, as Tony well knew, when incisive activity beckoned, she did not hesitate.

"This shall not be permitted. I insist that the committee go on record immediately, deprecating any such ill-advised action by HEW. Moreover . . ."

Tony leaned back and listened. Elsie insisting led to Elsie doing, which was exactly what he, Ben and Lou Flecker had in mind. While Elsie was busy championing Mrs. Gregorian, she was not going to be circulating her bombshell Republican national health-insurance plan. And by the time the smoke cleared, Elsie's fervor might be channeled in the right direction.

The trouble with converts, Anthony Martinelli had always believed, is that they were too damned enthusiastic.

"Mighty convenient," said Congressman Oakes when he lumbered into the office a few minutes later with Lou Flecker.

"What's convenient, Val?" said Flecker. The House leadership was nagging him to cut Elsie Hollenbach off at the pass. The press was camped in his office, clamoring for revelations about Newburg. Flecker withstood the buffeting by living each moment as it came. He had no time for overtones, undertones or subtleties.

"I suspect you're setting a fire to fight a fire," said Oakes. He, too, was a convert, but nothing could make him a zealot. "Well, you may be wise."

Before Flecker could frame a tactful version of the majority opinion, Elsie evinced impatience with her colleagues' propensity to waste valuable time on nonessentials.

"I have asked Dr. Urquhart to join us," she said. "We have an appointment with Secretary Buckley at two o'clock this afternoon—"

"By which time there's likely to be another murder in Newburg, according to what I read. Poor Ben. Does he sound as if he's holding up, Tony?" asked Val.

Tony was a man who honored his obligations. "Ben sounds pretty tensed-up to me," he said gravely. "These murders aren't doing him any good. And if HEW smears Mrs. Gregorian, Ben's going to get it from both ends. He's caught in the middle, you might say."

"Ha!" said Elsie, rising. "I think it's time for us to leave."

As everybody obediently fell in behind her, Val Oakes offered Tony some advice: "Back home we always say that you can spoil a pie by putting in too many apples."

Unoffended, Mr. Martinelli promised to restrain himself.

Forty minutes later Joseph Buckley, Secretary of Health, Education and Welfare, surveyed his quarters with mixed emotions. There was the signed Presidential photograph. There was a vast rug with the department seal. Behind a distant door were a private dining room, a shower and a fully stocked bar.

Unfortunately, nearer at hand was the Subcommittee on Medicaid Abuse—minus Benton Safford but plus Dr. Alexander Urquhart.

"We are grateful you could meet with us at such short notice, Mr. Secretary," said Elsie meticulously.

"My pleasure," said Buckley, wondering how he could have avoided it. "Now, when you called this morning, you said it was in connection with possible disciplinary action against Mrs. Gregorian in Newburg, Ohio. I did look into the file. . . ."

"Splendid," said Elsie menacingly. For all practical purposes, L. Lamar Flecker had yielded her the chair.

"I see that there have been protests from some members of the public," said Buckley, concentrating on his documents. "That was before this second murder—"

This time it was Dr. Alexander Urquhart who pounced. "What members of the public?"

"There seem to be forty-three names. . . ."

"My bet," said Urquhart ferociously, "is that they're all AMA—and probably a form letter at that. If HEW knuckles under to pressure like that—"

Buckley's tenure in office had been relatively brief, but he was already inured to undeserved attack. With a fixed, pained smile, he forged ahead.

"Now, I have been in touch with Trumbull to double-check on the facts. Undoubtedly we could press charges against Mrs. Gregorian—"

"But you won't!" Urquhart thundered while Tony evaded Mrs. Hollenbach's gaze.

Buckley had many good reasons to cooperate when the Congress descended on him. But he was human, too.

"We read the papers," he said indignantly. "If we went after this Mrs. Gregorian, we'd get lynched. God knows, what's happened in Newburg is bad enough. The last thing HEW wants to do right now is rock the boat any more."

"Hmph!" said Urquhart, only partly reassured.

Val Oakes then proved that there is such a thing as bipartisanship in the national interest. While his Democratic colleagues sat mum, he said, "That stands to reason. You want to lie low—at least until Congress sends a national health bill to the President, don't you?"

"Yes, we do, Mr. Oakes," said Buckley, ignoring the charged

atmospherics. "Tell me, Congressman Flecker, do you have any predictions on when that's likely to be?"

Flecker manfully looked straight at Elsie. "If we don't get hung up with a lot of debate over last-minute bills, if we can hammer out a solid compromise in committee, if we can avoid one-man shows— well, I expect we may be able to report something out in two or three months."

"Not a minute too soon," said Buckley.

By common consent, no one replied until Elsie, with a grim little smile, spoke up: "I agree with you wholeheartedly."

She was not addressing the Secretary of Health, Education and Welfare.

". . . so we got things sewed up," Martinelli reported to Ben later that afternoon. "Elsie's back on the team. She's still out to revolutionize the health system, but she'll go along with us on starting at the beginning."

"That's one loose end cleaned up. I only wish we could do the same with the rest of them. You wouldn't like to come down to Newburg and look for some missing evidence, would you?" asked Ben, who had spent his lunch hour listening to Owen Jones' troubles.

"I've done my good deed for the day," said Tony. "What's all this about missing evidence?"

Ben described what the police had uncovered in Jim Rojak's apartment. Empty envelopes did not impress Tony Martinelli, and neither did love letters from Nesta Deachman.

"Not unless she was playing around with Karras, too," he reflected.

"Unlikely," Ben said.

But Tony liked his theory. "That way her husband just knocked off her boy friends, one by one. Try that on the cops."

Ben replied that the Newburg police were thinking along different lines.

"Thinking?" Tony scoffed. "It sounds to me as if they're chasing their tails. Look, Ben, you're not going to be stuck in Newburg until they come up with something, are you? We need you back in Washington for the conference committee on the tariff."

Recklessly, Ben promised to be back at work by Friday at the latest.

"Don't tell me, tell Madge," said Martinelli. "Every time I pass your office, she's sitting on the phone, canceling your appointments right and left. I think it's beginning to get to her. If you don't shake loose from Newburg, you're going to be missing one damned good secretary when you get back."

"Hmm," said Ben, idly visualizing Madge.

"Hey, I was just kidding," Tony protested.

But Ben was not thinking about Madge Anderson's loyalty when he hung up. He was thinking about something else Tony had said, something that touched off a sequence of random thoughts . . .

About a telephone call that Jim Rojak had not made . . .

About a threat more dangerous than blackmail . . .

About a diagnosis that was wrong from beginning to end . . .

23

Chief Jones was still at his desk when Ben marched into Headquarters. With him was George Doyle. A pall of blue cigarette smoke hung over them and Ben saw frustration and weariness reflected in their eyes.

"I won't disturb you for long, Owen," he said without preliminaries. "But I have an idea where Rojak hid whatever he picked up in Karras' office."

"Go ahead," said Jones indifferently.

Ben knew a tough audience when he faced one. Jones and Doyle had been grinding over the murders of Theo Karras and Jim Rojak for a long, profitless time. Ben decided to start strong, with the one inescapable question.

"Owen, why was Rojak planning to detour out to the Newburg Country Club the day he was murdered—just before he was due here at Police Headquarters?"

Jones studied him inscrutably. "To cancel his appointment with the tennis pro."

Ben glanced from him to Doyle. "When he could just pick up the phone?"

A sharply indrawn breath told Ben he had scored, and he pressed his advantage: "You use the telephone to cancel appointments, especially if you've got other important things to do. No, Rojak was heading out to the club for a reason. . . ."

He had their full attention as he outlined his argument. Neither Jones nor Doyle interrupted him once.

"Look, we know Rojak was planning to march in here with a piece of hard evidence. That was his passport to security. Well, where would he keep it? His apartment? With at least one woman running in and out? His office? We've seen how well that could keep out another doctor. No, he wasn't stopping at the country club to cancel his appointment. He was stopping by to pick up that evidence."

Jones was still dubious. "You sound awfully confident about your theory."

"It's more than a theory," said Ben gravely. "I just called the tennis pro myself. That appointment was for the same time as the meeting with Fournier. Rojak had already canceled. And I know another good reason that Rojak hid his evidence at the country club. . . ."

Doyle was ahead of him. With a sudden access of energy, he rose to his feet. "If you're right," he said, "we haven't got any time to spare."

"Why?" Ben asked. "Everything will be where poor Rojak left it—"

"I wouldn't bet on it," said Doyle. "Dr. Deachman got out of that nursing home of his this afternoon."

Owen Jones was already heading for the door.

The drive to the Newburg Country Club was an experience. Jones ordered an unmarked car that was just pulling up as the trio emerged. Ben hurled himself into the back seat and waited for sirens and flashing lights, but they didn't come. What did was a display of speed driving bordering on the homicidal. The driver, a young uniformed man, followed Jones' commands joyously, gunning out onto Main Street with a roar. After they had avoided a head-on collision by inches, Jones hitched himself forward:

"Okay, Warren, stop showing off your reflexes. Get us out to the country club as fast as you can—but don't kill anybody on the way!"

Warren slowed to sixty and even stopped for one red light. It was a memorable trip for Ben, who did not expect to survive.

"And, Warren, when you get out toward the club, take the Frontage Road shortcut. We want the service entrance."

Ben, who had been visualizing a gravel-spattering arrival at the stately portico, glanced interrogatively at Jones, who smiled.

"We don't want to scare anybody when we get there. Warren, you stay with the car and make sure nobody sneaks out back. George, you get around to the parking lot and find out from the attendant if Deachman's car is there. Ben, you and I—"

"So I'm a member of the force, am I?" said Ben, interrupting this show of strength.

"You sure are," Jones told him. "You're in this up to your neck. If we end up with egg on our faces . . ."

"Okay," Ben said, "I'll take my chances. What's the drill?"

"First," said Jones with a wry twist of the lips, "we find out if this trip was necessary."

Warren had pulled up behind the country club, beside four large trash bins. Without a word, George Doyle scrambled out of the front seat and set off, dog-trotting toward the parking lot. Jones, followed by Ben, mounted the steps and pushed open the screen door.

There were three white-clad figures in the kitchen, busy with preparations for dinner. The chef, brandishing a chopping knife, froze at the sight of intruders. At the salad counter a golden-brown youth was startled into juggling a head of lettuce. Only the black-haired woman at the steam table ignored them completely.

Owen Jones discovered quickly that none of them spoke English.

Cursing under his breath, Jones pantomimed a futile request for the club manager. Meanwhile Ben stepped around him to take measures of his own. Punching buttons until he heard a protest, he gave orders into the intercom:

"Tell the manager the police want him here in the kitchen, on the double," he barked.

The manager came bustling through the swinging doors in minutes. He was nervous about life in general and his kitchen staff in particular, toward whom he kept casting placating glances.

Jones silenced his dithering with a flip of his wallet. "Official," he snapped. "Is Dr. Deachman in the club?"

"Dr. Deachman? Yes . . . yes, I think I saw him."

"Where?"

"I believe he was heading for the locker room. But you can't—"

"Lead the way!" Jones ordered.

The locker room of the Newburg Country Club was down a long corridor which opened onto the putting green. Jones and Ben trailed the manager in silence.

"In there," said the manager, pointing to a large steel door. He seemed reluctant to accompany them.

Quietly Jones opened the door and stepped inside, with Ben at his elbow. They were assailed by the aroma of strong soap overlying the sweet-sour reminder of athletic gear and perspiration-soaked towels. Six stalls against the far wall stood empty. Before the rows of lockers were narrow wooden benches.

And near the showers was Dr. Arnold Deachman, surrounded by squash rackets, tennis sneakers and a duffel bag. He was rooting through an opened locker.

Jones, now directly behind him, asked, "Looking for something, Dr. Deachman?"

The man did not move. Ben saw his neck redden, but otherwise he might not have heard.

"That's Dr. Rojak's locker, isn't it?" Jones continued.

Slowly Deachman turned to face them. His mouth was distorted and there was a glitter in his eyes that reminded Ben of trapped animals. Then, as if a plug had been pulled, the tension drained out of him. Sagging slightly, he tried for his usual manner. "I have nothing to say. Nothing."

George Doyle, arriving late, flicked the folder from Deachman's nerveless fingers.

In it was a check for fifteen thousand dollars—made out to Theodore Karras.

Jones was remorseless. "You have plenty to say, Dr. Deachman. Where do you want to say it?"

Nesta Deachman opened the door when they arrived. When she saw her husband between Owen Jones and George Doyle, she turned white.

"What's happened?" she said, moving to bar the door.

"There's nothing to worry about, Nesta," said Deachman too loudly.

"Arnie!" she cried, her voice rising. "Are you all right? Oh, I knew you shouldn't have gone out so soon. I told you so. Oh, you should have listened . . ."

Deachman was shaking his head. "Nesta," he said imploringly.

She looked at him, then turned to Jones. "He's a sick man," she said as if Deachman were not present. "You shouldn't be bothering him now."

The tremor in her voice betrayed her.

Owen Jones, like a large, competent sheepdog, moved them all indoors.

"That's why we brought him home to finish our talk, Mrs. Deachman," he said, forcing her to step back. "We thought that was the best idea for all of us."

"What do you want to talk about?" she asked sharply. "Arnie, what have you been doing?"

Deachman's head jerked back as if he had been slapped, but Jones didn't allow him to reply.

"Your husband's been looking through Dr. Rojak's belongings, Mrs. Deachman," he said conversationally.

She bit her lip, and Deachman broke in. "Now, Nesta, don't get excited. Don't lose your head. They can't make you answer any questions until we get hold of a lawyer. . . ."

But as he spoke, George Doyle was carefully placing the check to Theodore Karras on the hall table.

Nesta drew a long, shuddering breath.

"And that's not all," said Owen Jones.

From his own pocket he drew out a letter on pink stationery.

Nesta Deachman could have been staring at her destiny. When she looked up at her husband, she spoke in a tone that froze Ben's blood.

"So you led them right home to me, didn't you, Arnie dear? Once you found out about Jim and me . . ."

Deachman's mouth had fallen open. Almost groggily he stretched out his hand toward the letter. Obeying a nod from Jones, Doyle let him inspect Nesta's handwriting.

"You—and Jim?" he repeated dully. "You and Jim?"

Trembling, he began to read.

She watched him contemptuously.

"My God!" he said finally. "My God!"

He let the sheets fall to the table, to the floor. "You slut," he said in a monotone. "You cheap slut. After everything I gave you . . ."

"Gave me?" She laughed harshly. "You didn't give me anything. I earned it, baby, I earned it the hard way. God only knows how hard."

As he stared at her, she crossed her arms. "At least Jim was a man!"

"You—" But even in a rage Deachman remembered they were not alone. He bit down hard, his mouth a clamp.

"Afraid?" she taunted. "You're a terrible coward, in addition to

everything else. Everything scares Dr. Arnold Deachman, from performing in bed—"

Deachman choked and would have lunged at her if Doyle had not
crowded him into the wall.

"Oh, sure!" she crowed. "Hit me! That's all you're good for, hitting women. You don't know what else to do with them, do you,
Arnie? And you're too much of a coward to hit anything but a
woman, aren't you?"

He was struggling ineffectually against Doyle's bulk.

"Shut your mouth!" he yelled in a frenzy.

"Try and make me, Arnie! Try and make me! You couldn't, and
you know why? Because you're a stinking little coward. Even too
scared to do anything about Karras. You left the dirty work to me,
didn't you, Arnie?"

He moaned and Nesta stopped, cupping her hand over her mouth.

But it was far too late.

"Nesta Deachman, I arrest you . . ."

"You mean it wasn't any of the doctors? Nesta Deachman was the murderer all along? And her husband didn't even know?" Tony Martinelli still could not believe it.

"Oh, Deachman found out pretty early in the game," Ben corrected. "But he wasn't in on it with her."

The members of the subcommittee had been pelting Ben with questions from the moment of their arrival at 8 Plainfield Road. The first news stories to reach Washington had merely reported that both Deachmans were in custody and murder indictments were expected. This, while it had not been nearly enough to slake the curiosity of Ben's colleagues, had been enough for the Speaker, who recognized a heaven-sent moment to resume hearings in Newburg.

On the surface, the gathering at the Lundgren home was an ideal coming-together of people who wanted to know something and people who had all the answers. Unfortunately, Ben had learned years ago that orderly discussion was impossible during one of Fred's famous barbecues. Janet, for some reason, could produce a five-course meal for sixteen people with no disturbance beyond the steady chug-chugging of the dishwasher. But when Fred was overcome by a desire to feed his friends with his own hands, the upheaval stretched far and wide.

Looking around the backyard, Ben recognized all the usual symptoms. Charlene Gregorian and Michael Isham, who had been invited especially to hear Ben's recapitulation, were nowhere in sight. Charlene was probably still chopping the immense salad due to receive a dousing of Fred's house dressing. It was fifteen minutes since Mike had volunteered to help Lou Flecker remove the piles of debris husked from the corn now roasting in the coals. As for Val Oakes, he had taken one look at the shambles and promptly created a makeshift bar. This necessitated frequent trips to the kitchen, and every time he padded off he sternly commanded Ben not to say one word until his return. Only Elsie and Tony had the good sense to join Ben in deck chairs and let the whirlwind rage around them. Elsie was apparently resigned to never hearing about the murders, but Tony was sending off sparks of impatience.

"Well, you could have fooled me," he kept saying. "I had that Deachman dame pegged as the kind who gets other people to take the risks."

"God knows that's what she wanted," Ben agreed. "But the people she knew weren't very cooperative."

Before he could develop this theme, there was an interruption.

"Now, there you go again, Ben," Val Oakes grumbled as he emerged from the kitchen door carrying an ice bucket in one hand and leading Mrs. Gregorian with the other. "And what about poor Charlene here, who has the most right to hear the whole thing?"

Charlene, of course, had been closer than the Washington contingent to the rumors and the speculations flying around Newburg for the last twenty-four hours. But, far from being better informed, she was suffering from additional misconceptions, and Ben had to start by shooting down all her ideas. No, he told her, Rojak had not been Nesta's partner in crime, Howard White had not tried to steal Rojak's body and pretend he had fled town, Costello had not . . .

"In fact," he concluded, "you don't seem to have heard one accurate detail. I don't know what's happened to your grapevine, Charlene, but there was no conspiracy or—"

"Wait a minute, Ben!"

This time it was Michael Isham, rounding the corner of the garage and dangling a redwood chair from one powerful fist as if it were a handkerchief. He planted it with a thud, straddled the seat and rested his elbows along the back.

"All right. Let's start at the beginning and go on from there," he suggested.

Ben glared at the assembly. "Look, I'm only going through this once. I am not going to start, stop, go back, fill in, every single time somebody wants to look at the coals or get ice. Now, first of all, is everybody here?" He spotted an absentee. "Where's Lou?"

Janet appeared. "That's all right. Lou said to go on without him. He's gotten a call from Washington." She preened herself slightly. "It's the Speaker, and he remembered me when I answered the phone."

Val was more than equal to the occasion. "Only natural he should," he said. "Gus knows where the real political talent in this family is."

Janet acknowledged the compliment. With a deft twirl she rearranged the tray of snacks she had brought so that the cashews were now in front of Val. Ben got the peanuts.

"And don't wait for Fred," she added, as if the Lundgrens had not already pumped Ben dry. "He's put the steaks on, and he's not interested in anything else."

"So we're all here and nobody is going to make a move," Mike Isham said threateningly. "Now, Ben, I suppose this mess started with Karras filing suit against White."

Ben realized that Isham was cueing him not to begin with the arrival of a packet of HEW documents in the Soczewinski mailbox. Charlene's ebullience had not been completely restored by the good news carried from Secretary Buckley by Elsie and Val. She still had moments of guilt when she blamed herself for having delivered Theo Karras into the hands of a murderess.

Nonetheless, Ben shook his head. "You have to go further back than that. Probably to the day that Nesta Deachman decided to have an affair with Jim Rojak."

"What's so special about *that?*" Tony argued. "Married to Deachman, she was bound to play around somewhere."

"It's not the situation that was special. It's the effect it had on a very cold, avaricious woman. Because Nesta Deachman wanted money and pleasure, and for a while it looked as if it was going to be a case of what Nesta wants, Nesta gets. She'd set her sights on Deachman and she'd made him divorce his wife to marry her. Then, when she got tired of simply spending money, she set her sights on Rojak and he obligingly became her lover. By this time she had delusions of grandeur. Once she had gotten her hooks into Deachman, she'd had no trouble converting that hold into marriage, and she thought it was going to be just as easy the second time around. But Rojak made no bones about telling her that he wasn't interested in wedding bells."

Elsie Hollenbach had been listening to the recital with pursed lips. On the one hand, she was the last woman in the world to encourage discussion of infidelity. On the other hand, she might well claim to be the group expert. The late Henry Hollenbach had been adept at letting his playmates go just so far and no farther.

"That is not an unusual occurrence," she said with a finality that nobody dreamed of questioning.

Ben hurried on. "Yes, but it was the first blow to Nesta's confidence. She had been pretty careful about her relationship with Rojak. But when he flatly refused to marry her, she realized how many risks she had taken. And I imagine there was no lack of people she'd antagonized who'd be happy to publicize any indiscretions they got wind of."

"And how!" Mike Isham proceeded to list some of Nesta's enemies. "You know, the Deachman divorce made big waves, and it isn't as if the family had moved away. Margaret Deachman still has plenty of friends who'd love to catch Nesta in the wrong bed, and Deachman's kids have always had their knives sharpened for her."

Ben had not known these points, but they came as no surprise. From what he had seen of Nesta, he could easily believe she had left a trail of ill-wishers. "Exactly. When Owen Jones found one of her letters to Rojak, he said that she was willing to trade in a rich old man for a rich young man, but she had no intention of losing them both. Well, Rojak's ultimatum made it important for her to consolidate her hold on Deachman's affections. Then she got her second shock. You may not remember that Great Lakes started to threaten cancellation the minute Karras filed suit."

"How in the world could we forget?" Elsie reproved him. "Lawrence Fournier mentioned it the first time we met him at the HEW office, and we know he told the Newburg Seven, because that's why the police regarded Howard White as a leading suspect."

"All right, Elsie. I didn't mean you. But you can see what happened next. The doctors spilled out their troubles to their wives, and Nesta faced the prospect of being stuck with the old man when he was no longer rich. That wasn't her style at all."

"For God's sake, Ben," Tony Martinelli said, "you don't have to tell us that. But how did she get from there to murder? A chippie like her, you'd expect her to pry as much cash and jewelry out of Deachman as she could and then take off."

"You forget she was still seeing Rojak. What's more, she was taking the time of day from him. On the afternoon before Karras' murder, Rojak told her that he wasn't waiting to be sued. He was going to buy Karras off. That impressed Nesta as the height of worldliness. She couldn't help comparing her lover's active approach to Deachman's passivity. Then, a couple of hours later, she had a brainstorm. She had the answer to all her problems. *She* would bribe Karras. Luckily, her husband had just deposited sixteen thousand in her account for a fur coat. When the whole transaction was over, she would tell Deachman, thereby earning his undying gratitude."

Janet shook her head in sisterly criticism. "You don't know much about Arnold Deachman, do you? He's not the undying-gratitude type."

Ben agreed that he might have overstated the case and would have gone on, but there were other objections from the floor.

"The little lady wasn't interested in gratitude," Val pointed out. "She just wanted her husband to be a money-maker."

"Sixteen thousand? For a license to practice medicine?" In his own way Michael Isham was shocked. "Was she cheap or plain crazy?"

"Do you want to hear this story or not?" Ben demanded. "I'll rephrase that. Nesta wanted to keep Deachman sweet and she wanted him making a medical income. So, once she had her brilliant idea, all she needed was opportunity. It came that very night when Deachman was called away from a party they were attending. Nesta knew he'd go straight home from the hospital and she could figure on an hour to herself. She called Karras and found out he was still in his office. Then she left the party, drove downtown and made her first big mistake. She took the gun out of the glove compartment and carried it with her."

Charlene stared at him. "You mean she thought Theo was going to attack her? Where in the world did she pick up a notion like that?"

"Oh, no—" Ben began before he was overcome by a spasm of coughing as a cloud of acrid smoke drifted across the lawn. The alarmists in the group looked wildly at the house and the garage. They expected sirens any minute.

"That's just Fred," said Janet on a note of long-suffering. "He must be turning the steaks."

Only Tony was bold enough to venture a comment. "Christ, Janet, you must have to have the house painted every year."

"Never mind about that," Charlene said impatiently. "I want to know why Nesta Deachman was packing a gun."

"Because she was wearing diamonds, carrying a wad of cash and driving an expensive doctor's car. When she had to walk a block in a rundown neighborhood at night, she wanted protection."

Michael Isham laughed jeeringly. "Come on, Ben. Act your age. She's just trying to establish there was no premeditation."

"Well, that's her story, and Owen Jones believes it. And it makes sense. Her only source of information about Karras was the doctors, and they all assumed that any lawyer who had the nerve to sue them must be out to feather his nest. Nesta says she didn't expect any trouble from Karras beyond his trying to jack the price up."

Things were worse than Isham had thought. "You mean she's *talking?*" he asked in horror. "All this stuff is coming from *her?*"

"She was until her lawyer got hold of her," Ben explained. "Anyway, according to her, she swept into Karras' office with a check for fifteen thousand dollars, flung it on the desk and told him he couldn't have more because that's all she had. That's where she had her second stroke of bad luck. Because Karras had gotten a telephone call from Rojak just before she arrived."

Tony Martinelli's bright eyes were gleaming. "I'll bet he thought it was some kind of badger game," he said knowledgeably. "That's how it would have struck me."

"More or less. Karras thought Nesta and Jim Rojak were trying to frame him on a bribery charge so they could have him disbarred or pressure him into dropping the Soczewinski suit. He went up in smoke. But he was an old-fashioned man. He didn't believe in fighting with the wives. Instead he said he was going to call Deachman and tell him what Nesta and Rojak were up to."

"Poor Theo!" mourned Charlene Gregorian. "In some ways he was awfully innocent. He probably thought of Nesta Deachman as a filthy capitalist, without ever noticing that she was a sex object."

"Well, you can imagine how his threat sounded to her. She thought he knew all about her affair with Rojak. She says she yelled at him not to do it, he simply reached for the phone and, before she knew what was happening, she'd taken out her gun and shot him."

"Rooty-toot-toot!" Mike Isham chanted lustily. "Then what did this charming doll do?"

Ben shrugged. "What do you think? She rushed out of there and high-tailed it home. Owen Jones admits his boys flubbed it the first time they questioned the Deachmans. The police were so used to wives trying to cover for their doctor husbands it never occurred to them it could be the other way around. And when Nesta Deachman told them she came home from the party to find her husband already there and in his usual frame of mind, there was no outright deception. She was the one with screaming hysterics, and Deachman was doing the covering."

In spite of Medicaid fraud and other provocations, a certain sympathy for Arnold Deachman was surfacing.

"So Deachman knew everything that night," Tony concluded.

"No, Nesta was in no condition to talk coherently. When she shot Karras, he fell over the desk screaming and spouting blood. She was in shock by the time she reached home. Deachman had to sedate her before he could get anything out of her. Then he did what he could. After he packed her off to bed, he got rid of the clothes and cleaned the gun."

Tony goggled. "You mean, he didn't ask why she had committed murder?"

"She wasn't in any shape to answer questions until the next morning," Ben replied. "By then she'd heard the newscast and she'd had time to cook up her story. She sold her husband a bill of goods— about how Karras first tried extortion, then physical abuse, about how she was so scared she had to defend herself. Then she gift-wrapped it for him by pointing out that she had gotten rid of the malpractice menace once and for all."

Elsie was hewing to her own concerns. "Does that mean that Deachman did not go into hiding to avoid our subcommittee?"

"That's right," Ben told her. "Deachman had bigger problems than us. He was convinced that Karras had been a crook, and he didn't doubt Nesta's good faith. So he gave her the best alibi he could. But he didn't want to hang around for a second session with the police."

Mike Isham shook his head in wonder. "You mean he was hoping against hope that this would be an unsolved murder?"

"He wasn't the only one," said Ben grimly. "Look at Rojak. Of course, you could say he was in a worse pickle. He arrived the next morning to find Karras with his brains blown out—and Nesta's check lying there in plain sight. On top of that, the police have discovered that he'd already contacted his broker to see if he could raise a hundred thousand fast. We'll never know what went through his mind, but the upshot was that he mailed himself Nesta's check—and kept his mouth shut."

"He did more than that," Charlene's teeth closed with a click. "He lied about Theo, making him out to be some sort of criminal."

Here Ben was in no doubt about Rojak's mental process. "You have to remember that Rojak was no dummy. If he passed himself off as somebody willing to spend a half-hour and a few thousand dollars on a two-bit chiseler threatening him with a nuisance suit, he was almost a casual bystander. But if he admitted that he had called Karras, begged for an early appointment and started collecting big money to save his medical license, he would sound like a man desperate enough to murder."

"Wait a minute, Ben." Val Oakes was lying back in his deck chair, his hands cradling a frosty glass. He didn't bother to open his eyes. "If Rojak was so all-fired keen on being a bystander, he could have left that check for the police to find."

"I guess Rojak decided he could always do that. But he was already up to his ears in a fraud scandal. If Nesta was arrested, he knew everything would come out—the affair, his own plan to bribe Karras. There's a limit to how much a man can tough out. He did start to arrange an escape route. But Rojak didn't want to be exiled to Kuwait on a salary except as a last resort. So he did what the other doctors were doing—prayed that Karras had enough sordid activities in his life to generate a bunch of suspects other than the Newburg Seven."

"Great," Mike Isham bleated sarcastically. "That left everybody pretending the pressure was off and they could go back to normal."

Suddenly Ben chuckled. "Everybody except Nesta Deachman. That woman has a real genius for rewriting history. In no time at all she forgot she'd gone hysterical and convinced herself she'd been man enough to do what Deachman or Rojak should have done. Considering what they both owed her, it was only right that they should go on protecting her."

Elsie Hollenbach had no difficulty recollecting the arrogant display by Dr. James Rojak in the Federal Building. "I don't imagine she had much success converting Rojak to that view. Wasn't she alarmed when he held on to the check?"

"Not really. It wasn't until her husband spelled out the implications at the Community Medical Building that she got worried. Deachman, of course, didn't know about the check, so he still didn't see what was coming. But Nesta promptly rushed off to Rojak for reassurance. He dumfounded her by announcing that the crunch had come. He was picking up the check at the country club and handing it over to the police."

Tony Martinelli knew this world contains very little hard-and-fast evidence. "Was the check good enough to nail her? Couldn't she claim she intended to take it to Karras the next day?"

Ben ticked off the damning points, one by one. "The check was signed by Nesta, it had Karras' fingerprints as well as hers, it was dated the day of the murder, it was numbered so that it came directly after a check Nesta gave to her hairdresser at five o'clock that afternoon. As a nice finishing touch, it even had a drop of blood."

"Wow!" Mike Isham whistled reverently. "No wonder she was willing to murder for that check."

"Rojak didn't help things any. Apparently he explained to her how she, being a beautiful woman who had killed in a panic, would get off with a minimum sentence. Then he waltzed off to be the first one in the lounge while Nesta prepared a death trap for him."

"Good heavens!" Charlene startled everybody by slapping herself noisily on the forehead. "No wonder she was able to do it. I had completely forgotten that Nesta had worked in that building when she was Deachman's nurse."

Ben grinned. "It took Owen Jones a while to remember that, but I'm willing to bet it was the first thing Arnold Deachman thought of when Rojak's body was discovered. He was finally admitting to himself that there was something fishy in Nesta's story. That's why he helped Howard White try to pass the murder off as a natural death. Deachman still didn't know about the check or the affair, but he knew he was married to a tigress. This time when he fled to his nursing home, he really was feeling sick."

Tony looked at it from another point of view. "Well, Nesta must have been pleased that at least one of her men was still covering for her."

"Nesta was mad as hell," Ben corrected him. "As long as Deachman stayed in bed, she couldn't get at that check in the locker room. She finally stormed into Riverside Manor and abandoned all pretense with her husband. For the first time, he heard about the check. And she told him that they were in this thing together, so he had to stop taking tranquilizers and rescue her."

"But he was too late," said Janet with a sigh of satisfaction. "Just think, if he'd gone out to the country club twenty-four hours earlier, we still wouldn't know who the murderer was."

It was a daunting thought that Ben was able to dispel.

"Don't be so sure of that. Once Owen Jones found out about the affair, he was slowly zeroing in on Nesta. The police had finally realized that she was the one who had Deachman's car on the night of Karras' murder—the car with a gun in the glove compartment. And Owen never really bought the theory that Rojak secreted evidence incriminating some other doctor. Rojak didn't sound like the kind who'd protect anyone else unless there was something in it for him— like hiding a discreditable relationship. Then, when Owen had time to think about Rojak's murder, he couldn't miss the smell of intimacy. It's all very well to say that other doctors knew about the allergy shots, but how much did they know? Only that Rojak was enthusiastic about a new regimen. And having a nurse remind him not to forget his shot didn't help much. Only Rojak's office staff knew the details—and, of course, someone who was spending a lot of spare time with him. Nesta was in his apartment occasionally when a shot was due, she had even prepared his needle for him—just like his office nurse, she knew how many cc's he took."

Tony Martinelli was discontented. "You make it sound too easy, Ben," he grumbled.

"But the clincher was the hiding place for the check," Ben swept on heedlessly. "Even if the cupboard had been bare when we got there, that was a giveaway. Why would Rojak put his evidence in a locker room which all the other doctors visited? It didn't make sense unless the murderer was a woman—particularly a woman who had access to Rojak's apartment. Nesta was the only suspect who couldn't put her hand on that check without help. And it was her undoing."

"It sure was," Isham said with professional detachment. "They've got her cold now. And she can babble all she wants about not knowing what she was doing with Karras, the trap for Rojak was about as cold-blooded as you can get."

A momentary chill fell on the company at this reminder of Nesta's calm vigil as she waited in the doctors' lounge for Jim Rojak to deal out his own death. Then Val Oakes, seldom at a loss for the appropriate Biblical injunction, bestirred himself.

"Vanity of vanities—all is vanity," he intoned. "If that little lady hadn't thought her love affairs were as important to Karras as they were to her, two lives would have been spared."

Isham let a moment pass, then continued his review of the legal action to come. "And I suppose they'll drop the charges against Deachman. Any jury would sympathize with a husband in his predicament."

"They already have," Ben reported.

"And thanks to your efforts—" Isham bobbed his head in acknowledgment at Elsie and Val—"I can stop worrying about Charlene."

"Absolutely," said Elsie, unbending. "Joe Buckley ended by saying that a few more enterprising civil servants like Charlene and we'd have a better health system."

"Did he really call me that? Enterprising?" asked Charlene, blushing with pleasure.

She was too pleased for Ben's peace of mind.

"For Lord's sake, Charlene," he cried, "don't push your luck and get any more ideas."

She stiffened with offended dignity. "I have lots of ideas. But I could never do anything about them," she added regretfully. "Not after what happened to Theo Karras. Even if I could be certain that—"

Her further plans were drowned out by someone who had no attention to spare for murders, or Medicaid fraud, or national health plans.

"*Come and get it!*" boomed Fred Lundgren. "The steaks are ready!"

As they all rose and began drifting around the garage, Val Oakes paused at the bar for a fresh drink to carry with him. Under Elsie Hollenbach's dispassionate gaze, he felt compelled to justify himself with yet another injunction.

"Man does not live by bread alone," he told her.